IN OUR BLOOD

A JAKE HAWKSWORTH THRILLER

WILLIAM J. GOYETTE

outskirts
press

Outskirts Press, Inc.
http://www.outskirtspress.com

ISBN: 978-1-4787-9759-3

PRINTED IN THE UNITED STATES OF AMERICA

for SUE, CHRISTIE & LEXI
My loves. My life.

PROLOGUE

They'll never see it coming.

A lazy finger brushed across a blurred photo of an attractive couple hurrying across a hectic urban street.

Not in a million years.

He studied their eyes, imagined himself peeling back the eyelids, crawling through. Really digging inside their heads.

Not even after the last drop of blood has drained from their bodies.

The man in the photo was attentive, purpose in his frozen stride. The woman appeared distant, oblivious to the traffic buzzing around her. She gripped her companion's arm more out of necessity than affection.

His eyes flicked across more images of the couple. Split-second glimpses of their lives–together, alone, or with a young boy and girl. His attention shifted to a narrow slit of a window, the only source of light in an otherwise bleak space. Rain slammed the weathered panes at an impossible angle, painting an angry ripple effect on the bed beneath. The woman sprawled across it stared blankly at him.

"What are you looking at?" His gaze slid back to the photographs, to the woman frozen in time, His Fair Maiden, each snapshot an open window to her soul. She was a doting yet ferociously protective mother. As a wife she was efficient, dutiful, if somewhat apathetic. She was kind and respectful as a rule, but had no patience for fools, and made little effort to hide it. She took painstaking care of herself. Not, he sensed, for her husband or anyone else, but out of a selfish need to preserve the beauty she'd always known, yet also knew was on temporary loan.

He riffled through the photos. *Ah, there you are.* His favorite. Caught in close-up. Apprehension, bordering on fear, chiseled into the subtle lines book-ending her mouth that only made her more real, more potent.

What are you thinking, My Fair Maiden?

A leisurely finger massaged the contours of the face, circled the full lips, caressed the silken hair. He stood abruptly, moved to the bedside, shoved the photo into the face of the woman twisted among the covers. "Why don't you take care of yourself like this?" he said. He got no response. Not that he expected one.

After all, she was dead.

He was lulled by the *tap-tap* on the window above the ghastly corpse, the diminishing rain the only witness to his crime. Tears slid down the slick panes, mourning the woman because nobody else would.

But they'll all care about you, won't they? He positioned the photo of His Fair Maiden so it shielded the blanched face of the woman on the bed.

I've got a big surprise in store for you.

You'll never see it coming.

PART ONE

The Black Serpent
Fall

CHAPTER ONE

There is nothing quite as maddening as being shaken from a restless sleep by your ring tone. It cries out for immediate attention, until it is either answered or silenced. The latter is the choice of most.

Unless you're a cop.

A thickly roped forearm emerged from a sea of wrinkles. Fumbling fingers connected on the fourth shout-out. The too-small device slipped from too-fat fingers, drum-rolled on the floor. Cursing, pawing the floor blindly, at last hitting pay dirt. "This better be good."

Sleep was a precious commodity these days. Without Sheila's rhythmic breathing on his back, nights were endless and vacant. His right index finger clawed at the right thumb, picking at the rough, calloused skin until it bled. It was one of two compulsions he had no control over. He'd tried to stop, had even worn gloves in desperation. But the gloves had to come off at some point, and when they did, the disfigurement resumed.

"We've got a Sally over here at Cobb's Corner."

Jake Hawksworth groaned. "Too early for games, Kyle."

"Come on, Jake. It's an easy one."

Jake usually got a rise out of the Name the Crime Game. He and his partner used names of ghosts from their pasts, old girlfriends or drinking buddies, and linked them to on-the-job situations, especially the gruesome ones. A floater was a Teddy, named after Jake's high school pal who drowned in a local swimming hole. A missing person was a Rita, in honor of a girl a much younger Jake had almost married while on a bender.

Listening to her shrill voice was enough to make you want to run away.

Not all of the game's subjects were as wry as Rita.

Take Louis, for example.

Louis Henderson, Kyle's father, was killed in a botched robbery at a 7-Eleven when Kyle was ten. Though Kyle never confirmed it, Jake suspected this was why his partner had chosen a career in law enforcement. Hell, if Jake had a face like Kyle's, he'd have gone the modeling route. Fewer doughnuts. Better pay.

When Kyle added the man's name to the game, Jake tried to dissuade him. After all, the purpose was to blow off steam, not reopen unhealed wounds. Kyle insisted. A tribute to the old man, he said, and every fallen cop before and after him. The name had not yet come up in the short time Jake and his partner had been playing the game. Not yet.

Free drinks at O'Callahan's were at stake. As enticing as another victory sounded, Jake's brain ached. "I give."

A heavy sigh puffed through the receiver. "Sally. My first–"

"–lay," Jake finished. *Let the kid have some fun. Not his fault you're an asshole.*

"And?" The kid taunted him, the lilt in his voice signaling sure defeat.

"And…" Jake paused. It was a stupid game. One he'd invented after his wife scolded him for a lack of interest in his partners' personal lives. *This one's for you, Sheila.* "You said she was the worst lay you ever had. Like sleeping with a sack of potatoes, if memory serves me right."

"So then, what's a Sally?"

Jake imagined his partner in fist-clenching, teeth-grinding anticipation. "Let's just call it a draw."

"Bullshit," Kyle said. "Looks like you're buying tonight."

"Okay, you asked for it, partner. I'm gonna go out on a limb and say we've got a Sally who's dead in bed."

Silence. Followed by an overdramatic sigh. "Damn." More silence. Licking his wounds. "Anyway, Chief says to get your ass over here."

Jake hoisted creaky legs to the creaky floor. "My ass is on the way."

He scribbled down the address and padded to the bathroom. The mirror on the wall was no dream child of Walt Disney. And the muddled reflection frowning at him held no claim to The Land's Fairest. Hell, even Dopey had him beat there.

He wasn't handsome, never had been. Every school has that fat, homely kid who hides behind a clown mask. Back at Jefferson Heights a thousand years ago, that clown had been Jacob Francis Hawksworth.

As he entered his twenties, Jake went from flabby to what he liked to call stocky. His face took on a new shape, the absurdly wide nose that dominated it upstaged by a granite slab of a jaw that looked as if it had been Play-Doh'd on as an afterthought. Eyebrows thick enough to be moustaches topped off brooding eyes. A great look if you're a gangster.

Or a homicide cop.

Now, more than thirty years later, he gazed sullenly at a face that looked an awful lot like that fat, awkward teenager again—with a lot less hair and plenty more wear and tear.

The shower was soothing but Jake's head throbbed. He dressed quickly, skipped the shave. He collected his wallet, keys, and a handful of aspirin, and stepped out into the November air, as raw and ugly as his right thumb.

Rick Smolinski, Jake's neighbor and worthiest adversary in The Great Lawn War, was raking the last of the year's leaves, those rogue hangers-on that so desperately fight their inevitable fate. Rick claimed bragging rights to the best land-scaping on Edgewood Drive. At one time, there was no contest. When Sheila died, the lawn died with her. The flowers withered, the manicured lawn succumbed to brownish spots, like cancerous growths.

Jake cut a clear path across the city. While the rest of the free world enjoyed their coveted weekend sleep, he was going to work.

He defied a NO PARKING sign, pulled out a notepad and pen, scribbled initial observations of the ramshackle apartment building, nodded to a neatly pressed officer, and went inside. The steady drumbeat in his head came right on in with him.

Two more officers with spit-and-polish uniforms and regulation haircuts sipped coffee from Styrofoam cups. Jake wondered how long it had been since Yours Truly had cared about his appearance. Probably the day after Sheila's funeral, he decided. One of the officers, who appeared to be just shy of his sixteenth birthday, motioned Jake up a narrow staircase. Jake was greeted by his partner of almost two months, Kyle Henderson.

Henderson was young enough to be his son. Though Jake found him to be overzealous and oversensitive, he was also honest and reliable, if that judgment could be determined after a mere eight weeks. Kyle's chiseled face and athletic build scoffed at their thirty years. His coal-black eyes had an alertness Jake had never before seen.

"Jake."

Jake turned to the distinct voice of Frank Geoffreys, Chief of Detectives. Frank's ever-serious expression made him look like a man who is forever constipated. He thrust out a lengthy arm. Jake gripped the man's baseball mitt of a hand, well-worn leather laced with thick blue ropes straining beneath transparent skin.

"Good to see you, Jake," Frank said in the deep monotone that had become his trademark. There wasn't a cop in the district who hadn't tried imitating the inimitable Frank Geoffreys. "How's Nikki?"

Jake nodded. "Doing well–considering." Geoffreys opened his mouth to reply but Jake deflected him. "Who found the body?"

"Neighbor. Over there." Frank thrust a sausage finger at a snap-in-two woman hunched in a chair. "She noticed an odor coming from the apartment," Frank said. "The door was unlocked so she went in."

"M.E. been called?"

"On her way now," Frank said. "Ident's inside."

"Let's go have a look see," Jake said. He and his partner entered the door labeled 2B.

Crime Scene Services buzzed about with their high-tech equipment, doing their high-tech thing. Jake scrawled rapid-fire notes on pen and paper, old school all the way. He noted the stench that attached itself to everything in the apartment, burrowed into every nook and cranny. Some things you never forget. The smell of a putrefied body is one of them.

"When are you going to get yourself a tape recorder?" Kyle asked.

"Don't like the sound of my own voice."

A CSS officer with an impressive camera motioned them to a door with a thousand-year-old paint job. "Vic's in the bedroom, Jake. Looks like she put up quite a fight out here, though," he said. "Just let us know when you're all set in there."

Jake scanned the living room, decorated in Early White Trash. Overturned table. Discarded lamps. Threadbare sofa cushions folded up on one another like a big-old-fat-old house of cards. It was impossible to tell where the occupant's mess ended and the perp's began.

Jake surveyed a snap-together wall unit that housed a jumble of tattered books. Tawdry romance novels. Obscure detective pulp. A perfectly aligned row of shiny hardcovers caught his eye. The same author's name ran up each of their glossy spines. Every book written by the guy. Jake knew this because he had the same collection on a shelf in his house.

"She must've been a fan of McCauley's," an ID officer said. "How about you," he added. "A fan, I mean?"

"Who isn't?" Jake said. He winked at his partner. "Let's go meet your girl Sally."

CHAPTER TWO

Carla Mendez was a wilted flower that has hung on long past its season. White-with-specks-of-gray hair was pulled back so severely, her eyes seemed to stretch halfway around her head. A neatly pressed housecoat worked overtime to fill out the skeletal frame it dripped from.

"Mrs. Mendez," Jake said, "you said that Miss Thomas had a guest staying with her. A man. Can you remember what he looked like?"

The tiny woman let out a puff of air, deflating her fragile body even more. "I'm sorry I haven't been much help. It's just, after seeing Donna that way..."

"It's okay, Mrs. Mendez," Henderson said. "Take your time." Women melted when Kyle flashed those pearly whites. Even old coots in housecoats.

Carla Mendez returned the smile, smoothed her dress. "Thank you, Detective."

Jake stifled a groan.

Carla turned to Jake. "Yes, I think I can remember what he looked like."

Jake nodded. "Great. If you wouldn't mind coming down to the station..."

"Beg your pardon?" Carla crowed. "What for?" Her wrinkled face wrinkled up even more, if that were possible. Thin parched lips folded into one another.

"It would be a tremendous help, Mrs. Mendez," Jake's partner said. "If you'd feel more comfortable, I can accompany you."

The wrinkles smoothed, her lips unfolded and curled up.

"Then I'd be delighted," she said. "Shall I get my purse?"

"We'd like to ask a few more questions first," Jake demanded.

"If you must." Carla's lips vanished again.

"How long was this man staying with her?"

Carla looked to the ceiling as if the peeling paint held the answer. "Oh, I'd guess around a month, give or take," she said.

"When was the last time you saw him?"

"Maybe a week ago."

"Did you ever speak with him?"

"Oh, no. I was a bit frightened of him."

"Why's that?"

"The eyes," Carla whispered, pointing at her own hollowed out sockets.

"What about them?"

Carla cackled. "Well, it's probably just my imagination. They were actually very beautiful. Sky blue. Like Paul Newman's. Oh, I just adore his films. Was he Butch Cassidy or Sundance? My memory just isn't what it used to be."

"I believe he was Butch Cassidy, Ma'am," Jake said.

One thing Jake had learned over the years was to be patient with witnesses. Let them tell their story at their own pace. The problem was, he had about as much patience as a teen's dick on prom night. "I'm not sure I understand," Jake said. "If his eyes were beautiful, why did they frighten you?"

"It's hard to explain," Carla said. She looked to the peeling paint for more answers. "There was something beautiful and sinister about them at the same time. Do you boys remember that *Life* magazine cover of Charles Manson?"

Jake nodded. How could anyone forget that picture? He had never seen anything more terrifying. Outside of his own morning reflection.

"That's what he looked like," Carla said. Her eyes widened,

mouth collapsed into her face. Cheeks swelled. A puff of breath escaped. "Long hair," she continued, "scraggly old beard. And those eyes." Carla's own eyes narrowed. "Do you think he's the one who did that awful thing to Donna?"

"We're not ruling anything out yet, Mrs. Mendez. But we'd like to find him so we can speak to him. Do you remember ever hearing his name?"

Carla frowned. "I'm sure Donna mentioned it."

"Can you remember?"

"I'm thinking," the tiny woman barked.

Kyle chimed in. "Sometimes if I run through the alphabet, it helps me recall names."

Carla clapped her hands together. "What a wonderful idea, young man," she said. She began reciting her alphabet. "A... B... C... hmmm... C... D..."

She approached the last vowel. This wasn't working.

Now I've said my ABCs, I haven't got a clue for thee. "Why don't we try a different..."

"Hold on, Jake," Kyle said. "Mrs. Mendez, I noticed you paused at the letters C, L and P."

"Did I?"

"You did." Kyle coaxed her like a mother praising her just-potty-trained toddler. "Why don't we try those again?"

"Well, okay. Let's see. C. Carl. No. Charles. Chuck." Blood flooded into her face, pumping life into the ghastly gray mask. "I can't remember."

Kyle lulled her with his voice. "Take your time. Why don't we try L?"

Carla sighed. "Okay, young man. I'll try." Jake's impatience clicked up a notch. Carla closed her eyes, searched the black-ness for the name. "Larry. Lou. Louie. Lance. Lenny." Her eyes snapped opened. "That's it!"

Jake leaned forward. "Lenny?"

"No. Lance," she said proudly. "That's it."

"Are you sure?" Jake asked.

Carla shot daggers at him. "Of course I'm sure." Her wrinkles softened. "Wait a minute. No, that's not right."

Kyle Henderson rose. "That's okay, Mrs. Mendez. Maybe it'll come to you later. Why don't you get that purse and we'll give you a lift downtown."

"Oh, alright." Carla Mendez swooned over the man who was young enough to be her grandson–great-grandson, if Jake could go out on a limb.

Kyle helped the shaky woman to her feet. She looked as delicate as those dandelion puffs Jake used to pluck from his great-granddaddy's field. *What are they called?* Carla shuffled off in search of her purse. Jake was sure if he blew on her, she'd fragment into millions of tiny pieces and float up to the cracked ceiling, just as sure as those dandelion things–

What the hell are they called?

–were going to blow clear across old great-granddaddy's field and off into the cerulean Iowa sky.

Carla turned her head, the withered face transformed for a moment into a schoolgirl pining over her professor. The door frame swallowed her up.

Kyle grinned from ear to ear. "Jealous, Jake?"

"If you'd like, you can ride in the back seat with her, Casanova," Jake whispered, in case those old ears still worked. "Just be careful with that support hose. Hear it's a bitch to get off." They roared, and abruptly stopped as Carla Mendez reentered the room toting a purse large enough to hold all six New England states, Rhode Island tucked neatly into the side pocket.

Carla furrowed her brow. "Just what are you boys up to?" she asked. Then: "Oh, by the way, I remembered the name."

"You did?" Jake said, his eyebrows mixing with his hairline.

Carla beamed. "Yes. It wasn't Lance. It was Chance."

"What kind of a name is that?"

The old woman giggled. "I asked Donna the same thing. You know what she said?"

"What's that, Ma'am?"

"She said you're taking a chance if you get involved with him."

CHAPTER THREE

Amerian Airlines Flight 103 banked sharply to the left as it made its final approach on Logan Airport. In a cookie-cutter-friendly-yet-authoritative voice, the captain thanked everyone for keeping him in a paycheck, and then announced the weather conditions in painstaking detail.

Save your breath, Flyboy. It's Boston. It's November. It's cold. End of story.

Drew McCauley shifted in his overpriced first-class leather seat and glanced out the window at his overpriced first-class view, the same view those suckers in coach were going to get in about two seconds – *but we get to see it first!* The plane's shadow smudged the bleached-to-perfection clouds.

I'm just a smudge within that smudge, he thought.

He turned his attention to the manuscript stacked neatly beside the laptop (a ritual he had adopted after writing his second novel–*watch the stack grow, feel the progress*) and thumbed through his working draft.

Chance looked at his watch. 2:05. Like clockwork, the snot-nosed rich kid walked out of his snot-nosed, ivy-covered school. He always left fifteen minutes before all the other snot-nosed brats. Sure, they were all from rich, important families. But none were as important as this kid.

He was grossly overweight. How could someone get so fat in only thirteen years? His

standard-issue white shirt was untucked and
stained with ketchup and some shade of green,
probably remnants of his three boxed lunches.
Hard to believe this was Senator Redmond's
flesh and blood.

The kid wasn't vulnerable enough. Pathetic, yes. Vulnerable, no. Drew circled the second paragraph and shifted his eyes to the laptop (another ritual–*make the change while it's fresh, or else you'll forget*). He clicked on Chapter 7, selected the paragraph, and let his fingers speak.

The kid was thin and sickly. Thirteen? He
looked no more than ten. His standard-issue
white shirt was untucked and stained with
ketchup and some shade of green, probably the
result of being tripped in the cafeteria. He
was every bully's wet dream. Hard to believe
this was Senator Redmond's flesh and blood.

Better. But still not quite right. Asthma. That ought to do it. A kidnapped kid without his asthma medicine. This meant additional editing. But that was the fun part. Sometimes Drew sat back and let the characters edit themselves. Sometimes they even *told* him what they were going to do.

The flight attendant, far too pretty to be wearing that god-awful outfit, pleasantly instructed Drew to stash his laptop away.

Drew nodded. His eyes returned to the screen.

A stretch limousine idled on the curb. Blake
Redmond descended the marble staircase, lost
his footing. Books and papers littered the

curb. The driver jumped from the car and ran to the little twerp's assistance. Not the first time this scenario was played out, no doubt.

Chance sized up the driver. Pretty big guy. But caught off guard, he shouldn't be a problem. The limousine dissolved into a drab-gray horizon. The plan was set to go. Tomorrow afternoon. 2:05 sharp.

CHAPTER FOUR

Jake and his partner hiked the long, confining corridor leading to the Medical Examiner's office. Cadent steps on highly polished linoleum disrupted the building's customary silence. The antiseptic odor of death hung heavy in the air, cramming itself up Jake's nostrils, down his throat, crawling deep down inside him, a smell all the scrubbing in the world wouldn't wash off.

"You think Mrs. Mendez will be able to produce a good composite?" Kyle Henderson asked.

"I'm not sure she knows what day it is." A set of imposing steel doors beckoned them. "This way."

"Tell me, Jake," Kyle said, "how did the M.E. get the nickname Chilly?"

"You've heard. I suppose it's because of her cold detachment to the slabs of meat she dissects every day. She'll slice open your chest, stop to take a bite from her liverwurst sandwich, then go right back in and rip out your heart."

Kyle's eyes and mouth collapsed into his nose.

"And I mean literally, not figuratively," Jake added.

A weighty silver door welcomed them into The House of Horrors, as Chief Medical Examiner Amy "Chilly" Lin affectionately dubbed it. Chilly held an iPhone in one hand and waved them in with the other. Jake watched with amusement as his partner scanned the room. A kid in a candy store.

Jake recalled experiencing the same semi-erotic sense of awe the first time he had entered a coroner's space, umpteen years ago. The glassy stainless steel viewing table. The massive scale at the end of a thick chain. The lingering scent of Doc Weston's cheap after-shave. Doc Weston had recently passed, Jake recalled from the obits. Ninety-two years old. The old man had consumed himself with Death every day for sixty-some-odd years. Until, inevitably, Death consumed him.

Amy Lin bounced toward them. Kyle's probing eyes scrutinized the scale. "It ain't for weighing Swiss cheese," Jake said.

"How are you, Jake?" Chilly Lin's reed-like arms poked from an oversized, unbecoming lab coat. Jake guessed her age to be somewhere in the high thirties, though she'd take a scalpel to him before revealing that information. Her strict demeanor and severe bun contradicted her buoyant disposition. Chilly pivoted on sneakered heels. "Who might this be?"

Jake's partner stepped forward, arm outstretched. "Detective Henderson, Miss Lin."

She laughed heartily, a man's laugh, if truth be told. "Call me Chilly, Detective. Everyone else does. Do you have a first name?"

Henderson's face was an explosion of crimson fireworks. "Kyle," he mumbled.

Chilly nodded. "An honest name. I'm not much for formalities, Kyle. Anyway, nice to meet you." She turned her attention to Jake. "How's Nikki?"

"Tuition's putting me in the poor house." Then he added: "She's doing great. Thanks for asking. What do you have for me on the Thomas woman?"

Chilly gave them a follow-me. She tugged on a gleaming stainless door and slid out the very dead Donna Thomas. Kyle took a step backward.

"You okay, partner?"

Kyle nodded. His ashen face disagreed.

"You'll get used to it," Chilly said in a cheery tone. "If you don't, there's always the old nine-to-five." Kyle managed a weak smile.

"What can you tell us?" Jake said. He winked at Chilly.

Chilly's face was serious, as deadly serious as Sister Mary-Alice coming at a twelve-year-old Jake, wooden ruler slapping against her massive palm with each determined step. "Well, she was definitely dead before rigor mortis set in," Chilly said. Jake nodded pensively.

"Wait a minute," Kyle said, his eyes a sea of confusion. "Doesn't rigor mortis *always* set in after death?"

Chilly frowned. "Does it? I once had a gentleman in total rigor, and he was talking a blue streak. Then he sat up and jumped right off the table."

"You're not serious are y-"

Jake howled. Chilly chimed in.

"You're pulling my leg," Kyle said. "Right?"

Jake howled loud enough to wake the dead.

Donna Thomas was displayed before them. Jake imagined her eyeballing him through opaque eyelids, probably heavily mascaraed in life. Eyeballing him as if to say, *Like what you see, Fat Boy? Well, there ain't no chance in hell that a fat ol' slob like you is ever goin' to make it with me, not over my dead body! Now what are you standin' there for, go find the fucker done this to me!*

Jake studied the bruised body. He was a voyeur, the guy who slows down at a crash scene, sneaks a peek when his neighbor's shades are up. There was no dignity in death. You were merely a specimen to be poked and prodded, sliced and diced, the butt of dead jokes from insensitive lab assistants. And cops.

But not in Chilly's home. Chilly respected every poor soul who came across her table. Anyone who ignored this rule was ejected from her House of Horrors. Sal Martino, veteran officer and resident dickhead, had been ejected so many times for his lewd comments that Chilly had posted a picture of his mug on the wall with a note that read: *Be kind to the dead. Or you may be reincarnated as him.*

A Y-shaped incision marred Donna Thomas's doughy skin, made pastier by disturbing reddish and purplish splotches. "Find any prints on the body?" Jake asked, knowing it was a long shot.

"As you know, latents are extremely difficult to recover from human skin."

"Why is that?" Curious Kyle asked.

Chilly smiled patiently. "Welcome to Fingerprint 101. Assuming the assailant touched her with uncovered hands, recovery would still be tough. You see, human skin is very porous. And sweat and other oils produced by the skin don't make my job any picnic."

Jake pointed to bruising around the woman's neck. "Was she strangled?"

Chilly nodded. "Uh-huh. But that isn't what killed her."

"How can you tell?" Kyle asked.

Chilly ran a gloved finger across the woman's neck. "See the bruise pattern here? Indicates manual strangulation." Her gloved hand moved to the face. "The insides of her eyelids show signs of hemorrhaging, another indication of asphyxiation."

"So how do you know she didn't die from asphyxiation?" Kyle asked.

"Tiny lesions on her brain tell me she was probably deprived of oxygen for a significant period of time."

"You think he strangled her slowly," Jake said.

Chilly nodded. "He was savoring it." Her hand glided elegantly down to the woman's left wrist. "The ligature marks on the wrists and ankles are all ante mortum. The deep cuts indicate she struggled against the restraints for some time."

"Then how did she die?" Kyle said. The kid was squirming now, probably had a hard-on.

"Blunt force trauma," Chilly said in a pleasant voice.

Funny, Jake thought, not three words that ought to be said pleasantly.

Chilly's gloved hand directed their eyes again. "See these parallel contusions on the right side of the face?" Jake and his partner leaned in for a closer look.

"What were they caused by?" Jake asked.

Chilly shook her head. "I'm not sure. But the blood has been pushed up and out, causing central clearing around the point of impact. If I were to take a guess, I'd say she was struck with some type of stick. Perhaps a baseball bat or something similar."

"We didn't find a baseball bat or anything resembling one in the apartment," Jake said.

Chilly pulled a crisp sheet over Donna Thomas, sparing her soul any further embarrassment. "Of course you didn't. This guy cleans up after himself." Then she added: "Besides, maybe he's planning on using it again."

CHAPTER FIVE

"What's the deal?" Gerard "Bud" Boudreau asked, impatience creeping into the edges of his voice.

The couple seated across from him melted into the murky wallpaper that held this shithole together. The man tore himself from his dreary wallpaper world and joined Bud's dreary real world. "Heller says I can trust you," he said. "Two-hundred percent."

Bud nodded. "I don't even know your name."

The woman extricated herself from the wallpaper, coughed up a lung.

"I told you those things'll kill you," the man said. That said, he slid a pack of Marlboros from the pocket of a threadbare coat. "Smoke?"

"No," Bud said. "Gave them up a coupla years ago."

"Good for you. Now, back to the business at hand." The man jammed the Marlboro between an unkempt moustache and beard. The lighter licked at the stick, offering Bud a first glimpse at the mystery man's face. What was free of scruff was pallid. Careless black hair obscured one eye. The other was a striking blue, a bottomless pool of secrets.

"I'm Chance." Then as an afterthought: "And this butt fiend here is Lynette." The woman with hair the color of a rotting pumpkin scowled. Chance offered a steady, confident hand. Firm grip, Bud noted.

A waitress joined the party. "Anything else?" she said. The overdose of makeup couldn't mask the deep creases scarring her face. Her only saving grace was a nice pair of legs, most of which were exposed.

Chance nodded. "Another round, Jess."

So, Chance was a regular in this dive. Jess smiled. Two teeth missing.

Praise the Lord for those legs!

"And whatever my friend Bud here is drinking," Chance added.

"Bud."

"Pardon?" Jess said.

"I said I'll have a Bud," Bud replied.

Lynette laughed. "And I'll have a Lynette," she said. "Get it? He said–"

A taut fist exposed itself, hung there a few inches off the table, a silent warning. A fist Bud suspected was well trained in keeping its women in line. Lynette slumped in her seat, pouted, the child who didn't get that toy she'd been eyeballing in the grocery checkout line. Lovely Jess scurried away on those lovely legs.

"Where'd you get the name Chance?" Bud asked.

Lynette looked at Chance. He nodded and she crowed, "Because you're taking a chance if you get mixed up with him." The couple laughed. Bud hated inside jokes, especially when he wasn't in on them.

Chance leaned in close, tossing that thing called personal space right out the window. A mix of scotch and nicotine came right on in with him. Lynette tore a cocktail napkin into jagged strips.

"Okay, here's the deal," Chance said. "Ever hear of Drew McCauley?"

The name rang a bell. Bud shrugged.

"You never heard of the guy? The one-and-only-goddamn-master-of-suspense?" Lynette stopped shredding. Chance's face cracked open, then the smile, surprisingly white, tucked itself back up into his face. "You've got to know your subject. Research is key."

"What are we researching?"

"The author. Or more specifically, his kid."

Lynette had returned to her special talent of seeing how thinly she could shred a napkin. She was pretty good at it. Years of practice, no doubt.

"Wait a minute–how did a kid get into this?" Bud said.

"He's the one we're going to grab."

The words registered slowly, each one dissolving into Bud's head, the last one slapping him in the face. "Kidnapping?"

A well-scrubbed couple glanced their way. Chance eyed them and their gazes melted into their cheap Chardonnays. "Well hell, why don't you just post it on your fucking Facebook?"

"Sorry." Bud half expected steam to come shooting out of Chance's ears, like that fat guy in the funny pages his daddy used to read to him over Sunday breakfast at Stella's Eats so many lifetimes ago.

Chance eased back. "Okay, let's move on." Just like that. As if the scene they'd just played out had rewound and erased itself. "Here's the plan. We take the kid. Daddy pays up. The kid goes free. We get stinking rich. Any questions?"

Lynette awoke from her trance. Nestled up to her man. Her knight in shining armor. Supplier of her next fix.

"Yeah, I've got a question," Bud said. "How do you propose we take this kid? You make it sound so easy."

"Details, details. Remember, I've done my homework. And it *is* so easy."

"Okay, genius, and how much money are we talking?"

"How does two mil grab you?"

Two million bucks. Nothing to it. A hell of a lot more than

the five hundred bucks Bud had netted from that liquor store in Cleveland. Or that fiasco in Kansas City three years ago that had cost him nine months of daylight.

"You in or out?" Chance said. "I need an answer. Now."

"I'm in," Bud said. "One more question."

"I'm all ears."

"What if the guy won't pay?"

"He'll pay."

"How can you be sure?"

Chance's reply was matter-of-fact. "Because I know him better than he knows himself."

CHAPTER SIX

Drew McCauley rolled a weary neck as he exited the freeway, glad to be home. Sure, the accommodations were first-rate, as they always were when he blessed the writing world with his presence at one of those pricey seminars all the wide-eyed McCauley wannabes had anticipated for months. Once upon a time, he had enjoyed the attention. Now it was just old. Like so many other things in his life.

But that was a conversation better left for Seth to analyze to death. Seth Greenbaum, his shrink of three years. The only person on the planet who even had an inkling as to just how screwed up The Master of Suspense really was.

Drew turned onto Cliffside Drive. Stately colonials stood at attention, each boasting an impossibly perfect lawn. The urge to toss his Starbucks cup onto one of these pretentious lawns was overwhelming.

Being away did have its upside. Without fail, Anna Banana would be waiting in the driveway, ready to attack him before he had both feet out of the car. And there would be Paige, a few feet away, sporting that arms-crossed-back-arched stance and icy gaze, ready to ruin it all.

She still looked like the beautiful, spontaneous girl he'd married fifteen years ago. When was it that something sucked the life out of her and injected her with a truckload of bitterness?

He maneuvered the Rover down the serpentine driveway that sliced its way through landscaping expensive enough to feed several Third World countries. The massive house loomed before him, filling every inch of eyeshot.

No Anna Banana. No Paige. His pulse quickened.

The two men tag-teamed it with a well-nicked pair of Oberwerk binoculars. A black Range Rover inched up the driveway.

"I thought this is the part where they play happy family?" Bud said.

Chance frowned. "They always come out. Always."

"You said you knew their routine inside and out."

"Are you challenging me?"

Bud didn't want trouble with this guy. Something was not right about him. "Maybe one of them is sick or something," he said apologetically.

"Maybe," Chance muttered. "Now what's going on?"

Bud pressed the binoculars to his face. An attractive brunette emerged from the house and hurried over to the man. If there was a color called Fear, her face was painted in it. Two coats. The woman pointed toward them. Bud ducked.

"She can't see us," Chance said. "We're a hundred yards away."

"Then how do you explain that?"

"Maybe she saw a wolf or something."

"Or maybe that kid saw you when you went down to get a closer look."

"She didn't see anything. Anyway, we're still on for tomorrow."

"And what if their routine changes for tomorrow, too?"

Chance appeared unruffled. "We adapt."

"Slow down," Drew said. "What did Anna say she saw?"

"A man. Up there." Paige McCauley pointed to the dense forest that curled upward at the lawn's perimeter.

"What would anyone be doing way the hell out there?"

"I don't know, Drew," Paige said in her I-know-everything-and-you-know-shit tone, "but Anna isn't one to make these things up. Ben, maybe. Not Anna."

"She's five. Probably just saw an animal or something. I'm sure it's nothing to worry about," he said in his reassuring voice. He pulled her close. The embrace felt like one you'd give a co-worker at his wife's funeral–uncomfortable, forced, and in no way sensual.

Paige managed a smile, no small feat these days. "You really think so?"

Drew lied. "Of course. Let's get inside. I know someone who's just waiting for a tickle sandwich." Paige managed a laugh. For a brief moment that crazy, silly, unpredictable girl–the only girl he'd ever loved (hell, maybe the only girl capable of loving him)–had given the alien clone that held her hostage the slip.

Paige's laughter was distant now, drowned out by the rhythmic pounding in Drew's head. Goose bumps tap-danced up and down his arms. Just like they had a week earlier when he thought *he* had seen movement beyond the trees. When he felt that someone had been inside the house. No telltale signs. Just familiar little things that seemed slightly askew. His underwear drawer, writing desk.

Paige rushed off in search of Anna. Drew breathed in the sweet smell of home. His pulse slowed, his heart nestled back into place. He dropped his overnight bag, looked out the bay window. His heart tore from the gate again. Though he couldn't be certain, he thought he saw a man lurking just beyond the tree line, staring directly at him.

CHAPTER SEVEN

The room is always empty, except for a moon-drenched bed placed dead center. He moves. Slowly. Arms weightless. The bed grows nearer. He moves. Effortlessly. The bedspread rises. He pulls it back. Opens his mouth to scream. His beloved Sheila. Arms outstretched. Blackened eye sockets. Toothless grin. Translucent skin. Deflated breasts. Thousands of worms spill from the hollow grin. From the blackened eye sockets. Slithering down the mottled gray breasts. Across the bloated stomach. He opens his mouth to scream...

"Dad?"

Jake took in the face floating above him.

Nikki Hawksworth planted a loud kiss on her father's forehead. She swiped at her mouth in mock disgust. "Ooh, you're all sweaty, Dad." 'Dad' was the term of endearment Nikki had knighted Jake with when she only recently had outgrown 'Daddy.'

"Bad dream," Jake said. "How was the game?" He rose from the sofa, fluffed the squashed pillows.

"We killed 'em." Nikki tugged at Jake's shirtsleeve. "C'mon, let's go. I'm starving!"

Get your ass in gear, Jakey old boy.

Nikki bounced off toward the kitchen. Her rare visits breathed new life into the house–a house Jake once rushed to, now simply a stopover for a sleep, a shower, and a shave. There is lonely. And then there is the kind of lonely that burrows deep inside you, unpacks its bags, and stays long after its invitation has expired.

Jake pulled on a fresh shirt, splashed on a generous helping of Old Spice, and met his daughter at the front door. "Sure you want to be seen in public with an old goat like me?"

"Correction," Nikki said. "Handsome old goat. Now let's go eat!"

Jake and Nikki Hawksworth dined on pepperoni pizza and garlic bread. At an adjacent table, a young couple tried in vain to convince their son of about six to eat his dinner. He shot them with a toy gun, crawled under the table, took aim at Jake.

"BANG! BANG! You're dead, mister!" He emptied his plastic death machine on Jake.

"David, that's not very nice," David's father said in a not-stern-enough voice. The man, a young Ronald Reagan look-alike, struggled to pull the boy back into the red vinyl booth. His wife, who looked quite unlike the former First Lady, fretted over an infant pulling a Linda Blair with her baby food.

"Makes you want to run right out, get married, and have kids, doesn't it?" Jake said.

"Was I that bad?"

"Worse."

Nikki laughed. It was good to see her laugh again. With her infectious smile, Nikki could brighten the darkest of days. Except one.

Though not considered beautiful by today's bleached, plucked and tucked standards, Nikki made a striking presence. A toothy grin dominated her face. She was tall and had a healthy, athletic frame. And though she usually donned sweatshirts and jeans, her mother's undeniable grace was subtly evident as she nibbled on her bottom lip, ran a long finger around the rim of her glass. Her pony-tailed brunette hair swung from side to side, keeping cadence with a voice Jake never grew tired of listening to.

They talked about school. Nikki was a second-year law student, captain of her volleyball team and part-time tutor. She briefed Jake on her workload, said it was heavy. She talked about a guy named Chip, said they were "just friends," then went on at length about him. At last, the subject Jake had been avoiding.

"Any leads?"

"Nothing, honey. Nobody's come forward."

"Someone will, I know it," Nikki said.

Jake squeezed her hand harder than he meant to. "Mom wouldn't want us to dwell on this. We may never catch him. You have to accept that." Nikki's eyes begged him to make the pain go away. If only someone could make his go away.

Sheila and Jake Hawksworth had been out celebrating their twenty-third wedding anniversary. Dinner and the opera. A six-pack and a ballgame would have been just fine with Jake, thank you very much.

It was unseasonably cool for July. A million stars danced across an ebony backdrop. The city breathed loudly around them. Sheila was stunning in a black sequined cocktail dress and shawl. Brilliant diamond earrings only enhanced her elegant face.

A young couple breezed past. The man whispered to a leggy blonde keeping pace beside him. Jake was sure the woman mouthed *gorgeous* as she and her partner moved forward, a healthy bounce in their step.

Fifteen minutes had passed since the valet left to fetch the car. "Where the hell is that kid?" Jake grunted. "I'll get the damn thing myself. He just blew a great tip."

"Jake, don't let this ruin our night," Sheila said. "It's been wonderful." Then she added: "You've been wonderful." Her enunciation was impeccable, a far cry from Jake's untamed Boston accent. He'd been blessed–or was it cursed?–with his mother's Irish-Boston influence over his father's more refined British sensibilities.

Sheila was always the optimist. Jake recalled their wedding day when the band's equipment failed after the first set. While Jake drove himself into a frenzy, Sheila sent for a phonograph player and record albums. The crammed reception hall awaited the arrival of music; without missing a beat, Sheila kicked off a sing along.

This optimism ultimately led Sheila to pursue her dream of working with handicapped children. A fierce need to enhance her students' limited abilities grew to a manic obsession as Sheila pressed the youngsters to overcome their weaknesses and strive for greatness. Her expectations fell short and, for the first time, pessimism cracked her tough exterior. In time the crack healed, though scar tissue remained, as Sheila came to accept the limitations life cruelly dishes out.

"God, you're beautiful."

"Oh, Jake," Sheila said, though she clearly savored the compliment. "Go get the car and take me home to bed."

Her brazenness shocked Jake. A gentle breeze carried him along. Glancing back, he was transfixed by the vision beneath the yellowish glow of the lamppost, which cast a dreamlike haze around Sheila's statuesque figure. White slivers shimmered in her jet-black hair, pulled smartly off the silky face it framed. Determined eyes were set apart by a thin blade of a nose. Her subtly shaded mouth turned up in a radiant smile. She wore very little makeup. It wasn't necessary. Sheila's skin had ceased to age a decade ago, as if frozen in a cryogenic state.

"I'm expecting a big tip, lady," Jake called out. Sheila waved him away in mock disgust. It was the last thing Jake ever saw her do.

He had been gone two, maybe three minutes tops. He edged the car to the curb, noticed a small huddle formed around a dark object. Nausea rocked him as the scene frozen in place before him dissolved, then clicked sharply into focus. Sheila. Had she fallen? Passed out? He pushed a small elderly man aside and discovered that his guesses were dead wrong.

Sheila's body was a shattered sight. A doll that's been discarded because its face is cracked, its limbs broken. A cruel slash marred her forehead. Her mouth was agape, left leg turned in an impossible position.

Jake heard a scream, realized it was his own. The elderly man mumbled something indecipherable to Jake. Someone said something about a speeding car. A woman with high hair shook her head.

When the lights came back on, Jake was slumped in the back seat of a police cruiser. The romantic glow of the lamppost was disrupted by the intrusion of red and blue flashes. Jake's eyes searched for the vision of beauty beneath the yellow light. What they found was a dark roundish spot on the sidewalk.

Ambulance chasers milled about. A somber officer informed Jake that Sheila had been transported to the hospital. A multitude of injuries. Chief among them, a broken neck. Sheila would linger for weeks, feeding off machines until they could no longer feed her.

Through the crowd, Jake spotted the valet, a lanky teenager ridiculously clad in red vest and bow tie. "SONUVABITCH! Where the hell were you?" Jake squeezed the kid's celery stalk of a neck until it turned the color of eggplant.

The libidinous valet, Jake would later learn, had gone off for a little parking of his own. The events of that cool July night resulted in the loss of a part-time job to an oversexed teenager and the loss of a lifetime love affair to a fifty-six-year-old man.

They finished the pizza in silence. The couple with The Gun-Toting Tot From Hell had gone, but the aftermath was devastating to the pimply-faced waitress surveying the damage.

Nikki Hawksworth glanced over at the mess, smiled and said, "Do you really want grandchildren, Dad?"

CHAPTER EIGHT

Seth Greenbaum scribbled his final notes and closed the case file. He glanced at his Rolex. Damn. 10:42. And on a Saturday night, no less.

If the cancer doesn't kill you, these late hours will.

The city screamed six stories below. Filled with beautiful people, rushing to dinner dates, the theater, meetings with friends. Gorging themselves, drinking themselves silly, fucking each other's brains out. He ought to know. He'd been one of them himself before The News. Disease-free people, shoving their weekly responsibilities under the bed, out of sight, if only for a while, never for a moment thinking that The Grim Reaper, cloak and all, could be standing right on their doorstep, waiting to deliver the ultimate message, signed, sealed and delivered. Fuck 'em. Every last Gucci-wearing, Botox-injected, cosmetically enhanced one of them.

Seth stretched and moved across the room. He poured himself a generous glass of scotch. It was soothing as it made its way through his infected body. The strange thing was, he didn't feel sick. It had been more than three months since he had received his sentence. Still, he felt healthier now than he'd felt in years. *Maybe I can trick my body into believing it's not sick.*

Seth clicked off the overhead lights. He didn't blame Leon for leaving. Perhaps he'd have done the same if the tables were turned. Right now, instead of going home to a world of silence, he should be down in the Cayman Islands with Leon.

He recalled how great life had been before the diagnosis. How, at just thirty-four years of age, he'd built a lucrative practice and found his Prince Charming. And there was no ugly stepmother to fuck things up.

Here he was, the clinical definition of a basket case, treating the mental stability of people of wealth and power. Senators, authors, heads of Fortune 500 companies. Dropping three bills an hour to seek advice from someone ten times more fucked up than they'd ever be.

Something cold and hard stung his right temple. Hot breath on his neck. He felt his body tense, his loins tingle.

"Move and I'll blow your brains all over that imported leather couch." The voice was deep, low, meant business.

A warm sensation moved down Seth's left leg. "Take whatever..."

The cold metal pressed deeper into his temple. It traveled across his cheek, rested on his lower lip.

If the cancer doesn't kill you, a bullet ripping through your brain will.

The intruder grabbed his left arm and directed him toward the desk. "Sit."

The bluish haze from the laptop silhouetted the man against a gleaming city skyline. If he weren't absolutely terrified, Seth would have found the image breathtaking. He sat motionless waiting for the next command.

The man lingered for a moment, perhaps savoring the smell of fear. He waggled the gun at the laptop. "Are all your patients' files kept on that?"

"Yes," Seth whispered. "There and in those file cabinets on that wall over there."

"Anywhere else?"

"Some audiotapes."

"I want to see everything you have on Drew McCauley."

Seth shifted in his seat. This reminder that he had pissed his pants sent a rush of heat across his cheeks. "I can't do that. It's privileged information."

Cold metal shattered Seth's right cheek. He cried out to the bustling street miles below, to all those beautiful people eating and drinking and laughing, laughing at him for crying and for pissing himself, laughing because they weren't the ones with a gun shoved into their faces.

"Privilege is overrated," the intruder said.

Fire spread across Seth's face. He sank into the chair.

"I want every tape, every case study, every memo, every fucking e-mail from, to and about him," the man said calmly.

Seth ignored the throbbing in his face, focused on the task at hand. He printed all the documents on McCauley along with the case file. He placed a sleeve of miniature cassette tapes on the desk.

"Would you like to see the files on his wife?" Seth asked. Give him what he wants and then some. Sure it was unethical. But when you're on the wrong end of a gun, ethical means dick.

"She's a patient of yours?"

Seth sensed excitement in the man's voice. *Make him happy and he'll go away.* "Yes. For about eight months now. I'll pull up her files if you'd like."

"I'd like."

Seth collected the data he had on Paige McCauley and set them down on the desk beside her husband's file. "That's everything. Please don't hurt me." The last part slipped out.

The man moved into the shaft of moonlight that split the room in two. Seth caught a glimpse of his face. A shock of thick hair fell across most of it. An unkempt beard and dark sunglasses concealed the rest.

"I said if you cooperated I wouldn't hurt you, didn't I?"

Seth nodded. The nerve endings in his face cried out. He

sobbed quietly. He'd done everything the man wanted. And more. Kissing his ass had paid off. The sooner the guy left, the sooner he could get to the hospital. If he was lucky, they could make his face look as perfect as it did fifteen minutes ago.

"Get on your knees," the man ordered.

Panic washed over Seth. "What?"

"Do it. Now." Seth complied. "Put your head facedown on the chair." Seth paused. "Do it." Seth obeyed. The smell of imported leather invaded his senses. Footsteps moved toward the door.

He's leaving.

Seth listened to the sounds of the night, sounds he'd never noticed before. Car horns chattered from light years away. The laptop hummed a soothing hymn. A plane roared in the distance, taking more beautiful people to faraway paradises, to the Cayman Islands, to see Leon. His breathing was slow and rhythmic against the leather. Dead air. The guy was gone.

His head jerked back. A powerful hand twisted itself around his hair. He tried to push himself up. His face was forced into the padded seat cushion of the chair he had sat in every day for the last three years. A second hand wrapped itself into his hair now, pressed his face deeper into the cushion. The crushed cheek sent alarms to his brain. His brain ignored them. It was begging his lungs for air.

He clawed at the powerful hands. He was drowning. He recalled his last evening with Leon. Just before the news had come. They'd talked of all the places they'd travel to. Venice. The Far East. The Arctic Circle. The Grand Canyon. Funny, of all the exotic places he'd been to in his life, he'd never seen the Grand Canyon. What sense did that make?

Leon was gone now and Seth was gliding through a tunnel of dark. A pinpoint of light in the distance. His cheek no longer hurt. He was weightless, an invisible force nudging him toward the white dot, gently, like a dad prodding his frightened child to uncurl those toes from the pool's edge and plunge right on in. The dot grew closer. He plunged right on in.

CHAPTER NINE

Drew had been sitting at the computer for three hours and damned if he'd edited two pages. He still couldn't believe Seth Greenbaum was dead.

Thora Camden, The Best Damn Agent On The Planet, had called him with the news. So young. So brilliant. The details of Seth's death were sketchy. An apparent suicide, Thora suggested.

Drew had seen Seth only two weeks ago. Like most sessions, this one ran over. Drew sensed this occurred with patients Seth favored. On most occasions, their sessions were relaxed, almost too laid back for the money Drew was shelling out. But Seth had been different last time. Distant, distracted.

If Seth's death wasn't enough to cloud his mind, Drew couldn't shake the feeling that someone was watching his every move. *Could it be him? No, he's dead. Jake assured me of it. But they never found the body.*

Drew focused on the beckoning screen. He wished he felt as confident about the book as Thora did. What seemed formulaic to Drew was what Thora called marketable. Well, she ought to know what sells. It was she who took a chance on Drew's first novel, *Forbidden,* a potboiler about a teacher's obsession with a student, when everyone else wouldn't touch it with a fifty-foot pencil.

Thora Camden was loud, outspoken and one hell of a businesswoman. She used her six-foot, three-hundred-pound stature to full advantage. After all, who would risk not allowing The Great and Powerful Thora to speak?

Thora could smell a best seller if it was buried under ten tons of shit. Drew had produced fifteen of them in the twelve years since *Forbidden* topped the charts. *Random Acts, Chance Encounter,* and *Merciless,* to name a few. And he had Thora to thank for each and every one.

As for his current best seller-in-the-making, Thora said, "It's a real page-turner," and added, "Hell, you may even want to use that as a title."

Page-turner sure beat *Snatched,* Drew's working title for his latest "masterpiece of suspense," as the book's jacket would surely declare. Still, Drew had his doubts about what he considered to be a typical kidnapping yarn complete with ransom drops gone bad and the stereotypical bad guy with a soft spot for the kid in peril.

Snatched (soon to be renamed *Page-turner* if Thora had her way) had a couple of semi-interesting plot twists; yet none that would make your jaw drop. Sure, the asthmatic kid in need of his medicine made for edge-of-your-seat suspense, but Drew found that by Chapter Ten he despised the little twerp. He was tired of the kid whining and crying for his mommy.

For Chrissakes kid, pull yourself together and do something!

By the time Drew reached Chapter Sixteen, he decided this spoiled brat needed to be taught a lesson. The first draft had the kidnappers chopping off the kid's right hand and mailing it to the stereotypically rich parents (who, in true stereotypical fashion, never had time for the little bugger until threatened with losing him).

This latest plot development did not sit well with Thora. "Nobody wants to read about a poor defenseless kid having his hand chopped off," she said.

"How about just a finger?" Drew pleaded, fully aware of the damage this massive woman could inflict upon him.

In the end, Thora agreed to a toe, "but just the baby toe, that way no one will be any the wiser when he has his shoes on."

A baby toe it was. A fair compromise. Thora didn't know it yet but the baby toe was just a primer for what Drew had planned for the little pain-in-the-ass come the final act.

He clicked on the icon labeled Chapter 16.

Blake Redmond sat on the rumpled cot, hugged his knees tightly to his chest. His right foot throbbed. He removed his sock. A bandage covered his five toes. Funny, it didn't look like five toes. Must all be squeezed together. He unwound the bandage. Red spots stained the white gauze. He unwound faster. The bandage fell away. Blake screamed.

He rewrapped the foot, as if covering it would bring back the missing digit. He sobbed loudly, rocked back and forth. A memory of his mother wiggling his toes popped into his head.

This little piggy went to market, this little piggy stayed home, this little piggy had roast beef, this little piggy had none, and this little piggy cried...

"My piggy," Blake cried. "What have you done with my piggy?"

Drew laughed in spite of himself. Worst piece of crap he'd written. Maybe he could call the book *The Little Piggy That Got Away*. He wondered what Thora would make of that. A knock at the door jolted him.

"Come in."

"Hey, Dad," Ben McCauley said. "Sorry to bother you."

"Never a bother, Champ. What's up?"

"I'm heading to soccer practice. Mom and Anna went shopping."

Drew glanced at his wrist. 1:04. "You eat?"

Ben nodded.

"Hey, you didn't see my phone, did you?"

"No. Why?"

"Can't find it. I've looked everywhere."

Ben shrugged. "Dunno. Anyway, gotta go."

The man in the forest.

"I'll drive you."

Ben frowned. "I always take my bike."

"Thought we could catch up. You know, guy stuff."

"You okay, Dad?"

"Yeah, just that we don't talk much these days."

"Dad, I really gotta go. I'm gonna be late."

The man in the forest.

"Like I said, I'll drive you." Drew lied. "I heard a report of some wild coyotes in the area."

Ben rolled his eyes. "Yeah, right. Are you high, Dad?"

"Hey, don't cop an attitude with me." Nothing he hated more than kids disrespecting adults. "Either I drive you or you don't go. End of discussion."

Ben opened his mouth to argue but all that came out was a sigh, followed by a defiant "Fine."

"Be right down," Drew said. He traded sweats and a tee for a sweater, jeans, and baseball cap. He knew how Ben felt. Hell, he'd been fifteen once. But what was he supposed to say? That someone might be stalking them? Anyway, he didn't owe his son an explanation. Goddammit, he was the boss.

Drew bounded down the stairs. "All set to go, Champ?" No answer. He grabbed the keys, a jacket, and headed to the garage. The car was empty. Ben's bike was gone.

CHAPTER TEN

Blake Redmond plodded down the school steps. 2:05. His favorite time of day. When he could escape the teasing, the cruel jokes. Until tomorrow.

The limousine idled on the curb. Cars shot past. He could just run out in front of one of them. Who would really miss him anyway?

Richard didn't get out of the limo and open the door like usual. Blake always thought this to be silly anyhow. He could open his own door, even if Mother and Father thought this to be improper.

He grabbed the handle and flung open the massive door. See, nothing to it. He tossed his book bag onto the leather seat and slid inside. "Better not tell my mom I opened my own door, Richard," he said.

The man in the driver's seat turned his head.

"You're not Richard," Blake said. He reached for the door latch.

"And you're not going anywhere," the man said, pointing a shiny gun directly at Blake's face.

Route 9 is a scarcely traveled road, cutting through a two-mile stretch of dense woods. Joggers seek alternate routes rather than enter The Tunnel, as locals know it, because of thickly shrouded, intertwined trees that are nearly impenetrable to sunlight. But to a fifteen-year-old who is late for soccer practice, it's a great shortcut.

Ben McCauley entered The Tunnel at a good clip. The blackness swallowed him up. But it wasn't the darkness that made The Tunnel so frightening. It was the silence. Like entering a soundproof room. The perfect setting for bad stuff to happen. Like a scene out of one of Dad's books.

He was going to catch hell for taking off like that. What was the old man's problem, anyhow? Coyotes? Ha! Besides, what would the guys think if their captain drove up in Daddy's car? And Sandra Simmons would be on the next field over. How lame would that be? There'd be hell to pay, but no matter what the punishment was, it sure beat ruining his reputation.

The Tunnel seemed darker than usual, more closed in. The ceiling of trees sagged like a clothesline after a heavy rain, outstretched limbs ready to snatch him up and devour him whole. Mom hated driving through The Tunnel and it sent Anna Banana into total hysterics. Ben used to wonder why they made such a big deal about it. Until now. He pedaled faster.

He rounded a bend. A car on the shoulder ahead. He sped by, noticed a woman in the driver's seat. He thought to turn around and help her. After all, she was in The Tunnel. Then again, she had a cell phone in her hand. Someone was probably already on the way. Besides, what was he supposed to do, put her on his handlebars?

❧❖❧

Ben was lost in thoughts about Sandra Simmons and how hot she looked at last week's game. Funny, a year ago, girls were the mortal enemy. But lately he'd been thinking a lot about them. One in particular. And she no longer seemed like the enemy.

The bike eased into the curve in the road. A van ahead. Turned sideways. Right smack dab in the middle of the road. Two broken down cars in a row. He hardly ever saw two cars at all along this stretch. Sketchy. He slowed.

A flash of color to his right. He recalled being airborne then crashed face-first into the pavement.

His first thought was that a deer had run into him. Then he saw the large man on the ground beside his wreck of a bike. His face felt moist. The man on the ground stirred. A car door slammed. Footsteps pounded to his left.

The approaching man yelled for the other man on the ground to "get the little bastard." Adrenaline overtook pain. Time to get the hell out of here. A thousand knives stabbed Ben's legs. The large man sat up. The other closed in. Ben bolted for the forest.

The thick underbrush ripped angrily at the thin sweats barely protecting his body. His right arm screamed. His back, his legs, even his hair hurt. Razor-like thorns tore into his tender skin. Decaying tree limbs grabbed at him, desperate to touch the only sign of life to ever cross their path. His knee connected with a low-lying branch. He lurched forward. The ground fell out from under him. Branches snapped like toothpicks. He seemed to fall forever then slammed into something hard. Phantom trees encircled him, studying the foreign object heaped at their feet. The trees went fuzzy, and were washed away in a sea of gray.

Ben had the sensation he was floating. A massive chest heaved against him. Trees passed overhead. He cocked his neck and saw the man who carried him, the man who had knocked him off his bike. The man's neck was as thick as the ages-old trees that whizzed past them. The face was leathery, etched with deep creases and pockmarks. He looked like a bad guy from one of those old spaghetti westerns Ben used to watch with his dad on weekends.

Ben closed his eyes. Play dead. The pain pumping through his body was so unbearable he wished he were. He needed a plan. But what? There were at least two of them, maybe more. They were bigger, stronger. But he had something this big, fat, sweaty hulk didn't. Speed. Ben was sure he could outrun the hulk through the tightly packed forest. If his own body wasn't broken.

They moved through the woods, snapping and crunching with every step. The toes in Ben's right foot tingled. Spasms shot up his back into his neck. His arms felt like they had been wrenched from their sockets.

The thinner man said, "There's the road." Ben's heart quickened. He hoped his body had some life left in it. The snapping stopped. They were on pavement.

Don't open your eyes! Stay still!

"Get the van," the hulk said. He lowered Ben to the ground. Hurried footsteps moved away. Labored breathing beside him. Ben opened his eyes.

The thinner man trotted toward the van. The hulk was on his knees, clutching his chest. Ben knew this was the only chance he was going to get. Once they got him in the van, that would be it. He rose without a sound.

Run! No, go slow.

He inched away, amazed the hulk hadn't noticed. The hulk appeared to be in tough shape. The thinner man was almost to the van. A shrill ringing sound broke the silence. The thinner man pulled a cell phone from his pocket.

He turned in Ben's direction. "Lynette says a car's com–hey–HE'S GETTING AWAY!"

Lynette. The woman in the car. Ben's legs didn't fail him. He shot off in the direction of the woman's car. A door slammed. An engine revved. The hulk raced toward him. Tires squealed. The van bore down on him. Ben rolled onto the shoulder. The van brushed by him.

Ben struggled to his feet, was broadsided again by the hulk. An enormous hand smothered his mouth. The hulk squeezed his body so tightly Ben was sure his heart would pop right out of his chest. Just when he thought his lungs would explode, the massive hand relaxed. The thinner man swept up the bike and said to the hulk, "Get him in the van."

A black Range Rover rounded the bend behind them. Dad! The thinner man with long, scraggly hair gunned the van. The Rover morphed into a tiny speck, and then disappeared.

CHAPTER ELEVEN

Jake pressed a fat, calloused thumb to the doorbell gingerly, afraid even the slightest pressure might level this house. Strips of paint hung from weather-beaten shingles, shivering in the cold breeze. One half of the façade was painted a mossy green, the rest a dull white, as if the house had been carelessly tossed in the wash with the wrong color load.

A lock slid away and, with some effort, the door opened. Lydia Marsh smiled and said, "Good afternoon, Detective Hawksworth. Won't you come in?"

Jake stepped out of the chilly November air. The interior was no great shakes but, unlike the exterior, it was immaculate. Lydia Marsh guided him to a bright floral sofa. "Coffee?" she asked.

"No thank you, Ma'am," Jake said. "I'll try to be quick. I'm sorry to put you out as it is."

Lydia disappeared into a threadbare armchair. "It's no bother, really. I'm just not sure how I can be of any more help to you, Detective," she said. She looked older than her fortyish years, as if someone had carelessly scribbled on her face with an indelible wrinkle-making pen.

"Sometimes people recall things later," Jake said. "I know we've been through this before, but I was wondering if you could take me through the scenario one more time." He'd spoken with every witness to Sheila's death two or three times. And not one new lead had surfaced.

Lydia sighed. "I'll try."

The doorbell chimed. Jake thought he saw the house shudder.

"If you'll excuse me, that will be my son," Lydia said politely and hurried off.

Jake surveyed the room. A dog's breakfast of furniture was further offset by gaudy drapes. All the elbow grease in the world couldn't mask the water stains that marred a highly polished coffee table. A truckload of games, puzzles, and books teetered precariously in two of the room's four corners.

Muffled voices exchanged goodbyes, then Lydia reappeared. An impish boy with ears that looked ready for flight hid behind his mother. He reminded Jake of a deaf child Sheila had once worked with.

"Alex, you remember Detective Hawksworth, don't you?" Lydia asked. Her breakable hands moved in unison with her voice. The boy peered around his mother's waist, studied Jake. Alex Marsh furrowed his brow. He moved his fingers feverishly. The mother and son conversed silently, then Lydia turned to Jake and smiled. "Alex says he remembers your shiny badge."

"Would he like to see it again?" Jake wished he could ask the boy himself but he couldn't even sign *hello*. He flashed his badge.

The boy's hands spoke again. "Alex says he wants to be a detective one day."

"Tell him I'll bet he'll make a good one."

"I'll do that, Detective," Lydia said. "If you'll excuse us, I'll get Alex set up in front of the TV so we can talk. He's very good at reading lips. Sometimes he even shuts off the Closed Captioning."

"He seems like a very bright boy, Mrs. Marsh," Jake said.

"Yes, I'm very proud of him. He's my man of the house now." Sadness interrupted the woman's determined eyes. Alex Marsh waved to Jake and his mother hustled him out of the room.

At last she returned. "Sorry to keep you waiting, Detective. Now, what can I do to help?"

"Just tell me everything you remember leading up to the accident."

Lydia closed her eyes. They snapped open. "I remember seeing your wife standing on the curb beneath a lamppost. She was hard to miss. She looked like a movie star."

"It was our anniversary," Jake said. *You can't do this.* "Go on."

Lydia squirmed in her chair. "Alex and I had just come from our support group and were waiting for a cab. I was admiring your wife's outfit when I heard a squealing sound and turned. The car took the turn much too fast for such a busy intersection. The next thing I know, people are running and screaming. My son and I became separated. I panicked."

Jake fought back the demons clawing their way to the surface. "Then what?"

Lydia sighed. "I looked up in time to see the car racing away. Then somebody said a woman had been hit. That was when I saw your wife." Lydia's eyes welled up. Her chin dropped to her chest. "I'm so sorry."

Jake glanced down at his notes. "You said the car was a dark blue sedan, maybe a Toyota Camry?"

Lydia wiped her eyes. "Dark blue, yes. It was either a Toyota or a Honda. They all look the same to me."

"I know I've asked you this before," Jake said, "but can you remember a license plate number? Digits, letters?"

Lydia shook her head. "No. I've racked my brain trying to visualize it but everything happened so fast. And being separated from my son, well, that made me crazy." Then she added: "If there's one good thing I can say about Alex being deaf, it's that he was lucky enough to not have to hear that sickening sound I heard when the car…" Her hand shot up to her mouth as if trying to stuff the words right back in. But it was too late. They'd spilled out and made one hell of a mess.

Jake excused himself and followed Lydia Marsh's shaky finger to the bathroom. The reflection in the medicine cabinet begged for help. *Pull yourself together, Jakey old boy.* At last, he gave up the battle. He wept for Sheila. He wept for Nikki. He wept for what might have been. But mostly he wept for himself.

CHAPTER TWELVE

Paige McCauley clicked on the windshield wipers. The rain came in spits at first, then hammered the windshield as it fell slantwise from the sky. Raindrops gathered in clusters, clung to the glass like an angry swarm of bees. With a sweep of the wipers, they dispersed and a new swarm assembled.

"How's the leg, honey?" Paige asked.

"Okay, Mommy," Anna said through sniffles. "It just hurts a tiny bit now."

When it rains it pours.

A simple trip to the supermarket had turned into The Day From Hell. For starters, the shopping cart had a bum wheel. Just like last time. Rows and rows of perfectly good carts, and Paige always seemed to find the faulty one. Of course, the wheel didn't act up until it was half filled with colorful boxes and bottles and cans. Damned if she was going to transfer all those groceries.

To make matters worse, Paige ran–literally–into Nan Reilly with her shopping cart. The last person you wanted to run into when you had to be somewhere in the next decade. Nan rambled on in her I-know-something-you-don't-know voice about Liz Brunner's surgery and the alleged affair between Eleanor Lydon and her gynecologist. Paige knew there was a great joke somewhere in that. She came back to Earth when she heard Ben's name.

"Did you know your little Benny has a crush on that Sandra Simmons?"

"No, Nan, I didn't," Paige said.

"Nan rested her hand on Paige's. "Well, I think it's sooo cute!"

Paige pulled her hand away. The reflex startled her as much as it did Nan. "Listen, I've really got to... pick Drew up..."

"Fine," Nan barked. She spun her shopping cart around, all wheels in perfectly good working order Paige noted, and left a trail of anger in the cereal aisle.

Rudeness wasn't Paige's style. But it did get rid of Nan. Hell, maybe she'd try it more often. Paige maneuvered the shopping cart around a corner. Anna shuffled along beside her, gripped Paige's pant leg. The bum wheel jammed. Paige forced it forward. Anna let out a piercing scream.

She'd caught her leg on a metal support jutting out from a frozen foods case. The frantic store manager tried to avoid a potential lawsuit with a chocolate chip cookie from the bakery case. This quieted Anna but the gash looked bad. Two hours and three stitches later, Paige and Anna left the emergency room and headed for home.

Drew traveled south on Route I180. He should have caught up with Ben by now. Unless Ben took Route 9. *The Tunnel. Damn.* He turned the car around.

Where was the turnoff? Trees passed slow motion-like. He was in a dream; the kind where you try to run but go nowhere, all the while knowing some horrific monster is just over your shoulder, waiting to swallow you up.

The sun blinked, its shift nearly over, and then bid Drew farewell as he entered The Tunnel. A car up ahead. He slowed. A woman with pumpkin-colored hair waved a cell phone at him–*where the hell is my phone?*–and signaled that she was okay. Something felt wrong. He rounded a bend and glimpsed a van exiting The Tunnel.

Then it happened. Beads of sweat pushed their way out of his forehead. His hands quivered. Lungs collapsed into one another. Drew slammed on the brakes. He clawed at his chest, half expecting his heart to bust right through and land in his lap.

Work through it. Just like Doctor Pankowski showed you. Capital of Maine. Augusta.

Spell it backwards. A-T-S-U-G-U-A. Capital of Idaho. Boise. Spell it backwards. E-S-I-O-B. Capital of Montana. No fucking idea. Capital of Arkansas. Little Rock. Spell it backwards. K-C-O-R-E-L-T-T-I-L.

Drew got through the whole Eastern seaboard and about half of the Midwest before the attack receded. His heart slowed. Breathing came more easily. He pushed soggy hair off his face, regained his composure, pulled back onto the road. The practice field was just up the road. Ben would be there and everything would be okay.

But Ben was not there. Tommy Andrews bounced a soccer ball off his knee. "Tommy, you seen Ben?"

Tommy shrugged. "No, Mr. McCauley. Everything okay?"

"Yeah, everything's fine. Good luck this weekend."

Tommy nodded. "Tough team but I think we can take them. You coming?"

"Wouldn't miss it for the world. Now get back to practice, you slacker." Tommy waved and jogged off.

Okay, he took I180 after all. Should be pulling up any second.

The sky went gray, then melted into blackness. The rain moved in with a vengeance, pounding the car. Shrieking cheerleaders took cover in a concession stand. As quickly as it came, the storm went, blue skies tucking the clouds away in their back pocket. Drew left the practice field and traveled the length of I180. No Ben. He raced toward home.

CHAPTER THIRTEEN

Paige hunched forward, focused on the centerline between sweeps of the windshield wipers. Her fingers gripped the steering wheel so tightly, she feared they'd fuse themselves to the leather. At last the torrent slowed, the relentless pounding on the roof reduced to a steady din. Then, as if a main valve had been shut off, the rain stopped.

Paige relaxed her grip, eased back in the seat. She called Drew's cell for the third time since leaving the supermarket. Voicemail again. "Damn it, Drew, pick up."

Anna giggled. "Oh, oh, you said a bad word, Mommy."

"Sorry, honey. Mommy won't do it again."

"When are we gonna be home?" Anna asked in that I'm-one-minute-away-from-losing-it tone.

"Almost there. Why don't you read your book?"

Anna was no longer one minute away from meltdown. "I don't WANNA read my book. I WANNA go HOME!"

The throbbing in Paige's head reached a crescendo. She tried to soothe Anna with a song but once Mount Anna erupted, there was no stopping her. A couple of miles to go. Paige had endured Mount Anna for much greater periods of time than this. She could handle this one standing on her head. But, damn, her head pounded.

The sign for Cliffside Drive was a welcome sight. Anna's wailing had reached epic proportions. Paige started down the twisting drive. Anna continued her serenade. They rounded a bend. Paige slammed on the brakes. The seatbelt pinched her chest. She peered out the windshield. She screamed. Anna stopped wailing. Paige looked with horror at the object lying in the driveway.

She screamed again.

Sheer terror propelled Drew, leaving run-through red lights and near misses in his wake. At last, he maneuvered the snaking driveway. He braked hard, narrowly avoiding Paige's car. Paige and Anna stood in front of the car. His wife's eyes were wild.

Drew jumped from the car. "What's wrong?"

Anna tugged at Paige's hand. "Mommy, let go. You're hurting me." Paige released her grip. Anna ran up the driveway.

Paige fell to her knees. "Ben."

Ben's bike lay in a heap in front of the car. The rear wheel was bent, the seat cockeyed. Paige had hit Ben. But where was he?

Drew knelt beside his wife. "Honey, it was an accident. Where is he?"

"Where's who?"

"Ben."

"Do you think I–"

"Well, isn't that–"

"DADDY!"

Drew shot off toward the house. His heart tunneled through his chest.

Anna stood stock-still, her finger directing Drew to a Polaroid snapshot taped to the door.

"No."

Paige came up behind him. "What is it?" She reached for the photo.

"Don't touch it," Drew barked.

Ben. Mouth gagged. Eyes wide with horror. Paige gasped.

Her purse exploded in song. She fumbled for her iPhone. "Hello?" Her eyes met Drew's.

He grabbed the phone. "Who is this?"

The voice was muffled. "Shut up and listen. We have your son. We haven't hurt him. Not yet."

"You son-of-a-bitch! If you lay a finger on him, I'll…"

"QUIET! Listen and listen good. Understand?"

Drew felt his body deflate. "I'm listening."

The voice crackled through the phone again. "You're going to get together two million dollars. That should be pocket change to someone like you. And I think you're smart enough to figure out in what denominations. Then you'll wait for my instructions. And if you bring the cops into this your son will be buried in that soccer uniform of his."

"How do I know he's even alive?"

"A thing called Trust."

"I need time to get that much money together."

There was a pause followed by the man's final comment: "Time is not your friend right now. I'll be in touch."

The cell cried out from Jake's pocket. Jake juggled grocery bags, slid the key into the lock. The phone cried out again. "Hold on." One of the bags slipped from his grasp. The one with the eggs. Jake yanked the cell out of his pocket. "This better be good. You just killed tomorrow's breakfast."

"Jake. It's Drew McCauley."

Drew McCauley? Jake hadn't heard from him in ages. Aside from the sympathy card after Sheila's death. "Drew, what a surprise. How the hell are you?" *Funny, I was just admiring your book collection in a dead woman's apartment.*

"I need to see you right away."

"What is it?"

"Can't talk about it on the phone. Can you meet me?"

"I suppose so, if it's important. What's your address?"

"Not here. Can you meet me at The Black Raven in, say, an hour?"

"Sure," Jake said. "Black Raven. One hour."

"Thanks, Jake," Drew said.

The line went dead. What the hell was that all about? His wife? Kids? Jake was pretty sure he had two. Or was Drew in some kind of trouble himself?

I helped you out once kid. I'll help you out again if I can.

Jake grabbed a fistful of paper towels and mopped up the uncooked omelet running across his foyer.

CHAPTER FOURTEEN

```
Blake Redmond waited until he heard the door
lock. He removed the blindfold and let his
eyes adjust to the dim light that filtered
through a boarded up window.

The small room was musty, like he imagined
his basement would smell, were he ever al-
lowed to go down there. Mother always said
it would do a job on his allergies. She said
that about everything.

He sat on a small lumpy cot. No pillow. No
blanket. Nothing but a pile of books tossed
into a corner. Blake buried his head in his
knees and sobbed.
```

Muffled voices drifted down the hallway, slid under the door. The room was dark but enough light trickled in from an overhead transom for Ben to make out the basic setup of the room. A beat up dresser on one wall. A crooked painting— of what, Ben couldn't tell. He squinted. Maybe a barn in a field? Or a ship on the ocean? That was it, except for the rickety bed he was handcuffed to.

The handcuffs bit at his wrists. His body still ached. He want- ed to sleep but didn't dare. The voices got louder. Ben strained to make out what they were saying. No such luck.

Why him? What did they want? Probably money. Isn't that

what all kidnappers wanted? He knew Dad had a lot of it. At least that's what all the kids at school said. Mom and Dad never talked about it. Except when they lectured him about working hard to get what he deserved. Builds character, he could hear Dad say. Ben would give anything to hear him say that right now.

If it were money they wanted, Dad would pay. And he would be let go at some shopping mall. That's how the kidnappings he'd seen on TV always seemed to work. Except for one thing. In all those TV shows, the kid was always blindfolded. He'd seen their faces. Not long enough to really study them. But long enough to give the cops a pretty good description if he had to.

The door swung open. A dark figure stood in the doorway. Too thin to be the hulk. The man emerged from the darkness. Long hair. Scraggly beard. Jeans, black boots, shirtless. He moved toward Ben.

Ben pushed himself as far back as the cuffs would allow. His eyes attached themselves to the floor. Maybe the man would forget he'd seen his face.

"Look at me, boy."

Ben's eyes remained fixed on the floor.

"I said look at me."

Ben looked up at his captor. With the mess of hair and grimy face, the man looked like someone who has been lost at sea, washed up on a deserted island, a regular old Robinson Crusoe. This Crusoe reeked of beer and cigarettes. A woman appeared in the doorway. The one from The Tunnel. The man turned, revealing a tattoo on his back just below the left shoulder. A black serpent snaking through a human skull. Muscles flexed and the serpent came to life.

"Get out," the man said. The woman stuck out her tongue,

disappeared. Crusoe turned to face Ben. "You do what we say, nobody gets hurt. Understand?"

Then why don't I have a blindfold on?

Ben nodded.

The man smiled. "We'll get along just fine." He moved toward the door. What he said next sent shockwaves through Ben's body. "Your daddy looked just like you when he was fifteen, Ben."

CHAPTER FIFTEEN

Jake entered The Black Raven, an upscale pub he rarely frequented. Leather and scotch hung heavy in the air. He scanned the handsome décor for an old friend he wasn't sure he'd recognize. To his left, four nipped and tucked women chattered mindlessly over glasses of red wine. Probably tossed their brats at their overworked husbands before the poor saps even had a chance to set down their briefcases. Now the hens were crowing over which one had the lousier mate.

"... watches his goddamn football six days a ..."

"... leaves his dirty underwear all over the ..."

"... think he's having an affair ..."

The last snippet piqued Jake's interest. His eyes scanned the busy pub, but his ear kept close to the action. Three of the manicured and pedicured and whatever-else-they-could-cure women pushed their faces closer to the woman whose story obviously beat out their football and laundry woes. She related the sordid details in a hushed tone, forcing Jake to lean his body in.

"... secretary with tits popping out of her blouse ..."

"... business trip, my ass ..."

The woman with the unfaithful old lout (who was probably boffing his secretary in their bed right now while the kids watched age-inappropriate movies on Netflix in the next room) stopped talking and pressed her lips together. Her eyes locked with Jake's. "Enjoying yourself?"

"Sorry, Ma'am," Jake said. "I'm just looking for a friend."

The other vipers pursed their lips together with the precision of synchronized swimmers. Toss him into a tank of hungry sharks and Jake would fare better than with this hairsprayed quartet. They'd need new manicures after clawing his eyes out. The lead viper spit fire at him. "You were just looking to get your rocks off."

Movement at the back of the dimly lit pub distracted Jake from his tongue-lashing. Drew McCauley waved to him. Saved by the bell or, in this case, the hugely successful author. Jake returned the wave and slinked shamefully past the women, their freshly painted claws clicking against the table's polished surface.

"All alike, every last goddamn one of them..."

Jake licked his wounds and made his way to the far corner of the joint. Drew McCauley rose from his chair. An attractive brunette remained seated. What was her name again? Drew was taller than Jake remembered but hadn't lost his youthful looks. "Good to see you," Jake said, embracing his friend. "You look good."

And he did look good. Better than Jake had ever seen him look. Life is good when you're pulling in seven figures. But Jake sensed that if he were to peel back the ruggedly handsome face, he'd find the gawky teenager with bad acne cowering underneath.

"You look good too, Jake," Drew replied. "This is my wife, Paige."

Right. A writer with a wife named Paige. Don't that beat all. "Nice to meet you, Ma'am."

Chestnut hair dripped listlessly down either side of her face. Subtle worry lines edged remarkable emerald eyes. Were it not for her hastily thrown together appearance, Paige McCauley could easily blend in at a Cover Girl convention.

Perfect teeth turned up into a half smile. "Likewise," Paige said. "Drew speaks very highly of you. Said you helped him through a difficult time when he was younger."

Drew's body tensed, his eyes locked on Jake.

She doesn't know. You never told her.

"Yes, you could say that, Ma'am," Jake said.

"Please, call me Paige. Drew told me about your recent loss. I'm very sorry."

"Thank you, Ma'am."

"She must have been very special to you."

Jake nodded. "That she was. And she was one helluva mother too." Those remarkable emerald eyes welled up. "Did I say something to upset you, Ma'am?"

"It's our son," Drew said. He produced the snapshot.

Jake gazed at the horrific photo. In the Age of Super Technology, it amazed him that anyone still owned a Polaroid camera. "When?"

"This afternoon. On his way to soccer practice," Drew said. "They want two million dollars. Jake, he said any cops and they'll kill him." Drew filled Jake in on the rest of the conversation. Then he said, "Tell us what to do."

"You have any other children?"

"Yes. Anna. She's five," Drew said.

"Where is she now?"

"With a friend. She's safe." Drew put his hand over his wife's. "We made sure nobody followed us."

"What makes you think someone would be following you?"

"Someone's been watching us," Paige said. Her eyes darted around, as if that someone was in the pub watching her right now.

"Ben's bike was left in our driveway," Drew added. "Pretty banged up too."

A too-cheerful waitress appeared. Jake ordered coffee all around. When the waitress was gone he said, "Let me call my superior–"

"No!" A delicate hand shot to Paige McCauley's unglossed mouth. "I'm sorry. But he said no police or else…"

Jake took in the seemingly perfect couple seated across from him. Their seemingly perfect world was falling apart right before his eyes. "I really think you need to let pros handle this."

Drew shook his head. "I just want my son back. I'll pay whatever they want."

Still as stubborn as Jake remembered. "Drew, you have to trust me. Can you do that?"

"Here you go." The waitress plunked down three mugs and filled them like a pro, not a drop spilled. Her name was Candy, if the nametag didn't lie. "Anything else?" Candy asked.

Jake smiled. "We're good. Leave the pot?"

Candy blushed. "Sure." She giggled and turned to Drew. "Excuse me…" She tugged at her apron nervously. "You're Drew McCauley, right?"

Drew smiled graciously at his gushing fan. "Yes."

Candy said, "I told my girlfriend it was you. Winner gets their pick of shifts this weekend."

"Looks like we have a winner, Candy," Jake said.

Candy giggled. She'd gone past star-struck straight to stalker. *Just ask for the damn autograph already.*

"Would you mind… I mean could I–"

Go on, ask him.

"–have your autograph?"

Bingo.

Drew patted his shirt. "Sure. Do you have a pen and paper?"

Candy, old pro that she was, pulled a Number Two pencil from her high hair and tore a sheet from her little notepad quicker than a gunslinger at high noon. Drew scribbled with all the neatness of a doctor. Candy tucked the pencil back into her head and said, "Thank you. Is there anything else I can get for you today?"

"We're all set," Jake said, not bothering with pleasantries.

"Okay," Candy said, oblivious to Jake's growing impatience. "I'll be right over there if you need me." She walked away with the pot, returned, set the pot down, giggled, then hurried off.

Jake shook his head. "Bet you get that all the time."

"Naw," Drew said, but Paige's bobbing head told Jake differently. "I don't care how big you are, a writer can walk through Times Square without so much as a second glance. Unless he's King or J.K. Rowling."

"Or the master of suspense, the dashing Drew McCauley," Jake added. Candy cleared a table nearby, eavesdropping. Jake waited until she left, then said: "Now, where was I? Oh yeah–trust. Do you trust me?" Drew nodded. "What about you, Mrs. McCauley?"

Her remarkable eyes searched for an answer. "I don't know." She looked at her husband then locked gazes with Jake. "You really think it's the right thing to do?"

Jake nodded. "I do. But time's ticking."

Paige McCauley stood abruptly. Instinct brought Jake to his feet. "Please," she said, waving him to sit. "I'm just going to the ladies' room." She disappeared into the crowd buzzing around the bar.

Jake listened as Drew offered a detailed account of the day's events. Then Jake grabbed the bull by the horns. "She doesn't know how we met, does she?" he said. Drew's gaze fell to his coffee. "The answer's not in that coffee cup, my friend."

Drew furrowed his brow. His boyish good looks faded before Jake's eyes and a tired old man now stared across the table. "Some skeletons are better left buried."

Jake could still read his old friend like a book. "You think it's him, don't you?"

"No. He's dead, remember?"

"Presumed dead," Jake said. "They only recovered two of the three bodies. Just assumed the other body was swept away in the tide."

Drew lifted his mug with an unsteady hand. "You think it's him, Jake?"

"Naw. Besides, it's no secret that you don't do your grocery shopping with food stamps. Probably some dirtbag looking for a quick payday."

Drew nodded. "Yeah, you're probably right. Anyway, it's been a couple of years since he went missing."

"Here comes your wife." Jake stood. "Listen, we're going to get Ben back. Jot down your phone and address." Drew scribbled on a cocktail napkin adorned with, what else, a black raven. Jake stuffed it into his pocket. He extended a hand to Paige. "Nice to finally meet you," Jake said. "I'll be back in touch as soon as I can."

Paige McCauley's delicate hand gripped Jake's. Its strength surprised him. "Thank you, Detective Hawksworth," she said. She turned to Drew. "Did you tell him about the book?"

"What book?" Jake asked.

"Just a crazy coincidence, is all," Drew said. "The novel I'm working on. It involves a kidnapping."

"Of a young boy," Paige added.

"Who knows about this?" Jake said.

"Only a few people," Drew answered. "My agent. And a couple of people over at the publishing house. These are associates of mine. Friends. People I trust."

"You're right," Jake said. "Probably a weird coincidence. But I'm going to want to talk to these associates of yours just the same. In the meantime, I'll send someone over for the bike."

"You will help us get our son back, won't you?" Paige McCauley asked. She rested a hand on Jake's hand. The strength it had exhibited earlier was gone. Her skin was as smooth as the porcelain dolls Sheila once collected. But she looked far more fragile.

Jake put on his best face. "He's going to be just fine." The weary woman looked as if she almost believed him.

Jake dialed up Frank Geoffreys. Frank's wife answered in her usual cheerful manner. "Hi, Trish. Jake Hawksworth. Listen, I'm sorry to be calling so late but it's rather important. Is Frank there?"

"Hello, Jake," Trish Geoffreys said. "Not a bother at all. I'll see if I can drag his butt off the couch. Hold on. Nice talking to you."

"Same here, Trish." Jake heard muffled voices.

"Jake?" Frank said.

"Sorry to bother you at home like this, Frank."

"Everything all right? Nikki?"

"She's fine. Frank, listen. I have a favor to ask."

"Shoot."

"Do you remember Drew McCauley?"

A long pause. "The writer," Frank said at last. "The one you—what about him?"

"I got a call from him today. Son's been kidnapped. He wants my help, Frank."

"Did you put him in touch with the—"

"He wants me to help him."

"Jake, you're Homicide," Frank said.

"I promised McCauley I'd be there for him."

A loud sigh. "Jake, you have more on your plate than you can handle. And now the Thomas case."

"I'm all over that, Frank. And it'll be a good chance for Henderson to get his feet wet."

"Jake, this is out of your league. Alan Weeks is the best man for this kind of thing." Dead air followed by another sigh. Then: "Here's the deal."

Gotcha.

"Alan Weeks will run this show. If you want to lay low in the background on your own time, and if it's okay with Weeks, I'll allow it. On your own time." That ever-serious Frank Geoffreys tone kicked in. "Understood?"

"Understood. Thanks."

"And Jake, one more thing."

"Yeah, Frank?"

"Weeks gets to call all the shots. Any problems, you're out. Plain and simple. You're to be invisible."

"You'll never even know I was there, Frank. Thanks again. Tell Trish I'm sorry I bothered you."

"Goodnight, Jake."

"Goodnight."

Jake stripped to his boxers and fell heavily onto the bed. That nightcap he promised himself was waiting downstairs. But downstairs was a thousand miles away. His eyes wavered, then snapped shut.

CHAPTER SIXTEEN

The Hostage Rescue Team assembled at the McCauley residence three days before Thanksgiving. Diligent agents buzzed about the house and its perimeter, setting up surveillance, tapping phone lines. All the usual holiday preparations.

Jake gazed out the window. A heavy rain blurred the landscape. A hand touched his shoulder, wrenched him from his stupor.

"Jake."

He turned. "Well, well, look what the cat dragged in. How have you been, Alan?" The two men embraced.

"It's been what, four years?" Special Agent Alan Weeks said.

"Six," Jake said. "You look good." At six-four and then some, Alan was a towering presence. His graying flattop added another two inches to his height and was as starched as his suit. A mile-wide grin washed over his face.

"And you look like you haven't been sticking to that exercise regimen I put you on," Alan joked. Alan was referring to a training program he had created for Jake, which consisted of jogging, weight lifting, and diet. Jake stuck to it the best way he knew how. He jogged to the fridge, lifted whatever food he could find and washed it down with a Diet Coke.

The two men swapped war stories. Alan offered his condolences on Jake's loss. Sheila had been close to Alan's ex-wife when he and Jake both worked out of Precinct 3. So close, in fact, that Sheila knew of Connie's extramarital affairs long before Alan ever suspected a thing. Drew entered the room. Jake waved him over.

"Drew, I'd like you to meet another old friend of mine, Special Agent Alan Weeks." Drew gripped the taller man's hand.

"Call me Alan," Weeks said. Never one for formalities, Jake noted.

"Alan is one of the best," Jake said in the most reassuring voice he could muster. "He's handled many similar cases."

"And how many children have you gotten back alive?" The voice behind them belonged to Paige McCauley. She was at the end of her rope and made no attempt to hide it.

Drew moved toward his wife. "Honey, this is Special Agent Weeks. He's going to help us get Ben back."

Paige pushed Drew's hand away. "He didn't answer my question."

"Paige, please..."

Alan Weeks put up a hand. "It's okay, Mrs. McCauley is right. I didn't answer her question." Alan looked Paige squarely in the eye. Straight shooter all the way. "Ma'am, I'm not going to lie to you. These situations don't always have happy endings. But I can tell you this. We are prepared to take every precaution to ensure your son's safety."

"My wife didn't want you involved," Drew said.

"And you, Mr. McCauley?" Alan asked.

Drew shrugged. "I'm not sure what I think anymore. I just want my son back."

Alan nodded politely. "I understand. But let me assure you, you're doing the right thing. When folks try to handle matters such as these on their own terms, things can sour very quickly."

Jake interrupted. "Drew, it's important that we don't let this leak out. If the press gets hold of this, you may as well send in the clowns because we'll have a three-ring circus on our hands."

"I called Ben's school," Drew said. "Said he has the flu and will be out all week."

"Good," Alan Weeks replied. "We don't need any outside interferences."

"So, what next?" Paige asked.

"We wait," Jake said.

CHAPTER SEVENTEEN

Bud traveled the long narrow hallway to the last door on the right. He unlocked it, pushed it open. The air was damp, coated in mildew and the faint odor of urine. The boy recoiled. Bud tossed a paper bag onto the bed. "Eat."

The boy remained still, eyes fixed on the floor. Bud pulled a cheeseburger out of the bag and held it out. "I said EAT." The boy didn't budge. Bud had never liked kids, not even when he was one himself. And he certainly wasn't going to let himself feel sorry for this snot-nosed brat who, until now, had everything handed to him on a silver platter.

Bud shoved the burger into the boy's face. "Eat it or I'll make you eat it." The boy paused, then snatched it away and put it to his mouth. He sniffed it, took a small bite. "Don't worry," Bud said, "I didn't poison it. Daddy's not gonna pay for a dead kid."

"My dad will give you whatever you want," the kid said. Ketchup hung off his lip. "If you let me go, I promise he will."

Bud roared. "What do I look like, an idiot?" *Don't answer that.* "You're right about one thing. He'll pay, all right."

The kid sat up. "And then he's gonna kick your ass."

"So, you're a tough guy. We'll see how tough you are after a few more days here." *That ought to set the tears rolling.* Instead the kid locked gazes with him. Defiant little bugger. But it sure beat having to deal with a crybaby.

A slamming door. Voices. Bud moved to the door. "You want trouble, you came to the right place," he said and snapped the door shut.

Chance intercepted him in the hallway. "I thought I told you not to talk to him."

Bud brushed by him. "I was just giving him something to eat, is all," Bud said. "If you're afraid I'm going to get all mushy over that kid, you can forget about it. Where's the beer?"

Lynette unpacked groceries and hummed a tune between hits off her cigarette. With that garish tangle of orange hair, she looked like Lucille Ball's ugly stepsister. Her body wasn't half bad if you could get past the face. But that was a big *if*.

"In the fridge," Lynette said. She resumed humming. An old Steely Dan song. What was the name?

It stirred up memories of a better time. Hanging out on A Street with the boys. Those long hot summer nights where you could always find a warm beer and a cold woman. Steely Dan wafting from a cheap transistor. Not a care in the world. And Lisa.

Lisa wasn't like the other girls he'd been with. They were nameless, faceless, wham-bam-thank-you-ma'ams. Not Lisa. She was different. Sure, she had a kick-ass body. But she was smart too. And she actually listened to what Bud had to say. Nobody had ever done that before. Ever.

Bud knew he was nothing to look at. And having dropped out of school midway through his sophomore year of high school, he was no match for her intellect. Still, she wanted to hear what he had to say. Go figure. Life was good. Until the drugs.

He tried to kick the habit. He really did. After all, he finally had something worth staying clean for. In the end, it was the habit that kicked him. Hard. Then, while serving eight months for possession, he got clean and sober. Lisa would be waiting for him. He was sure of it. And life would be good again.

"Here, catch!" Lynette shrieked.

An economy pack of toilet paper hit Bud in the face. Lynette cackled like the beady-eyed bird she was. Bud stared at the twelve rolls of toilet paper wrapped up in a neat package at his feet. Perfect. After all, his life was one heaping pile of shit.

CHAPTER EIGHTEEN

"Here we go!" Alan Weeks called out. Drew picked up the landline. Jake bemused himself that someone other than himself still had a landline.

"Hello."

"Got the money?" The voice was harsh, muffled. Like one of those voice changers you hear on the radio.

"I'm working on it, but–"

"How many badges you got looking at you?"

"None. I just want my son. You'll get your money."

"It better not be marked. None of that exploding dye shit." The line went dead.

A burly FBI agent with a thick unibrow and do-it-yourself buzz cut entered the room and said, "We've got the number."

"Great," Jake said. He marveled at how easy it was to trace numbers in this modern age. He scribbled the number down on a square of paper and looked at it curiously. "Why does this number look familiar?"

Drew glanced a look. "Because it's mine."

"What are you talking about?"

"It's my number. My phone's been missing for days." Fear exploded in Drew's eyes. "Jake, how did he get my phone?"

"Easy, Drew. Keep it together. For Ben. In the meantime, we'll try to zone in on your cell." Jake looked at his watch. Three minutes to noon. "How goes the money situation?"

"Almost all set," Drew said calmly, though he was visibly shaken.

Paige put a hand on her husband's. "Drew, we really should

call and check on Anna. She's going to be upset if she doesn't hear from us."

"Jake, is it okay if we call Anna?" Drew said.

"We've got to leave the line open."

"We can use my cell," Paige said.

"That okay, Jake?" Drew asked.

Jake nodded. He watched the couple rush off, the thought of speaking to one of their children bringing them a rush of relief.

"Hey, Jake."

Jake flinched.

"Sorry, big guy," Alan Weeks said.

"I guess I'm just a little jumpy right now. So, what do you think?"

Alan frowned. "If you're asking if I think we're going to get the kid back, between you and me, I don't know."

"That's not an option," Jake said. "I'm the one who talked them into this." He glanced across the room. Drew and his wife huddled together, speaking in hushed tones to their daughter. "Like I said, that is not an option."

Jake surveyed the room. It more closely resembled a museum than a home where children lived. Any warmth this house once had was gone, swallowed up by the gleaming mahogany floors and perfectly plumped pillows standing at attention on the sofa.

In fact, a long narrow table crammed with photos held the only evidence that a family lived here. Ben in his soccer uniform. Anna in a ballet costume. Drew and Ben atop a mountain. A close-up of Paige, stunning even with her tongue sticking out at the camera. A family shot taken on the beach, four brilliant grins beaming at Jake. Just your average ordinary family.

"Like that picture of Paige?"

Jake turned. The McCauleys' faces were suddenly more

alive, as if the mere sound of Anna's voice had recharged them. Jake's eyes fell again to the photographs. "Yeah, that's my favorite, I think. How's Anna?"

"Scared," Drew said. "But Thora–she's my agent and a close friend–is great with kids and is keeping her thoroughly entertained. Funny, Thora scares the living daylights out of most adults, but kids seem to adore her."

"Glad to hear she's in good hands," Jake said. "Which reminds me, I'd like to speak to Thora and anyone else who has knowledge of that book you're writing."

"Right, I almost forgot," Drew said.

"Would you like to see a copy of the book, Jake?" Paige asked. "I mean, would it help at all?"

"Can't hurt, I guess. And I have read all the others. It would be something to see Drew McCauley's latest masterpiece of suspense before the masses get their grubby paws on it."

"I only have the one printout," Drew said.

Paige frowned. "Drew, Jake's not going to steal your idea." She rolled her incredible eyes. "Drew is superstitious about his working draft. Nobody's supposed to read it, except for me, of course." Her sardonic tone hung uncomfortably in the air.

"She's my toughest critic," Drew said.

"And your biggest fan, I gather," Jake added. Paige smiled a half smile that dissolved into a half frown.

"You're right. I'm being silly," Drew said. "Of course you can take it. If there's even the slightest chance that it could help get Ben back, that's all that matters. I'll go get it." He rushed off, muttering to himself.

Jake turned to Paige. "How are you holding up?"

She shrugged. "Inside I'm screaming. Drew always says I'm the glue that holds this family together. More like the Crazy Glue, I guess." She smiled but Jake could see the pain in her eyes.

"So, is it good?" Jake asked.

"Is what good?"

"The book."

"Oh, that. Well, I haven't read the whole thing yet," Paige said. "Drew likes to spoon-feed me little bits at a time. He always leaves me dangling at the cliffhangers. Which is kind of exciting, I suppose. Wondering what's next to come. Though, I'm not sure I want to know what comes next in this one."

"What do you mean?"

"Well, this is the first time a child has played the victim and it makes me a bit uneasy," Paige said. "Sure, he's killed off plenty of people in his other books. But they were adults and usually deserving of their fates. This one, it just–"

"You're not giving away all my secrets, are you?" Drew said.

"You know I hate it when you sneak up behind me like that," Paige snapped. The temperature dropped a few notches. "I was just telling Jake about the book."

Drew's halfhearted laugh and downward glance only added to Jake's suspicions that this marriage was precisely how he liked his scotch, old and on the rocks. "Like I said," Drew stammered, "she's my toughest critic."

"Your prettiest too," Jake said, hoping to cut through the tension, though he doubted a chainsaw would do the trick. Paige's cheeks flooded with a healthy shade of pink.

Drew handed Jake a hefty stack of paper. "Read it and weep, my friend," he said. "Preferably not the latter."

Jake looked at the cover page. "*Snatched?* Catchy."

"Well," Drew said, "if Thora has her way, that title will be changing. Personally, I think it has a nice ring to it."

Agent Gil Burrows approached. Jake's dislike for Burrows was no secret. Jake could overlook some things. Incompetence was not one of them.

"Jake," Burrows said, "some woman named Carla Mendez just called. Says she has some vital information on the Thomas case. Said she'll be waiting for you."

Jake nodded. "Thanks, Gil." He turned to the McCauleys. "Listen, I need to take this. I'll be back as soon as I can. In the meantime, you'll be in good hands with Alan."

"We understand," Drew said. His wife's halfhearted nod shared his sentiments.

Jake patted the manuscript. "A little light reading for later. Hang in there. And, do me a favor, will you?"

"What's that?" Drew asked.

"Don't let Alan know you gave this to me," he said, patting the manuscript again. "Let's let him think he's in charge."

Paige leaned forward and kissed Jake lightly on the cheek. "Thanks for everything," she said.

The kiss lingered on Jake's burning cheek as he stepped out into the cold. This woman he barely knew was putting all her faith in him. He rubbed at his cheek, trying to erase the hope, the trust that this kiss represented. Because he wasn't sure he could fulfill the expectations locked inside it.

CHAPTER NINETEEN

"Where the hell is he?" Bud asked.

Lynette snapped her chewing gum. "Said he had to go out and take care of some things."

"What things?"

"Didn't say."

Lynette snapped her gum again. One of the 1001 habits she had that made Bud's skin crawl. He wanted to take that gum and wrap it around her neck a few hundred times. "I don't like this sneaking behind our backs shit."

Lynette cackled. "Afraid he's going to run off and leave you stuck with me?"

"Don't flatter yourself," Bud said. "I just think we should know everything that's going on, is all. Like, when are we going to set up the drop? I want this over so I can get the hell out of here."

"Why, got a hot date with your right hand? Or is it your left?" Lynette twirled the wad of gum around her finger, then jammed it back into her mouth. "Relax. It'll all be over soon. You'll get your money, we'll get rid of the kid, and you and me won't have to live under the same roof no more."

"What do you mean, get rid of the kid?"

"I meant let him go."

"You said get rid of him."

"Did I?"

"Chance said nobody was going to get hurt."

Lynette swung her garish hair from side to side. "All of a sudden we've grown a conscience?" She smirked. Another of those 1001 habits.

"Listen, you bitch!" The smirk folded up into the ugly crater. The bird cringed. "Kidnapping is one thing. But I'm not going to have any part in hurting a kid. You got that?" Bud moved closer with each word.

Lynette giggled. "Cool your jets. Nobody's going to get hurt. I'm just messing with you. Why don't you sit down in that chair and let ol' Lynette give you a backrub?" She slinked toward him.

Bud pushed her away and yanked open the door to the fridge. "Great, no beer. Just my luck." He reached for his jacket.

"You know the rules," Lynette said. "Chance says nobody goes anywhere without his say-so."

"Is that so?"

"Uh-huh."

"Well, I want beer." Bud headed for the door. Lynette came at him, nails at the ready.

"Chance says NO ONE LEAVES THIS HOUSE!" She clawed at Bud's face.

Bud had been taught to never hit a woman. But since when had he followed the rules? He backhanded her.

The bird held a shaky hand to her face, redness already taking shape on her sallow cheek. Her eyes alternated between anger and disbelief. "When Chance hears about this, he's..."

"HEY!"

Bud turned toward the silhouette framed by the doorjamb.

"If we're going to kill each other, how are we going to get this deal done?" Chance said.

Bud's brain couldn't believe what his eyes were processing. "What the...?"

CHAPTER TWENTY

Jake tossed Drew's manuscript onto the passenger seat and headed down the McCauley's endless driveway. For all that they had, Jake was sure they'd give it up in a heartbeat to see their son again.

He wondered what earth-shattering news Carla Mendez had for him. The only thing she had given them was a name, and a nickname at that. If it even was the right name. Her description to the sketch artist was sketchy at best. In the end, the rendering wound up looking remarkably similar to the Charlie Manson magazine cover she had spoken of.

Jake dialed up Kyle Henderson. "Meet me over at your girlfriend's place."

Pause. Then: "My what, Jake?"

"Carla Mendez's place."

"What's up, Jake? She remember something else?"

Jake laughed. "Something *else?* I don't think that woman would remember it was Christmas if the fat man fell down her chimney. Probably nothing. I'll see you there in a bit."

"Not if I see you first," Kyle said.

Jake's thoughts drifted to Nikki. And Thanksgiving. It was going to be a tough one. Sheila had always made a big deal of the holidays, but Thanksgiving was her favorite. She went overboard, cooking a feast large enough to serve the Mormon Tabernacle Choir and their extended families' families. Not that Jake ever complained. He couldn't get enough of his wife's famous cooking.

As luck would have it, he and Nikki had been spared the annual trip to Sheila's Aunt Sophie's in upstate New York.

Apparently, her hemorrhoids were acting up. Ironic. A pain in the ass with a pain in the ass.

He thought of skipping the holiday altogether this year, but Nikki would have none of it. Jake decided they'd have a small dinner for two. He'd take her someplace nice. Then she'd dropped the bombshell.

Her friend Chip–

What the hell kind of name is Chip?

–wasn't going home for the holiday break, and would Jake mind terribly if he joined them for Thanksgiving dinner? The idea made Jake uncomfortable but, then again, he ought to see what this Chip guy was all about before things got too serious. So, there you had it. A cozy dinner for three. Sure beat Aunt Sophie's hemorrhoids.

Jake pulled up to Carla Mendez's apartment building. No sign of Kyle. Jake climbed the steps and rang the bell. No response. Again. Nothing. He headed down the steps. A voice crackled over the intercom.

"Who is it?" Carla's shaky voice spit out.

Jake moved back up the steps. "Mrs. Mendez, it's Detective Hawksworth. Jake Hawksworth."

"Detective Hawksworth, what a pleasant surprise! Won't you come up?"

Surprise? Jeesuz, she doesn't even remember she called me.

Carla buzzed Jake in and met him on the second floor landing. "Why, Detective, it's so nice to see you."

"Excuse me, Mrs. Mendez, but you sound as though you're surprised to see me."

Carla Mendez furrowed her ancient brow. "Shouldn't I be, young man?"

Jake tried to contain his anger. "Mrs. Mendez, you asked that

I rush right over. Well, here I am."

Carla Mendez looked first at the ceiling, then at the floor, then directly into Jake's eyes. "I did no such thing, young man."

Jake felt his face flush. "Look, Mrs. Mendez, I'm really busy and I don't have time for games."

Carla Mendez was a wounded kitten in the middle of the road. And Jake was the eighteen-wheeler bearing down on her. Her eyes welled up. "Is that what you think, Detective? I'm just some lonely old lady with nothing better to do than call the cops for fun?"

Kyle Henderson thundered up the staircase. "Jake, what's up?"

"Mrs. Mendez says she never called."

"I didn't!" The old woman's voice was an unpleasant mix of surprise and hysteria.

"Kyle, I've gotta go," Jake said, making no attempt to hide his anger. "Can you make sure she's okay?"

"Sure, Jake."

"Thanks. I've got to get back to the McCauleys. Call you later."

Jake descended the stairs, leaving his partner to deal with the blubbering old woman. A rush of cold air welcomed him as he exited the stifling heat of the old building.

He settled into the warmth of his car and reached under the seat. He uncapped the bottle and pressed it to his lips. The whiskey soothed his throat. He closed his eyes and sat back. Picked feverishly at his right thumb until he broke skin. It hurt. But it relaxed him.

Maybe he'd been a little too hard on the old gasbag. She couldn't help it if she was senile. But dammit, he didn't have time for this shit. Kyle would smooth things over. Like he always did. And Mr. Jack Daniels would smooth things over here.

Like he always did.

Jake took a swig from the bottle, capped it and returned it to its hideaway. He started up the street. A large gangly dog appeared from nowhere. Jake braked hard. The manuscript riding shotgun spilled forward. The dog gave Jake an if-I-had-a-middle-finger-I'd-use-it glare, then trotted off.

Jake pulled over. He swept up the scattered sheets. Page numbers. Good. He began sorting the pages. Something caught his eye. Ice poured into his spine. The name danced across the page.

```
The leggy blonde pressed her body against
Chance's. Her fingers roamed across his
chest, down his stomach. She fumbled with
the belt buckle and unzipped him. They fell
onto the bed. Chance tore her blouse off and
groped for her breasts.

She said, "Why do they call you Chance?"

He smiled and said, "Because you're taking a
chance if you get mixed up with me."
```

Jake reread the passage. The initial conversation with Carla Mendez echoed in his head, pingponging off his eardrums.

"I remembered the name. It was Chance."
"What kind of a name is that?"
"I asked Donna the same thing. You know what she said?"
"What, Ma'am?"
"She said you're taking a chance if you get involved with him."

Jake turned the car around and raced toward Carla's.

CHAPTER TWENTY-ONE

"Are we good to go?"

"Yes," Drew said.

"Good. Now listen up, because I'm only going to say this once. Put the money in a duffel bag. I assume you have one of those lying around?"

"I think so–yes," Drew said. He wished Jake were here right now. Alan Weeks and his team seemed like decent enough guys. But did they really have Ben's best interest at hand?

The voice on the other end of the phone–no longer *his* phone but an untraceable burner phone–was quick and firm. "I'll call you back." The line went dead.

Drew looked at his wife. She'd aged ten years in two days. And she was still a vision of beauty. He didn't have to ask her what she was thinking. Her eyes held the answer. "Agent Weeks," Drew said, "I'm beginning to think this whole thing was a mistake."

Weeks brushed a hand across the silver flattop. "You have to trust us."

"Why? I don't even know you. Do you even care about my son or is this just another notch in your holster?" Drew knew he was out of line. And it felt good. He was sick of doing everything by the book all the time. Ben was alone and scared somewhere. If he was even still alive. To hell with right and wrong. To hell with Alan Weeks. And to hell with Jake for not being here.

The phone rang. Again. "Are you going to answer it?" Weeks asked.

Paige swatted Drew's arm. "Drew, get the phone." He didn't

budge. She said, "Either you get it or I will." Drew snatched it up.

"Did I catch you at a bad moment?"

"Just tell me what you want me to do."

"Great, a team player. Okay, listen up. Take the money to Southside Mall. Should be full of mothers with small children getting an early jump on their Christmas shopping. Keep that in mind in case you're thinking of straying from the plan. All those babies in strollers. Pity if they ended up missing out on Christmas."

"I get the picture. Then what?" Drew asked.

"There's a pay phone to the right of the information booth. Can you believe it? They still have pay phones at that shitty old mall! Wait there for my next call. In twelve minutes." *Click.*

Twelve minutes. Could they even get to the mall that quickly? And what if he refused to go? What would they do? Kill Ben? *Do I really want to take the chance?*

Weeks barked orders to his men. He gripped Drew by the arm. "We have to move," Weeks said. "Mrs. McCauley, you'll be safe here."

Things were moving too quickly. Drew needed time to think. But there was no time. He had about eleven minutes to get to that phone. He kissed Paige and rushed out the door on Alan Weeks's heels.

CHAPTER TWENTY-TWO

Paige paced the living room. What if Drew didn't get there in time? What if he did and the kidnapper never called? What if the guy got the money but decided not to return Ben? *What if Ben's already...?*

"Mrs. McCauley?" It was Special Agent Gil Burrows. "Are you okay?"

"Do you mean since you asked me ten minutes ago?"

Burrows smiled. "You've made your point," he said. "I'll be in the other room if you need anything." He appeared unfazed, turned and left. Probably used to dealing with whacked-out mothers on the edge.

Paige downed her coffee. How many cups was that? Six? Seven? Who the hell was counting? She plunked herself down in the comfort of her favorite chair. She tried to remember her last conversation with her son. Something about his last soccer game and would Dad be able to make it? Though Ben never said it, Paige knew his father's absences deeply affected him. Ben would casually scan the stands, pretending not to care. But Paige knew behind the stoic expression was a boy ready to explode. And she'd be the one left to clean up the mess.

Why hadn't Weeks called in yet? It had been more than an hour since they'd gone. Something was wrong. She knew. Just like, at age sixteen, she knew something had happened to her best friend, Sharon Fallon, that hot summer day in July of 1991. They'd planned on meeting at the bridge and biking over to the beach. Though she'd waited nearly two hours, Paige had known, had actually felt, that Sharon was dead five minutes past her scheduled arrival time. It wasn't until later that her parents confirmed what she had already known. Sharon had tried to beat a commuter train across the tracks at Sheffield's Crossing. Probably hurrying so she wouldn't catch the Rage of Paige for being late as usual.

A phone rang. Two more times. Why wasn't anyone answering the damn thing? "Agent Burrows, you might want to answer..." Paige stopped. Her eyes locked on the purse tossed carelessly on a table. Her iPhone. She lunged for it.

Please don't hang up. "Hello?"

"Paige."

"Drew?"

"Yeah. Listen to me."

"Drew, why are you calling me like this? You sound funny. Is everything okay?"

"Slow down. Everything went as planned. I need to talk to you. Alone."

"What do you mean? Where?"

"Meet me at the Seaview Motel over in Saugus."

"I can barely hear you. Where's Weeks?"

"I ditched him."

"What? Why? Drew, I don't under–"

"–Seaview Motel. I'm under the name Marshall Bingington." Marshall Bingington was the name of the protagonist in *Forbidden*, Drew's first novel.

"Now? But I can't just..."

"I'll be waiting." *Click.*

What did he expect her to do, just walk right out the front door and say she was going for a gallon of milk?

"Mrs. McCauley?"

Paige spun around. "Yes?" Her heart pounded in her eardrums.

Agent Burrows eyed her cell. "Did you just get a call on that?"

Think fast. "Yes. My mom. You know, the usual mother-daughter stuff."

Burrows frowned. He wasn't buying it. Could he see the sweat beads she felt popping up on her forehead? Someone called from the other room. "Stay here," he said. "I'll be right back."

Paige reached into her bag for her car keys. No, they'd see her trying to leave. She knew pretty much where the agents outside were stationed. Getting past them shouldn't be a problem. Once she made it to the tree line, she'd walk the perimeter of the property until she got to the main road. Then she'd call for an Uber. Drew must have good reason for ditching the feds and wanting her to do the same. She slipped out the back door.

CHAPTER TWENTY-THREE

Jake entered Carla's apartment building to find his partner bounding down the narrow staircase two steps at a time.

"You're a brave man, showing your face back here," Henderson said. "The old coot is furious."

"Give it a rest. I know who killed Donna Thomas."

"You do?"

"Well, not exactly," Jake said. "But I'm pretty sure the guy who did this is the same guy who took the McCauley kid."

"Jake, what are you saying?"

Jake shook his head. "I don't believe it myself. But some co-incidences are too coincidental to be coincidences."

"Huh?"

Jake handed his partner the manuscript page. "I need to get back into that apartment."

Carla Mendez fumbled with the set of keys. "I accept your apology, Detective," she said. "But you really should work on your manners. Ah, this is the one." Jake pulled away the yellow tape and entered apartment 2B.

"Thank you, Mrs. Mendez," Jake said in the gentlest voice he could muster. "We'll let you know when we're through." He handed Kyle a pair of gloves.

"What are we looking for, Jake?" Kyle asked. "C.S.U.'s been through this place with a fine-toothed comb."

"Maybe not fine enough," Jake said. "I think this guy was staying here with Donna Thomas." He motioned to the book-case. "Anything strike you as funny?"

Kyle studied the bookcase and its contents. "Miss Thomas wasn't exactly into the classics," he said.

"What else?"

"Well, there are a whole bunch of McCauley's books here."

"Bingo. Anything else about them?"

Kyle shrugged.

Jake ran his hand across the spines. "Notice how perfectly aligned they are."

"I don't get you, partner," Kyle said. "So, she was a neatnik."

Jake clapped his hands together. "But that's just it. Look around. The lady made Oscar Madison look neat."

"Who's Oscar Madison?"

"Never mind. Look at all the other books. They're a mess. But not McCauley's books. They're perfect. Even alphabetized."

"And talk about coincidences," Kyle said. "One of them even has the guy's name in the title." He rubbed a gloved finger across the book's spine.

Chance Encounter.

"Well, whattayaknow," Jake said. He pulled the book from its home between *Alibis All Around* and *Forbidden* and opened it. The inside of the book had been hollowed out. Scraps of paper fluttered to the floor.

Jake frowned at his partner. "Fine-toothed comb, huh?" He knelt to the floor and riffled through the Post-Its, file cards and folded up sheets of paper scribbled with notes. "Unbelievable."

"What is it, Jake?"

"Everything you ever wanted to know about Drew McCauley and his family. Their schedules. Even Drew's shirt size. This guy's done his homework."

"I guess you should thank Mrs. Mendez for calling you over here in the first place," Kyle said.

"She never called," Jake said. "I think he wanted me to find this. It's part of his sick little game."

"Jake, you talk like this guy knows you."

Jake nodded. "I believe he does."

CHAPTER TWENTY-FOUR

```
Blake knew he should try to find a way to es-
cape. He wasn't tied up. He was free to move
about the room. Instead, he just sat there.

The door. He hadn't even checked it to see if
it was locked. He should at least do that.

He rose from the bed and moved toward the
door. He reached out and gripped the knob.
Ice cold. Turn it. Go on, you big baby! But
what if they're waiting on the other side?
```

Ben's eyes traveled the length of the metal headboard he was handcuffed to. It curved and curled. He moved his arm up and around, following the shape of the metal frame until he reached the midpoint. Here the metal was thinner and soldered together. And old and rusty. He just might be able to loosen it.

He worked the joint as quietly as he could, rubbing the handcuffs back and forth across it. His arm tired quickly and the cuff chafed his wrist until it bled. At last, the frame started to loosen! He pushed and pulled and scraped. His wrist ached. A little more. The joint snapped.

Panic washed over him. What if they walked in right now? He looked up at the transom above the bed. If he stood on top of the headboard he could probably reach it. But would the rickety frame support his weight? Only one way to find out.

Ben slipped the cuff through the crack and heaved himself

up on top of the frame, distributing his weight the best that he could. The frame creaked. But it held. He grabbed the window crank and hoisted himself up. The panes were thickly coated with grime. He swiped at the glass. Daylight laser-beamed him.

His eyes gradually adjusted to the light. He could make out trees. A roofline in need of repair. Part of a sign emerged from behind the roof. Worn out green letters. Curly letters. The sun flickered like a candle in a breeze, making it impossible to make out the letters. At last, the sun slipped behind a cloud, giving Ben the break he needed.

GETY FROGGY.

In green curly letters. Why did it seem so familiar? He'd seen it before. With Anna.

Daddy, I want to go on the Fidgety Froggy! Right now!

The Fidgety Froggy! A babyish ride he wouldn't be caught dead on. He was at Clearview Amusement Park. Dad had taken them here two summers ago the week they went camping. On the only day it didn't rain, and right before it closed down for good. Ben remembered how upset Anna Banana had been when she found out the park was closing.

I want to ride on the Fidgety Froggy! Don't let it go bye-bye!

The window was small but he bet he could squeeze through it. When the time was right. Muffled laughter drifted under the door. He lowered himself down, looped the handcuff back through the metal framework, and adjusted it so the split was undetectable.

His eyelids were heavy, heavier than he could ever remember. He needed to sleep. But what if the frame pulled apart and they walked in? He had to stay awake. The room got fuzzy. Ben closed his eyes. The Sandman had won.

CHAPTER TWENTY-FIVE

Jake dialed the McCauley residence. Agent Gil Burrows picked up after one ring. "Gil, you know the drill," Jake said. "McCauley's supposed to answer."

"And if he was here, he probably would," Burrows said. "They're making the drop."

"Damn." Jake had promised Drew and Paige he'd be there for them. "You talk to Weeks yet?"

"Not yet. Should be calling in any time now."

"Where's it going down?"

"Southside Mall."

"Listen, I want you to patch me through to Weeks. I need to talk to McCauley. But first let me talk to Mrs. McCauley."

"She's gone."

"What do you mean, she's gone? A whole goddamn team watching her and you let her waltz out the door?"

"Back off," Burrows said. "We're in charge here, not you."

"And a fine job you're doing."

"Screw you, Jake. Maybe I'll give Geoffreys a call and see what he has to say."

Play their game. "I'm sorry, Gil. I was out of line."

"Way out of line."

Jake couldn't afford enemies right now. "You're right, Gil. I guess the pressure's just getting to me. Can I ask you for a favor?"

Burrows puffed loudly. "What?"

"Can you tell me where you think Mrs. McCauley may have gone?"

"How the fuck should I know? She got a call. Said it was her mother. A couple of minutes later she was gone."

Jake reached for the bottle under the seat. Empty. "Okay, Gil."

Silence. Then: "We're trying to locate her," Burrows said. "As soon as I know, you'll know."

"Appreciate that. In the meantime, I need you to put me through to Weeks." *Kill 'em with kindness.* "Please."

CHAPTER TWENTY-SIX

The Uber pulled up to the Seaview Motel. "Enjoy yourself, miss," the driver said. Paige thanked him and slid out. The car sped off, kicking up dust that hung in the frigid air.

Paige surveyed the place. Listless paint clung to rotted shingles. Forgotten hedges shrouded cracked, grime-slicked windows. What the hell was Drew thinking choosing this place? She'd heard stories about the "No Tell Motel." Prostitutes. Illicit affairs. Drug deals. If those walls could talk, a lot of high-powered businessmen would be doing some fast talking of their own. Why would Drew come here?

Is he familiar with the place?

She entered the motel's lobby, as spacious as a broom closet. Faux-mahogany paneling made it feel half that size. The pungent smells of cheap cigarettes and urine attached themselves to the paneling, burrowed into the moldy carpeting. The man behind the desk looked up from his skin magazine and smiled. If four teeth constituted a smile. This place was chock-full of clichés. Probably why Drew liked it so much.

"What can I do you for?"

"I'm here to meet somebody."

"Course you are. Ain't we all?" He snorted.

"It's not what you think."

Four Teeth leaned forward. He reeked of month-old beer and week-old perspiration. Or was it the other way around? "Don't worry," he said. "Your secret's safe with me." He snorted again.

"What room is Marshall Bingington in?"

Four Teeth leaned closer. "He your boss, Ma'am?"

"Listen..." She stopped. *Speak his language.* "You're a smart guy," she said. "Want to know what I have to do to earn my bonus?" The man snorted, brought his face inches from hers. A dog waiting for that steak to fall off the grill. "Closer." She put her lips to his ear. "Really want to know?" He nodded. "BE ON TIME! Now what room is he in?"

Four Teeth jerked back and nearly fell off his stool. Paige waited for him to go off on her. Instead, he smiled and said: "Room 103, Ma'am."

She paused at the door. What if the news was bad? If something had gone wrong, he would have told her on the phone. Unless the news was so bad it could only be said face to face. She knocked on the door.

A muffled voice. "Come in. It's open."

Paige let her eyes adjust to the darkness. Drew sat on the bed, hands buried in his hair. Paige fumbled for a light switch.

"Leave it off."

Paige rushed to his side. "Drew, are you okay?" She touched his shoulder. He flinched. "What's wrong?" Fear gripped her, squeezed every inch of her body.

His face turned upward, but the darkness erased his features. "Sorry to worry you," he said. "It's done. They promised to release Ben by this evening. But I just couldn't go home. Not yet."

Paige sat down beside him. "Do you think we made the right decision?" she asked.

"You mean the money?" he said.

"No. I don't care about the money. I mean getting Jake and his men involved. I mean, how much do you really trust him?" No response. Paige felt her muscles tense, as if they were being tightened by the turn of a crank. "You do trust him, don't you?"

His tender hand reassured her. "Of course I do. Don't you?"

"I don't know a thing about him," she said, "other than the fact that he helped you through a difficult time when you were a kid. Anyway, how did you manage to give Weeks the slip?"

"I could ask you the same question." He turned and kissed her. Hard. Ran a hand over a breast that hadn't been touched in what seemed like forever.

Paige felt that crank turn another notch.

"What's wrong?" he asked.

"I just don't think this is an appropriate time. Our son is God-knows-where and we're sitting in a roach-infested motel like a couple of high school kids. We should get back before they start wondering where we are."

He cradled her face in his hands. "I'm scared." He broke down.

He was supposed to be the shoulder for her to cry on. She stroked his hair. "I'm sorry, Drew. I know this has been tough on you. On all of us." She pulled his face to hers. Their kisses were manic, desperate. Who was she kidding? She needed this as much as he did.

He eased her back on the bed, his weight pressing down on her. His touch sent shockwaves through her. It had been months since they'd made love. Maybe it was the strain of the book. The kids. Or perhaps they'd just grown apart. She was as much to blame as he was. Maybe more. Now some maniac was threatening to tear her family apart. She was not about to let that happen. Not to her family.

"I love you," she said. "I always have. Even if it hasn't appeared that way lately."

"Show me."

They undressed in record time. Drew's body felt solid. He'd been working out religiously over the past few months. So much so that Paige had begun to worry that there might be someone else in the picture. Ben flashed through her mind. This was wrong. So wrong. But she couldn't stop herself.

His thrusts were deep, rough. Too rough. But she was on another planet. This was not the Drew she knew. But she liked it. And missed it. She clawed at his back. He moaned softly. They came together, a rekindling of sorts. Everything was going to be okay. She would keep her family together. That she was certain of.

They lay still, their low breathing playing a quiet duet. Paige waited for the silence to be disrupted by a headboard banging against their wall, a perk one would expect in a classy joint like this. The disruption never came, leaving Paige feeling oddly cheated. "I think we should bring Anna home," she said.

"Do you think it's safe?" he asked.

"The place is like Fort Knox. I can't pee without Burrows or one of his pals walking in on me. I miss her, Drew."

He brushed a hand across her cheek. "I miss her, too. But I think we should wait until we know it's safe. You think she's okay?"

Paige laughed. "I'd be more worried about Thora if I were you. Anna probably has her running ragged." She fell back onto the pillow. She thought about the lewd things that had taken place right where she lay. "Anyway, you're probably right."

"Of course I'm right." He kissed her and rose. "We'd better get back."

Paige nodded. A sense of security washed over her. Drew moved to the bathroom and clicked the light on.

Paige sat up. "What the hell did you go and do that for?"

"Do what?" he said. The dull light played across the ripples in his back.

"You know damn well what I'm talking about. What would ever possess you to do a stupid thing like that? You know how much I hate those things."

"Like I said, we'd better get back," he repeated. Paige stared with disgust at the tattoo, just below the left shoulder. A serpent, snaking through a human skull.

CHAPTER TWENTY-SEVEN

Blake Redmond wondered how many days he had been in this awful place. Three? Four? Two weeks?

He shivered and pulled the musty blanket over his legs. His breathing was labored. He really needed his Puff-Puff. Should he tell them about his asthma?

He'd be no good to them dead. He closed his eyes and concentrated on his breathing.

It was time. Ben slipped the handcuffs through the crack in the headboard and straddled the bed frame. He reached for the window handle and turned it clockwise. Nothing. Probably rusted shut. He turned harder. Still nothing. He widened his stance on the rusty heap and, with both hands, attacked the handle. It moved. Just a little. But it moved. He put everything he had into it. The window creaked open an inch.

The cold air felt good on his face. He studied the window. Fully open, he could definitely squeeze through. Then he'd be home free. Wait till he told Anna Banana that he'd seen the Fidgety Froggy.

Voices.

Ben frantically turned the crank counterclockwise until the window met its seal.

Voices. Right outside the door.

He jumped down from the frame.

I'm dead.

Keys jingling.

I'll never make it.

He looped the cuff back through the cracked rod–

almost there

–and slid a shaky hand up and around the curved iron frame, which seemed to have more twists and turns than before.

Key sliding into lock.

Made it!

Ben looked up at the transom. His handprint. Clearly stamped on one of the dusty panes! The door opened.

Don't look up!

A man entered. It was his father.

"Dad!" *Why does he look so angry? Aren't you happy to see me? How did you find me?* "Dad, what's wrong? Did the cops get the bad guys?" *Why won't you look at me?*

Dad opened a small black bag and pulled out a hypodermic needle. "Dad, what are you doing?" The man smiled at him. He looked like Dad. But this was not his father. The man moved toward him. The hulk appeared in the doorway.

"Hold him still," his father's clone said. The hulk rushed forward and pressed his weight down on Ben.

"You're not my Dad!"

The clone raised the needle to Ben's arm and said, "Nighty-night, Benny Boy."

CHAPTER TWENTY-EIGHT

The McCauley home was a tempest of emotion. Perspiration oozed from its walls, nerves rattled its windowpanes. Its foundation cracked, its support system weakened, it wavered precariously in the path of the approaching storm.

Drew tried frantically to locate his missing wife. Alan Weeks barked at his team in an adjoining room. Jake paced the living room. He'd give his left nut for a drink right now. Why the hell hadn't the kidnappers shown up for the drop? Maybe they got scared. Or maybe they knew they were being set up.

Drew moved toward Jake, purpose in his step. He looked like hell. "Paige's mom never talked with her today," he said.

"We'll find her, Drew."

"Where could she be? And where the hell were you when we needed you?" Drew crumbled. "I'm sorry–I didn't mean that."

Jake wrapped his arms around his friend and pulled him close. Just like he had when the verdict came down all those years ago. "Drew, there's something I need to tell you. Have a seat." Drew sat without objection. "You know that call I went out on?" Drew nodded wearily. "I think it was a ruse to get me out of here."

Drew's eyes narrowed. "Who would do that?"

Jake looked his friend in the eyes. "Your brother."

The words delivered one-two punches to Drew's windpipe. His eyes rolled around in their sockets, his puckered lips sucked on dead air. A gurgling sound, followed by a violent puff of breath. "Martin's alive?"

Jake nodded. "I think so. I found evidence today at a murder scene. Evidence I'm pretty certain leads to your brother."

"What kind of evidence?"

The door burst open, revealing a disheveled and frightened Paige McCauley. Portrait of a woman gone mad. "Drew, why did you run out on me like that?" she asked, her voice rising with each syllable.

"Wha... where have you been?"

"What do you mean, where have I been?" she whispered loud enough for the neighbors to hear. "Where have I been? I came out of the bathroom and you were gone. How could you do that to me?"

"Paige, what are you talking about? I've been with Agent Weeks all afternoon."

Paige laughed. A terrifying laugh. The kind that usually bounces off padded walls. "Are you saying you weren't just with me at the Seaview Motel?"

"Paige, I-"

"Then who was just with me twenty minutes ago–your twin?" Her lower lip quivered.

"Oh, God," Drew said. Jake caught him as he stumbled backward.

"What is it?" Paige said. Silence. "You're scaring me." Her eyes locked on Jake. "Jake, what's wrong? TELL ME!"

Jake helped Drew to a chair. "Paige, please sit down."

Paige clenched her fists. "I don't WANT to sit down, Jake. I WANT you to tell me what's going on." She was no longer dangling on the edge of hysteria. She'd taken a nosedive into the abyss.

"Yes." The answer slowly rolled off Drew's tongue.

Paige stepped back. "What?"

Drew stood on wobbly legs. Jake readied himself to catch his friend again. "Yes." Then the fastball between the eyes. "It was my twin brother."

Paige's eyes hardened. "You don't have a brother," she said to her husband's vacant stare. Jake looked away. He couldn't bear to watch the train wreck as it unfolded. "Jake." Her voice was soft now, the hushed tone one would use on a newborn.

Jake looked with pity at this woman he'd only just met. He wondered what the real Paige McCauley was like. He hoped to meet that woman when all this was over. "Yes, Ma'am?" He knew she hated him calling her that. But right now he needed to distance himself from her, treat her like any other nameless, faceless victim.

Paige stared him down. "You seem like a straight-shooter," she said. "Tell me, what is Drew talking about?"

Reality had not yet set in. Once it did, there would be hell to pay. Drew had betrayed her. Jake supposed he had too on some level. "I'm sure Drew has his reasons for not telling you."

"Telling me what?"

The phone rang. *Saved by the bell.* "Drew, get the phone," Jake demanded.

Drew was numb. He picked up the phone. "Hello." His eyes grew, as if air was being pumped into them. His free hand gripped his chest.

Jake grabbed the receiver. "Martin, I want to talk to the boy. Or should I call you Chance?"

"Nice detective work, Detective," the ghost from Jake's past said. "Where's my baby brother?" The voice sounded remarkably like Drew's.

Jake said, "I know it was you who killed Donna Thomas. I found the notes. Looks like you've done your detective work too."

"Well, well, Hawksworth. I guess you can file Donna away under Cases Solved and take a vacation for yourself."

"Why'd you kill the Thomas woman?"

"Let's just say she was collateral damage."

"You bastard, you can't hide forever."

"You're forgetting one thing."

"What's that?"

"I still have the kid. And that gives me the upper hand, wouldn't you say?"

"Martin, you don't want to hurt Ben. He's family."

"I HAVE NO FAMILY! You saw to that, didn't you?"

Jake wanted to reach through the phone and strangle the bastard. "Martin, whatever it is you want, we can arrange it. But you have to release the boy first."

Martin laughed. "Since you asked so politely, I'll give it some thought, Jake. You don't mind if I call you Jake, do you?"

"Call me whatever you want, Martin. Now about the boy..."

"By the way, sorry to hear about your wife. Hit and run, was it?"

Phantom claws ripped at Jake's chest. "Leave my wife out of this."

"You sure it was an accident?"

"What are you getting at?"

Martin laughed. "Nothing at all, Jake. Nothing at all."

"If you had anything to do with–"

"Why would I have any reason to hurt you?" Martin said. "Just because you put me away for half of my fucking life? I don't hold grudges, Detective."

"Martin, why do you continue to blame others for your actions?" Jake said.

"Spare me the psycho mumbo jumbo," Martin said. Then he added: "Oh, one more thing."

"What's that?"

"Tell my sister-in-law she was better than a whore on a holy day."

A horn blared three times from the driveway. "Ah, right on time," Martin McCauley said.

"Right on time for what?" Jake asked.

"I sent a little something over for my baby brother. Consider it an early Christmas present. Got to run." *Click.*

The front door opened. Two federal agents, guns at the ready, flanked a terrified UPS deliveryman. In his hand, a neatly wrapped box.

"The guy says he was paid a hundred bucks to deliver this package," Agent Ron Gibbons said.

The UPS guy, a small balding man who looked like he could use the hundred bucks, nodded dumbly.

"Do you remember what he looked like?" Jake asked.

The deliveryman raised a shaky finger at Drew. "Like him."

Drew rose from the chair and moved toward the man. "Give me the box."

"Drew, we don't know if it's safe," Jake said. "Nobody touches it."

Drew lunged at the bald guy. "I said give me the box!" The deliveryman tossed it at him like it was a hot potato. Drew read the small card tucked into the red ribbon. "Oh, God."

"Drew, what is it?" Paige asked. Drew's mouth was agape, his jaw melting off his face. "You're scaring me!" She snatched the note from his hand. "What does this mean?"

Jake didn't know what was unfolding, but it was bad. Really bad. "Paige, what does it say?" he asked.

She read the contents slowly: *I told you no cops, Baby Brother. One more word of advice. You should have rethunk Chapter 16.* "Drew, what's in Chapter 16?"

Drew's eyes disappeared behind weary lids. "No. Can't be. How could he know?"

"Know what? Drew, WHAT THE HELL IS IN CHAPTER 16?"

Paige grabbed the festive box and tore at the ribbon.

"DON'T OPEN IT!" Drew screamed.

Paige ravaged the paper. No one tried to stop her. They all watched in awe. Jake included. Paige opened the lid, pulled back the tissue paper. Her eyes fixed on the contents. The scream was bloodcurdling. The box slipped from her grasp. It tumbled like a die across a craps table, seeming to bounce forever before at last teetering on end. The object inside spilled out and rested on the gleaming hardwood floor.

It took a moment for Jake's brain to process it. Somebody gasped. Paige fell backwards. Jake's eyes told him what it was, but his brain refused to accept it.

A tiny human toe.

CHAPTER TWENTY-NINE

Finding an address for Thora Camden was easier than finding a plastic surgeon in LA. Only one person in the state with the name. What the hell kind of name was Thora? Sounded like the stage name of a female wrestler.

Ladies and gentlemen, weighing in at an impressive four hundred and fifty pounds, the great, the powerful–the obscenely obese Thora!

The sun drizzled into the horizon as he moved down the rural street. A man walking a mop with a collar approached on the opposite side of the road. *Act casual.* He cocked his head downward, slightly but not conspicuously, and waved. The elderly man returned the gesture and he and his sorry-ass excuse for a dog continued on their way.

The house was well lit and neatly kept, though smaller than he'd imagined. He saw movement behind one of the front windows. Thora Camden came into view. Unlike her house, she was much larger than he expected. Maybe she really was a female wrestler. She wouldn't go down easy. He'd have to take her out swiftly, before she had time to react. The kid would be a no-brainer.

He wondered how much Drew would be willing to pay for a package deal. The large silhouette disappeared from the window's frame.

He started up the driveway.

CHAPTER THIRTY

"There's another note inside the box," Agent Burrows said. Jake summoned a pair of gloves and gingerly picked up the small box that lay inches from the severed digit. He pulled out a square of paper and unfolded it.

"What does it say?" Paige asked, each word rising in tempo.

Jake paused then read the note. *Here's a present from your son. I'll deliver Anna's gift in person. Love, Uncle Marty.*

"He has no way of knowing where Anna is," Drew said.

Paige covered her face. "We talked about her."

"Who?"

"Me and... him. He knows she's with Thora."

"Get Thora Camden on the line, now!" Jake barked.

"Anna, dinner's ready!" Thora Camden stirred the sauce and gave it one final taste. "Perfect, as always," she said to the room.

"Can't I watch just ten more minutes?" Anna bellowed from the living room.

Thora rolled her eyes. "You said that ten minutes ago. Now please turn off that idiot box and come help me set the table."

"But it's my favorite show!" Anna's shrill voice rattled the teeth in Thora's mouth. Drew always said she was a handful. More like a truckful.

Thora stood in the doorway, hands on hips and said simply, "Now." Anna clicked off the television. Worked like a charm every time. Thora wasn't sure if it was the stance, the tone of voice, or the combination of both. Hell, if it worked, who cared?

"What are we having?" Anna asked in her whiny, I-miss-my-parents-and-want-to-go-home voice.

"My specialty, chicken and–"

The doorbell.

"Now, who in the name of Jesus can that be?" Thora pulled aside the heavy drapery and peered out at the front porch. "Anna, it's your daddy!"

Anna jumped up and clapped her hands. Thora's cell buzzed to life.

Thora motioned Anna to get the door. "Well, don't just stand there, young lady. Let your daddy in while I see who that is." Anna skipped toward the door. Thora snatched up the phone. "Hello?"

"Thora, listen to me," the voice said. Funny, it sounded just like Drew. But that was impossible. Drew was smiling at her from just beyond the door.

"Who is this?" Thora used the slightly annoyed tone she usually saved for telemarketers.

"Aunt Thora," Anna whined. "I can't get the door open."

"It sticks a little, honey. You have to turn the latch real hard, then tug on the door." The little girl's father waited patiently behind the door's glass panels.

"DON'T OPEN THE DOOR!" The words boomed through the phone.

"Who is this?" Thora demanded.

The answer sent invisible spiders running up and down her arms. "It's Drew. Do not open that door for anyone. Get Anna and hide. The police will be there in a minute. Do you understand?"

No, she didn't understand. "Listen, I don't know who you are and what you're trying to pull, but the man you claim to be is standing right at my front door. Now–"

A horrific gasp on the other end of the line stopped her. Then the voice said: "Thora, that man is not who you think he is. He's the man who has Ben, now he's after Anna. Please–"

"Aunt Thora, I got it!" Anna shrieked with delight. The latch turned. She tugged on the door. The man smiled at the little girl.

"Thora, DON'T LET HIM IN THE HOUSE!"

The man's eyes locked on Thora's. His smile curled downward. His pleasant eyes morphed into those of a panther's ready to pounce. The world was silent for a moment, as if the hand of God had placed a heavy finger on the planet's axis, stopping its endless rotation. Thora's brain told her to grab Anna and run. The door splintered, disrupting her thought process. A horrific cracking sound. A spray of wooden fragments.

Thora's protective instincts kicked in. She ran full-force into the man standing in the opening where her beautiful antique door used to be. They hit the concrete steps hard. She was glad she hadn't started that diet yet. Her weight was her greatest weapon. Thora landed hard on the grass, wet with the cool evening frost, the man under her crushing frame.

Sirens wailed in the distance. If she could just keep him down for another minute or so, they'd be here. She saw a glint of silver. Her right side burned. The gibbous moon went in and out of focus. She touched her side. It was warm and sticky. The man pushed her. She fell away.

He loomed over her, his face illuminated by the bulging moon that encircled his face like a glowing sombrero. His left hand made a fist and held something shiny. He moved in closer, the moon exploding behind him. The sirens were on top of them now. He raised the fist. Thora suddenly understood what the shiny object was and why her side was a six-alarm blaze.

So, this was it. She'd always imagined her death would be a bit more exotic. Maybe in the throes of passion. Or succumbing to snake venom while journeying up the Amazon. Not sprawled helpless on the tiny lawn that she could never quite perfect, no matter how hard she tried. The knife arced. In a last-ditch effort, she threw up her knee, a move she'd learned in a self-defense class a hundred years ago. The knee connected. The man fell sideways and landed with a dull splat.

Tires screeched in the driveway. Flashing lights bounced off the stars that looked down at her from their safe perch high above. Movement to her left. Two police officers stormed past her, guns drawn.

"Where is he?" the taller of the two asked. Thora opened her mouth to answer. A foggy haze enveloped her. The frantic voices of the cops became whispers. The moon grew like a balloon before her. It filled the sky, swallowed up the stars, then swallowed her up.

He hurdled a chain link fence, sidestepped soccer balls and toys strewn about a neatly manicured backyard. The moon and well-lit home made him a sitting duck. The sirens were faint now as he slipped through a row of hedges into another sprawling backyard. He stopped dead in his tracks. A doghouse. A large doghouse.

He stood motionless, gazed at the inky half-circle below a hastily painted sign. DUKE. *Shit.* Not likely Duke was going to be a toy poodle. He inched back toward the hedges. The wind beat at his back. Movement in a large bay window. An attractive woman carried a plate heaped with some sort of meat and set it down on a table occupied by a handsome man and three well-scrubbed children.

He studied their faces. They smiled and laughed and shared their days with one another. He played out their conversations as their perfect smiles moved silently.

How was your day, Dear?
Susie got all A's on her report card again.
Johnny scored the winning touchdown.
Hey kids, I have a surprise—we're going to Disneyland!

He noticed he was trembling. Not because he was cold. Because he hated these people. And everyone else like them. He was overwhelmed by a desire to kill the whole lot of them. He could too. Really, it would be easy. He could wait until they were asleep. He'd have to take out Dad and Duke first. The rest would be gravy. Hell, maybe he'd take out the whole fucking neighborhood while he was at it.

A Golden Retriever padded into view and the Cleavers welcomed it with the same enthusiasm one would show the Pope.

"Well, hello there, Duke."

The perpetually happy family chattered on silently, unaware that their worst nightmare was only twenty feet beyond their window. The youngest child, a boy of about seven, turned his head and gazed out the window. His cheerful face took on a new expression. An expression Martin knew well. Fear.

The boy raised a pointed finger. The whitewashed expressions vanished from the other Cleavers. Dad rose and flung open a slider leading to a deck large enough to entertain the entire city of Boston, and most surrounding suburbs. "Who's there?"

Martin bolted, letting the hedges swallow him up. Maybe

Mom would call the police. Or Dad would sic good old Duke on him. He decided that one day he'd come back and make good on his promise to put this anonymous neighborhood on the map. It would be talked about for years.

But not tonight. He had one other family to destroy first.

CHAPTER THIRTY-ONE

Jake hung up the phone. "Anna's okay. Thora's en route to the hospital. She's in tough shape but they say she'll make it."

"Take me to my daughter," Paige McCauley demanded.

"Take it easy," Jake said. "They're bringing her to you as we speak."

Drew moved toward his wife. "It's going to be okay," he said.

Paige shoved him hard. "Don't touch me."

Drew backed away, a wounded man.

"Why didn't you tell me you had a twin?"

"I thought he was dead. Until today."

Paige came full-force at her husband. "Was that before or after he...?"

Jake stepped between them. "Mrs. McCauley, please–"

She threw up her arms in mock surrender. "I'm okay. I'm okay." She walked away then turned back to her husband and said, "No, I'm not okay. I just had the best sex I've had in months with a man I thought I was in love with," she said. "Turns out it's his twin brother who apparently is a convicted felon and the kidnapper of my son." She added, "Now he can add rapist to his illustrious résumé. Is it going to be okay? No. Am I okay? No, I am definitely not okay."

"Paige, don't do this," Drew said. "I can't get through this alone."

"It's always about you, isn't it? What's best for you. Always has been. You should have thought about that when you and your buddy Jake were keeping your dirty little secrets." Then:

"Just one more question."

Drew shot Jake a look of desperation.

You're on your own on this one, pal.

"If he's your twin, why is he calling you his baby brother?"

"He was born three minutes before me. He always said that made him the big brother and that he got to make all the rules."

Paige moved as if to attack, then retreated. "It looks like he was right." She pivoted on one heel and was gone.

"You okay?" Jake asked.

"I can't put her through any more of this," Drew said.

"It's not your fault."

"Oh no, Jake? Did you know that in my original draft I cut off the kid's whole hand? Thankfully, Thora talked me out of it."

"You had no way of knowing what you wrote in a book would someday be used against you. This guy is sick. He's not like you and me. He's–"

"–my brother," Drew said. "My own flesh and blood. His blood runs through my body. Maybe that makes me just like him."

"You're nothing like him."

"How well do you really know me, Jake? You've read my books. Some pretty sick things happen in them. Things that come from this sick mind." He slapped himself on the side of the head. "Martin acts out what I only have the guts to write about. So I'm just like him, only a more pathetic version of him."

"He's the pathetic one, Drew. Using a helpless kid to exact his revenge on you. And what he did to Paige..."

Drew squeezed his eyes shut. "Don't, Jake."

"I'm sorry. But you can't just throw in the towel now. That's what he wants."

Alan Weeks stormed into the room. "Jake!"

"What is it, Alan?"

"He's back on the phone. Said he wants to talk to you. Only you."

Jake followed Alan's mile-long stride and snatched up the receiver. "I'm here, Martin."

"Nice talking to you again, Jake."

"Let's skip the foreplay and get it on."

Laughter. "Always the romantic, Jake. Okay, listen up. I'm going to give you one more shot at this. Blow it and the kid is dead."

"How do I know he's not dead already?"

"You'll just have to trust me on that."

"No."

Silence. Then: "What did you say?"

"You heard me. I want to talk to the boy or the deal is off." Weeks sprung a few leaks. Drew moved toward him. Jake put out a firm hand.

"Hawksworth, you're bluffing."

"Try me." Weeks was ready to pounce. Wait'll Geoffreys heard about this. "Put the kid on or I hang up."

It wasn't Weeks who lunged. It was Drew. "Jake, you son-of-a-bi..." He ripped the phone away from Jake. "Ben? It's Dad. Are you okay?"

Quiet sobs brought the room to a standstill. "They hurt me, Dad." The sobs grew.

"I know, Champ. You'll be home with us before you know it. Mom and Anna and I love you." He cradled the phone as though it were his only son.

An angry voice told Ben to say goodbye. "Hey, Dad?"

"Yeah, Champ?"

"When I get home, can we take a family vacation?"

"You got it, Champ. Anywhere you want."

"How 'bout camping again, like two summers ago?"

Drew looked dumbly at Jake and shrugged. "Sure, buddy. Whatever you want. Ben?"

"Put my pal Jake on, Baby Brother. Now."

Drew handed the phone over to Jake, his breakdown now a done deal.

"Jake, you there?"

"I'm here." *And you're lucky I'm not there.*

"Good. You're going shopping. Southside Mall, like last time. Only this time you'll be alone. None of your guys dressed up in a Santa suit or pushing a baby stroller. If I see anyone who even looks remotely suspicious, game's over."

Jake kept his temper in check. "When and where?"

Martin paused, then said, "Because I like you — take the holiday off. Enjoy a good old-fashioned Thanksgiving with what's left of your family. We'll go shopping Friday. Biggest shopping day of the year, you know."

"Why wait? Let's get it on right now."

"I said Friday." A hint of anger rose in Martin's voice. "One more thing."

"I'm listening," Jake said, defeated.

"Don't be stupid or you'll get more than a toe next time." The line went dead. The click echoed in Jake's ear.

All eyes were on Jake. He turned to Alan Weeks. "Alan, I'm going this one alone."

"Like hell you are. Geoffreys said–"

"I don't give a damn what Geoffreys has to say. You heard what he said. He wants me. Only me. I don't think he's bluffing."

Weeks moved toward him. "This is not your case, Jake." His face was a rich shade of crimson. Jake was sure his flattop bristled. "I'm in charge here and what I say goes!" Weeks stormed from the room.

Jake saw the look on Drew's face and prepared for round

two. "Okay, Drew, lay it on me. What's on your mind?"

Drew's jaw turned to stone. "What's on *my* mind?" he asked in disbelief. "What's on your mind, Jake? Where do you get off putting my son in danger?"

"I needed to know Ben was okay."

"And so you threaten to hang up? What if he did?"

"He didn't."

"And if he had?"

"I knew he wouldn't." *He wants to make you suffer for a while longer before he kills your kid.* "It was a hunch. You got to talk to your son, didn't you?"

Drew sighed and his body folded into itself. He lowered himself into an overstuffed leather chair. "I suppose I should thank you for that."

Jake shook his head. "No thank yous are in order. By the way, what was that thing with the family vacation?"

Drew looked at him with the same blank expression he had when Ben had mentioned the vacation. "What do you mean?"

"You seemed puzzled when Ben mentioned going camping again. Why?"

Drew's eyes flickered. "Oh, that. A camping trip. Over at Tomahawk in Clearview. Ever been?"

"Yeah," Jake said, "but that was probably before you were even in diapers. Did something unusual happen there?"

Drew's weary head shook like a Bobblehead staring through the back window of an old Buick. "No, nothing bad or anything. I just found it odd that he would want a repeat of that trip. It rained almost the entire week. You ever try camping in a tent during a torrential downpour, Jake?"

Jake laughed. "I'm more the cheap-motel-room-with-a-six-pack-and-cable-TV type of camper. Of course, Sheila was more the five-star-hotel-with-champagne-and-a-dinner-show type, so there you have it."

The tension rolled off Drew's shoulders, if only for the moment. They reminisced for a while about how each had met his wife, about the births of their children, about life in general. Then Drew said, "Drill Sergeant Weeks is ready to have you court-martialed. So what are you going to do now?"

Jake smiled weakly. "I'm going to get your son back."

Jake rapped on the door. No answer. Again. Nothing. "Mrs. McCauley, may I please speak with you." The door stared silently at Jake. "Mrs. McCauley, I know how upset you are. But right now we have to focus on getting Ben back." Nothing. He turned and walked down the hallway.

The lock disengaged. Jake turned. Paige McCauley looked like the victim that she was. The beautiful woman Jake had only just met was gone. In her place stood a hollowed out shell. "What do you want me to do?" she asked.

Jake knew she was standing here for one reason only. Her love for her son. "Talk to your husband," Jake said. "He wants to tell you about his brother and why he kept things hidden all these years. You may never forgive him for what he's done, but at least let him explain why he did it. Please, I'm asking you as his friend. And yours."

Paige buried her face in her hands. She stood motionless, a portrait of grief, then turned away. The door closed slowly. Before it clicked shut, a trembling whisper escaped into the hallway. "Tell him I'll be right down."

CHAPTER THIRTY-TWO

The wintry air stung Jake's face as he moved briskly through the quiet downtown square, usually bustling, now sprinkled with those lucky few who weren't joining those unlucky masses who were heading off to their Thanksgiving destinations.

When Jake left the McCauley residence, Drew was pacing the living room, preparing to face his wife. Jake had debated sticking around to support his friend, but he'd done enough damage for one night. He spotted a neon sign up ahead. Maybe there was a little more damage to be done after all.

The pub was dark, cramped, and loud. Stale beer lingered in the air. Just the way Jake liked it. He pushed past a group of tattooed punks and made his way to the bar. He motioned to the barmaid, a twenty-something with a perky smile. "Bourbon, straight up."

What was he doing hanging out in a bar with people young enough to be his own kids? The eyes of rebellious youth observed his every move. The door swung open. The cold breeze swept two women into the bar. The taller one looked vaguely familiar but Jake couldn't place the face.

She moved in his direction. Their eyes connected. She threw a friendly wave. He knew her. But from where? Maybe one of the countless cases he'd worked on over the years. Or one of the countless bars he'd frequented.

The girl approached, her cheeks burnished a healthy pink. "Hello, Mr. Hawksworth," she said cheerfully.

Still nothing. Familiar face. Familiar voice. But not a clue as to why. "Excuse me, miss," Jake said, "do I know you?"

The girl threw her head back and laughed. "I'm sorry, Mr. Hawksworth. I'm Nikki's roommate from last year. Karen. Karen Fisher."

Jake felt heat rise up his neck. He was in a college bar. With his daughter's friends. What if Nikki were to walk through that door? He'd have a hard time explaining his way out of this one. "Yes, of course. How are you, Karen?"

"I'm great," she replied. "What brings you in here?" She moved closer and whispered, "Are you working a case?"

"I was just... I really have to be..."

A voice rose up behind him. "Bourbon, straight up." Jake slapped a ten spot on the bar and left the drink. "I have to be going, Karen. Nice seeing you again."

"Tell Nikki I said hello," she called after him.

Jake made a beeline for the door. He didn't need to be running into Nikki's current roommate or, even worse, Nikki herself. He tore out of the pub, the smell of reckless youth clinging to his coat, the music's rhythmic beat still slamming around in his head.

He retraced his steps, found the warmth of his car. He sat, let the engine idle. It was time to stop. If not for himself, for Nikki. His fumbling fingers gripped the smooth cold bottle secreted under the seat.

He rolled down the window. Time to say goodbye once and for all to his old, and not so dear, friend. "Fuck it." He tossed the bottle, jammed the car into gear and punched the pedal.

The cemetery where Sheila rested was the only place Jake found solace these days. A brilliant bouquet of flowers leaned against the headstone. Nikki must have been by earlier. Jake was sure Sheila would be able to name each type of flower. He, on the other hand, couldn't name a goddamn one.

He filled Sheila in on the case then segued into Nikki's new beau, adding that he was the kind of boy Sheila would approve of. Then it was confession time.

"Baby, I wanted that drink so bad. To make me forget the pain. But now I'm beginning to see that I can't forget it. I just have to accept it. I'm trying really hard, but it's not easy. But I'll try. For Nikki. And for you." Jake waited for some sign that Sheila's spirit was there. Nothing mystical happened. Just a dog barking in some faraway yard. He wiped the moisture from his eyes. "Okay, love, I'm off to catch the bad guys. I won't let you down." He touched the surface of the headstone. A cold shiver ran up his arm.

Darkness blanketed the cemetery as he made his way back to the car. Not a soul in sight. Who (other than slightly-over-the-edge cops) would wander around a cemetery after dark anyway, much less one that was supposedly haunted?

There had been a number of sightings over the years. Always the same. A tall thin man clad in black, his features indistinguishable beneath a wide-brimmed hat. Most spotters recalled that The Tall Man did not attempt to approach them. Rather, he seemed to be trying to get away from them, as if *they* were the ghosts. And they all made one common and startling observation. The Tall Man didn't walk. He seemed to glide over the ground.

Jake had been through this cemetery on half a dozen occasions after the sun had retired and hadn't seen so much as a chipmunk, never mind a gliding apparition.

Movement to his right. A figure moving among the headstones. Dressed in black. A hooded jacket replaced the wide-brimmed hat The Tall Man had become infamous for. And this guy, ghost or no ghost, had his feet firmly planted on the ground. "Who's there?" Jake called out.

The figure paused, then bolted. Jake raced after it. He kept pace with it until they reached the outskirts of the cemetery, where the figure vanished into the shadows. Jake slowed and regained his breath.

Maybe The Tall Man was real after all. Okay, so what Jake had seen didn't have the right hat. Maybe The Tall Man had opted for a new look. Even ghosts have to keep up with the latest trends. Jake laughed at this thought. When you're an eternal soul, fashion comes and goes and comes and goes and so on and so on.

He cranked up the heat in the car and watched crystallized ice die before him. Could that have been The Tall Man? No. Most likely a homeless drifter or a grave robber. No such thing as ghosts.

Only horrors from the past that come back to haunt you.

Jake dialed up Nikki on the cell phone. It rang three times before an upbeat voice answered. "Hi, honey," Jake said. "Don't say anything, just listen. I'm giving it up. For good this time. You can hold me to that promise."

"I will," Nikki said. "You can count on that. Where are you? You sound far away."

"It's this crappy phone. I stopped by to talk to Mom. Those were beautiful flowers you left."

"What flowers? Dad, I haven't been to the cemetery in weeks," Nikki said.

Jake's blood ran cold. *Then who has been?*

His brain went into overload. He thought about Sheila down in that cold ground. He thought about the dark figure running through the cemetery. He thought about Drew and Paige and what they must be going through. He thought about their son, who may or may not be alive. And Nikki. Could he protect her from a similar fate? Then he thought of someone he hadn't thought about in nearly three decades.

Scott Dempsey.

PART TWO

One Less Bully in the World

Spring, 1989

CHAPTER THIRTY-THREE

The day Scott Dempsey died was an ordinary one in Riverton. Early morning commuters moved like automatons, hustling to catch trains and buses, cursing anyone who agitated their daily routines. White-collared men in wingtips and women in mannish suits stood stock-still like cattle, awaiting the familiar rattle of the ever-punctual train that would whisk them off to their alternate lives in the city.

Riverton was a bedroom community with little industry. The white collars journeyed to a metropolis of towering skyscrapers, the blue collars to the neighboring town of Scarborough. Scarborough's chief industry was textile. It employed more than half of Riverton's residents.

By day, the people of Riverton viewed life from vastly different perspectives. The banker looked up to gleaming steel and glass structures framed by azure heavens. A far more dismal sight welcomed the factory worker–colossal smokestacks spewing toxins into a muddy grey sky.

At day's end, their paths crossed in the speck-on-the-map town of Riverton. It was here that they shared the same crimson horizon, perhaps with different outlooks, but the same horizon nonetheless.

These paths were about to collide. Edward Dempsey, the quintessential starched-collar banker, and William McCauley, the everyman house painter, exchanged nods as each began his daily routine. Though the men were next-door neighbors and their sons played ball together, they had never spoken so much as a passing hello in the driveway or in the school bleachers.

On this sunny, ordinary morning in May, the two men climbed into their cars and drove off in opposite directions.

Less than a mile away, a rookie detective named Jacob Hawksworth was shoving a half-eaten bagel into his mouth as he reached for his keys, badge, and piece. Rollins was going to be all over him for being late again.

What all of these men didn't know, couldn't know, was that in less than forty-eight hours their lives would be forever connected.

CHAPTER THIRTY-FOUR

It was the kind of day one would describe as perfect. Powder blue sky peppered with bleached-to-perfection clouds. Slight breeze rustling full-bodied trees.

The stillness of this perfect morning was shattered by the clacking of a well-worn wooden screen door, its springs long broken, as it slapped drab clapboard in rapid succession. Two boys bounded off the precarious stoop, sneakered feet barely making contact with it.

"Pick up the pace, slacker!" Martin McCauley yelled. He smiled and left his lanky counterpart in his dust.

Drew McCauley smiled back. For the first time in a long time, he felt close to Marty. Marty was different these days. Friendlier. More patient. Mom had even commented on it over dinner the other evening. "Good to see you boys getting along like brothers should," she'd said.

Drew would be off to college soon. He supposed Marty was trying to make up for lost time before they separated. What surprised Drew was that Marty showed no hostility over his acceptance into three top schools.

What surprised no one was Marty's announcement that he wouldn't be applying to college at all. He was graduating high school by the skin of his teeth (thanks to countless hours of tutoring by Drew). Maybe he'd take a year off, see the sights–

of what, Riverton?

–then look into the Army. A little discipline might be just what he needed, Mom had confided to Drew.

The bus rose out of a fiery horizon. Jenny-Lou Farmingdale

whispered something to Shelby Stack (She Be Stacked to the entire senior class). Marty horsed around with Chet Lane and Scott Dempsey.

"Hey, shitbag," Scott said. Drew made circles in the sand with his sneaker. Sometimes if he ignored Scott, the bulldog moved on to another victim, usually Jenny-Lou. But today it looked like Drew was the lucky winner in the show of all shows, The Scott Show. "Hey, buddy, you deaf?" Scott taunted. Chet Lane snorted.

Drew sighed. "What?"

Scott was a big kid, not tall but muscular in places Drew didn't know muscles existed. His so-yellow-it-was-almost-white hair was cropped severely, making his enormous head all the more menacing.

He slung a heavy arm over Drew's shoulder. "She Be told me she wants you bad," Scott whispered. Chet snorted again. Marty looked mildly amused, mostly bored.

Drew tried to pull away. Scott tightened his grip around his neck. "Cut it out," Drew said. Scott's grip tightened.

"What are you, a pussy?" Scott chided.

Heat rose up Drew's neck. Scott relaxed his arm. Drew slipped out of the headlock. "Back off."

Jenny-Lou and She Be stopped their chatter. Chet snorted.

"What did you just say?" Scott barked.

"You heard me." A wave of heat flashed across Drew's cheeks. He was as surprised by his actions as everyone around him appeared to be.

"You're dead, McCauley!" Scott took a swing. Drew flinched. The punch never connected. Marty gripped Scott's wrist, twisted it behind Scott's back.

"Say Uncle," Marty said in a dead voice.

Scott shook his head. "Yeah, yeah, I give."

"You didn't say Uncle."

"Uncle," Scott said reluctantly. Marty released Scott from his arm lock.

The bus pulled up to the curb. Scott said, "You're lucky I didn't kick your ass." She Be and her friend climbed aboard. Chet and Scott followed.

A hand squeezed Drew's shoulder. "Looks like my baby brother grew a set of balls today," Marty said.

Drew avoided Scott until fifth period gym class. Scott kept his distance during a pick-up basketball game. He even said "Nice shot" when Drew sunk a basket. Coach Mosher, the quintessential gym teacher's gym teacher, told the class to hit the showers. She Be Stacked posed as the boys jogged by. But Drew's eyes were somewhere else. Sarah Delano. Sarah waved shyly as Drew passed by. He'd been trying to work up the nerve to ask her to the prom for weeks. What the hell, now was as good a time as any.

"Hi, Sarah." Her friends giggled and gave Drew the space he was looking for.

"Hi."

Drew's heart danced. "I was just wondering..."

Scott Dempsey pushed past Drew. "Go get her, Tiger."

Just ask her. Drew stumbled on his words. "Would you like to come... I mean go... to the... prom? I mean, with me?" *Smooth going, pal.*

"Okay," she said, then rushed off to join her friends. Just like that.

Maybe you're not such a loser after all.

Drew hurried through his shower and toweled off. He need-ed a few minutes to review his notes for the upcoming Trig test.

She'd actually said yes. Drew couldn't wait to tell Marty, who had convinced him that pigs would fly before any girl ever went to the prom with a loser like him.

He wrapped the towel around his waist and sloshed through the puddles of water spotting the cold concrete. He remembered hearing someone yell *GET HIM!* and was lifted off the floor. Scott, Chet and Lenny Higgins, the state's top-seeded wrestler, carried Drew to the locker room's entrance and pushed him out into the hallway. Scott snatched the towel. "You think she'll still go to the prom with you when she sees what she's getting?" The door slammed. The click as it locked was deafening.

Muffled laughs. Someone whistled. Drew stared at the peeling red door stamped with the words BOYS LOCKER ROOM. Funny, he'd never noticed the door was red.

Time stood still. Then a familiar voice said: "Andrew, take this." Mr. Leberman, his Trig teacher. Drew took the sport coat being offered.

Sorry, Mr. Leberman, I won't be taking the test today because I'll be busy jumping in front of a bus.

Then he saw her. Sarah. Her face a mix of shock, sadness, and disappointment, Drew supposed. Marty had been right all along. Pigs would fly before any girl would ever go to the prom with a loser like him.

CHAPTER THIRTY-FIVE

The sun chased Drew as he tore through the forest. It split the tree line, shooting spikes of light at him. The Trig test could always be made up. Besides, he'd already been accepted to every school he'd applied to. To hell with the test. He'd never be able to face Leberman again anyway. And Sarah. To hell with the prom. To hell with everything.

Where is it? Gotta be around here somewhere.

He'd go deeper and deeper into the forest until he became hopelessly lost, cut off from civilization.

There!

The awesome tree was menacing, dozens of arms ready to snatch him up and crush him in their grip. His eyes scanned the massive trunk. The initials D.M. and M.M. carved into it. One for him, one for his twin. How long had it been? Six, maybe seven years? Their last trip together to the cave.

He scanned the thick brush. His heart shuddered. The mouth of the cave.

The cave had been a place where he and Marty shared their secrets. A place where he could make the world go away. Its entrance seemed smaller now. Thorny vines warned intruders to stay away. Drew tugged at the vines, pricked his thumb. Blood rose from the wound. Just like it had the first time he had visited this place.

The first time he'd been to the cave, the clearing had been small and squarish, as if landscaped by someone other than

Mother Nature. It was edged in a crude tangle of undergrowth that cast long, menacing shadows. One particularly sinister silhouette, resembling a pointing finger, sent its silent warning. Sunlight skipped across a cluster of jagged rocks, skated off their sleek surfaces. Tucked inside the wall of rocks was a hole so perfectly round, it could have been painted on, perhaps by the phantom landscaper.

"This is it." Marty pulled a flashlight from a raggedy knapsack and shoved it into the cave. Dust filtered slantwise through the shaft of light. Tiny particles rushed toward them, tumbling over one another, 3-D-like, escaping whatever horror lurked in the darkness. The hole swallowed Marty up.

"Come on, Baby Brother." Marty's voice echoed through the blackness. "You're not afraid, are you?" The taunt repeated itself three times.

"Coming." Drew pushed his face into the hole. He could no longer see the dust particles, but he knew they continued their onward surge, could feel them bouncing off his cheeks. He fumbled for his flashlight, clicked it on, and inched forward. The ceiling brushed his crew cut hair.

He called out to Marty. Nothing. Again. Nothing.

Panic rattled him, like the time Marty locked him inside that old refrigerator in Old Man Riley's junkyard. It was only after Drew stopped screaming that Marty had opened the door. Drew wondered if Marty had let him out for fear that he'd killed his brother. But then, why had he been grinning from ear to ear?

The flashlight cut a swath, connected with a pair of eyes. Drew yelped.

"Shut up, you idiot," Marty said. "You're not wimping out, are you?"

"No," Drew said. "Let's just go. There's nothing here anyway."

"Crybaby. Anyhow, there's a hole in the roof right around the corner. C'mon." Splinters of light trickled in, connecting the fragments of Marty's face. "Here we are."

"Where's here?"

"My secret hiding place. This is where I come to think."

Must not come here often. "What do you think about?"

"Lots of things. And nothing at all."

The air was damp, as if a giant sponge had been squeezed out above them. The walls were wider and higher here, wallpapered in a greenish moss. Drew pointed his flashlight at a rusty metal toolbox propped against a wall. "What's that?"

"A surprise," Marty said. "Have a seat. You're my first guest."

Drew dropped his backpack and plunked down. Marty sat cross-legged before him, dragged the box over and pulled out a torn magazine. He tossed it at Drew. "Welcome to manhood, Baby Brother."

Drew opened the forbidden book, skipped over the pages with writing on them, stopped to gaze at the photographs of women in odd positions. Fleshy pillows and dark triangles filled the pages. Drew was falling in love with a brunette on page thirty-two when Marty snatched the book away. "Give it back!"

"Later," Marty said. He reached into his knapsack and produced a pocketknife. He flipped it open, ran his finger across the blade.

"Marty, careful. It's gonna cut you."

"*It* can't do anything."

"What are you gonna do with it?"

Their eyes locked. "What do you think I'm gonna do with it?" Marty asked.

Drew shrugged. *Kill me like you killed Molly Sheehan's cat?*

"I've called you here today to unite us in brotherhood."

"What?"

"A pact," Marty said. "A blood pact. Uniting two beings into one. Some shit like that. Saw it in a movie." Marty turned the knife slowly, caressed it. "Give me your hand."

"Why?"

"Afraid?"

"A little."

"Don't be. You're my baby brother. Would I hurt you?"

Drew lied. "I guess not."

"Then give me your hand. You're my flesh and blood. We have to join our blood so our flesh will be one."

"Why?"

Marty put on his shut-up-and-stop-asking-questions face. "Because, stupid, if one of us dies, he can go on living in the other."

"Nobody's gonna die."

"We're all gonna die someday. Tell you what. I'll go first." Marty slid the metal shaft across his left palm. A slash of red appeared. Marty sucked on the wound. He pulled his hand away, exposing a bloody grin. "Your turn," he said.

"No way. You're crazy."

"Don't you care about me?"

"Course I do," Drew said, "but..."

"Forget it! I thought we had a special bond, but I guess I was wrong."

Guilt was Marty's greatest weapon. Worked every time. "Okay," Drew said. "But do it quick."

"You don't have to look if you don't want to."

Drew felt his body spasm. His palm yawned open into a horrific scream, spit blood over his cupped hand, painted the dirt canvas. The cut was deeper than Marty's. Drew clenched his hand into a tight fist. This only increased the throbbing.

Marty gripped Drew's wounded hand and squeezed. Then

he whispered three words that dug deep into Drew's head, stamped themselves permanently on his brain, remaining dormant for decades, until they would be uttered once again.

"Blood brothers. Forever."

Drew applied pressure to his thumb and the bleeding stopped. He then finished clearing the entrance and squeezed into the dark corridor. Without a flashlight, visibility was zero. But he wasn't afraid. Nothing could compare to the horror of this afternoon. He swatted tears from his eyes, angry that he even cared enough to cry.

He crawled through the blackness. Something crawled across his hand. Where was that hole in the ceiling? Somebody could seal his eyelids shut and paint them black and he'd still have more visibility than he did right now. At last, a flicker of light invaded his world of darkness. Vines crisscrossed over the hole in the ceiling, an army of snakes. Drew crouched in the cold, cramped room that now felt oddly comforting.

He let his eyes adjust to the dark. The old rusted toolbox. Right where they had left it. He flipped it open and pulled out the flashlight Marty had had the good sense to stash there.

He rifled through the contents. Two Playboy magazines. A half-eaten roll of Necco Wafers. A hardened stick of Juicy Fruit. A deck of cards (missing the Ace of Spades, he recalled). A folded up piece of paper. He removed the square of paper and unfolded it. Marty's childlike handwriting decorated the sheet.

Today I thot about killing my brother. 7/11/83

CHAPTER THIRTY-SIX

The words played over and over in Drew's head.

Today I thot about killing my brother. 7/11/83

Their birthday. Their eleventh birthday. Drew searched the deep corridors of his brain for some memory of that day.

Huffy dirt bikes. Mine was black, Marty's blue. Marty loved that bike. We had a great day. Riding for hours. He was so happy. Why did he want to kill me?

Maybe it was a joke. Had to be. Sure, Marty had threatened to kill him dozens of times. But he never really meant it. Did he?

He and Marty are riding their shiny new bikes around the Bumpitty Road, a name given to the local granite pit by the neighborhood kids. It is a maze of hilly crisscrossing paths, great for stunts and popping wheelies. Jagged rocks and tree stumps dot the dirt paths, making the experience all the more dangerous.

They fly over the paths on their new bikes, dulled by chalky dust. Drew approaches the steepest hill. He slows, thinks about the grief he'll get from his brother. He pedals as fast as he can. He is airborne. The landing is going to be rough. He readies for impact. The front tire connects with a boulder and twists to the right. Drew flies over the handlebars, somersaults down a sharp decline. The bike comes down on top of him.

"DREW!" His brother is miles away.

He tries to sit up. His back screams. His brother's voice screams again.

"DREW!"

"DREW!"

Drew was awake. The balled up sheet of paper containing those ominous words leapt from his grip. How long had he been asleep?

"DREW!"

Marty's voice. No, couldn't be. Marty was at school, probably cutting class and having a smoke in the second floor boys' room.

"HEY, BRO! I KNOW YOU'RE IN THERE!"

Drew sat bolt upright. Marty was outside the cave.

"OKAY, IF YOU WON'T COME OUT, I'LL HAVE TO COME IN!"

Drew smoothed out the wad of paper, folded it into a little square and stuffed it back in the bottom of the toolbox. Marty appeared. As usual, his baseball uniform looked as if it had seen plenty of action.

"Thought I'd find you here. Missed you at practice."

Practice? "What time is it?"

"Almost dinnertime," Marty said. "Heard about what happened to you today, Bro. Sorry 'bout that."

"How'd you know I'd be here?'

Marty shrugged. "Guess I thought about where I'd go if I wanted to crawl inside a hole and die. Guess I was right."

"I'm not going back. Ever."

"Sure you are," Marty said. "You wouldn't do anything to hurt your scholarship."

"What if I said I didn't care about college?"

"I'd say you're lying," Marty said.

"What if I said I didn't care about anything anymore?"

Marty laughed. "I'd say you sound like me. Anyhow, I have

a surprise for you."

"What?"

"Guess who's outside?"

"Who?"

"Scott Dempsey."

Drew stood, forgetting how low the ceiling was. He massaged the bump that was already forming on his head. "We made a deal we'd never tell anyone about this place."

"Relax, Bro," Marty said. "He's here to apologize."

"Yeah, right. Scott wouldn't apologize if you held a gun to his head."

Marty shrugged. "No gun." He held up the Louisville Slugger he was carrying. "I could always use this on him."

Drew smiled. "Yeah, time for batting practice," he said. They laughed.

"You want me to?" Marty asked.

"Want you to what?"

"Crack him over the head with this."

Drew waited for the punch line. "Yeah, sure, Marty. Whack him good." Then: "You're kidding, right?"

"Of course I am. Whatta think I am, psycho or something?"

Kind of. "So why did you bring him here, anyway?"

"I told you. To apologize."

"Why would he do that?"

Marty swung the bat, missed Drew's head by inches. "Because I told him if he didn't, I'd tell everyone that he tried to grab me in the shower after practice."

"No shit. You really said that?"

"Uh-huh. He's going to tell everyone that you did it on a dare. You might even come out of this looking kind of on the cool side, Bro."

Drew wanted to hug his brother. But Marty would call him

Homo or some other name like that and then punch him in the gut. "Thanks."

Marty punched him in the shoulder. Hard. "What are bros for? Now let's get out of this shithole before it caves in on us."

Scott kicked up dirt with his cleats. He mumbled his apology to the ground. He swore he'd never bother Drew again, even extended a hand, which Drew brushed off.

"We better get home," Marty said. "Mom's gonna be pissed."

They walked along the crooked path, Scott in front, Marty pulling up the rear. Scott must have had good reason to think people would believe Marty's story about the shower. Otherwise, he'd never have apologized. Come to think of it, Scott and Chet Lane did seem awfully chummy during gym class and baseball practice.

Without warning, Drew was shoved hard. He hit the deck, took in a mouthful of dirt. He looked up. Marty raised the baseball bat. Drew let out a silent scream.

"Hey, Scott," Marty said. He took a batter's stance.

Scott spun around.

"Batter up!"

Scott registered the bat's movements with his eyes but his brain was late to react. The bat crashed into the right side of his head. A dull popping sound echoed through the trees. Scott staggered, raised an unsteady hand. A slow trickle of blood slid down his melon head. He tilted his head at Drew the way a confused dog does. He widened his stance, tried to brace himself. Time stood still as Scott teetered, and the whole world shook when he crashed to the ground.

Marty surveyed his work. "I'd say that was an in-the-park homer."

Drew didn't speak. Couldn't. His brain struggled to process

what had just happened. A minute ago Scott was apologizing. Now he was on the ground, not moving a muscle.

"What's your problem?" Marty said. "You said to whack him good."

Drew's voice clawed its way back up his throat. "Do you know what you've done?"

Marty frowned. "I did it for you, you unappreciative little prick." He threw the bat at Drew's feet. "Look at it this way. Now there's one less bully in the world."

Drew gazed at Scott's lifeless body, curled up in a fetal position. The only time Scott had ever looked vulnerable. "Is he dead?"

"Probably," Marty said. "That was one hell of a swing, if I do say so myself."

"They'll put you away forever," Drew managed to choke out.

Marty shook his head. "Uh-uh, I'm a minor."

"I read about a kid same age as us who killed a guy hunting," Drew said. He noticed his voice sounded higher, faster. "Told the police it was an accident, that he thought the guy was a deer. Turns out it was his girlfriend's father and she asked him to kill the guy. He got tried as an adult. Got life."

Marty took all this in with no expression. "No body, no crime."

"What's that supposed to mean?"

"It means we get rid of the body."

"We?"

"You're in this with me, Bro," Marty said. "You help me or I tell the cops you did it."

"THAT'S A LIE!"

"Your word against mine."

"I won't do it." The sun reeled in its warmth, disappeared

behind the tree line.

"You will. Or I'll bury you right beside your old buddy Scott."

Today I thot about killing my brother.

CHAPTER THIRTY-SEVEN

"He's not dead!" Drew said. Scott's battered body moved. Just a little. But it moved.

"He's dead," Marty replied. The body moved again.

Drew stared into the face of his enemy, no longer a threat, caked in a mix of blood and dirt. Scott's eyes opened, locked on Drew's. They were angry eyes, typical Angry-Scott eyes. Even after what had just happened. Still, Drew was relieved to be looking at those steely eyes. "See. He's alive. We need to get help."

Scott mumbled something incoherent, tried to sit up, fell over. He brought his hands to his head and let out a guttural groan. "Moddafupper," he muttered.

Drew leaned in. "Scott, can you hear me?" It was the first time Drew had ever hoped for a response from him. "Scott, what did you say?"

Scott sat up. He wrapped a meat hook around Drew's ankle. Drew came down hard, his head connecting with a tree root. Scott's face was the stuff nightmares are made of. Mud-smeared cheeks cracked open into a hideous grin. "I said, 'Motherfucker'." His baseball-mitt-sized hands clawed at Drew. Drew pushed himself back, tried to right himself. Scott reeled him in.

"I'm gonna kill you, McCauley," Scott said, his voice regaining strength. A thin red line slid down his enormous head.

Drew clawed at weeds, jagged rocks, anything he could grab hold of. Marty watched in amusement, arms crossed, like he was front-and-center at a Three Stooges film festival. The bat lay at his feet, clumps of dirt clinging to dots of blood the way breadcrumbs stuck to Mom's chicken as she rolled it through the batter.

Scott's strength was building. He hefted himself to his knees, attempted to stand. "When I get my hands on you, you're history," he said. He rose on unsteady legs.

"But... Scott... Marty... did it," Drew pleaded.

Scott's legs wavered but he remained upright. His baseball uniform looked like it had been through a grueling double-header. "I don't care if the Pope did it," Scott said, his voice weak but determined. "You're gonna pay." He steadied himself.

He attacked.

Drew remembered the blur of Scott's dirtied uniform as it rocketed toward him. Marty charging at Scott. Then he remembered the sound the bat made when it came down on top of Scott's head. Dad's walnuts. That's what it sounded like. The walnuts Dad used to crack open as he sat in his recliner, watching the Red Sox on a sticky summer night. Dad would toss his head back, drop the contents of the shell into his mouth, and crack another one. This would continue until the bowl was empty or Dad fell asleep, whichever came first.

That's what Scott's head was like. One big fat old walnut.

The only thing Drew remembered after that was the sound of his brother's voice calling to him as he raced through the forest. His brother's voice faded, then died.

Drew had no memory of how he got home, but there he was, standing in his driveway. Mom's Chevy wasn't there. The melting sun sat on its perch above him, taunting him, as if to say, *no matter how far you run, you can't get away from me.*

He looked around for signs of neighbors. Must be coupon day at the A&P. He slipped around to the back of the house. He slid the key soundlessly into the lock.

"Hello, Andrew."

The words slammed into his back, rattled his insides. Mrs. Dempsey. Should he pretend he didn't hear her and slip inside? Too suspicious. He turned and smiled. "Hi, Mrs. Dempsey." His heart flip-flopped in his chest. He glanced down, unable to look at this sweet woman who was in for a world of hurt.

Blood. On his shirt. On his jeans. On his hands.

Gretchen Dempsey looked comical in her gardening apron with matching hat and gloves. Bright red flowers spilled from the clay pot in her hand. Like the blood from her son's head. "Didn't you go to baseball practice today?" she asked. If she noticed the blood, her smiling face gave no indication.

"No, I don't feel very well." Sunlight was enjoying its last moments of life, that time of day when shadows play tricks on the eyes, make you think you see snakes in the grass or demons peeking from behind fences. Or blood all over your neighbor's clothes.

"Sorry to hear that, Andrew," Mrs. Dempsey said in her too-sweet voice. She placed the pot on the ground and took a step forward. She'd see the blood, and that would be that. But her face remained frozen in its always-cheerful expression. Drew studied her face for the first time. It was cracked in a million places, like an old leather shoe. Probably from all that damn gardening. He wondered how such a nice lady could give birth to such a horrible kid. He could always ask his own mother. He pushed open the door. "Andrew?"

His stomach jumped into his throat. "Yes, Ma'am?"

"Have you seen Scott? He said he'd come right home after practice to help me dig some holes."

He's dug his last hole, Mrs. D—pretty soon you'll be digging a big one for him. Drew lied some more. "No, haven't seen him all day. I really have to go now." One foot in the door.

"Looks like you've been digging some holes yourself, young man," Mrs. Dempsey said. She laughed.

Drew nodded, hurried into the kitchen and locked the door. He'd lock out the world so nobody could make him lie anymore. Mrs. Dempsey's laugh echoed in his head.

He peeked out the window. Mrs. Dempsey, no more than five feet tall, had returned to the task at hand. She struggled with an enormous shovel, a look of pure determination on her leather-shoe face. Drew wondered how she'd hold up when she found out her only child was dead.

Dead. Scott Dempsey was actually dead. Drew lurched forward and vomited on the linoleum floor.

CHAPTER THIRTY-EIGHT

Volunteers from three counties joined in the massive search effort. News reporters looking for that career-making story camped out in front of the Dempsey home, hoping to catch a glimpse of the parents or, better yet, snag an exclusive interview.

Drew watched the swirl of activity from his bedroom window. He hadn't spoken to Marty since leaving the forest. Maybe if they didn't talk about it, it would be like it never happened.

The door flew open. "We need to talk," Marty said. "Cops are downstairs talking to Mom."

"What do they want?"

"I don't know, but we have about thirty seconds to get our story straight," Marty said, his voice charged with fear.

"What *is* our story, Marty?"

"This is it, Bro. Moment of truth. Blood brothers, remember?"

Drew's chest hurt. Heat flashed across his face. "I dunno, Marty. I'm a god-awful liar. They'll know."

"MARTY? ANDREW?"

Drew froze. Mom. "Answer her," Marty said.

"You answer her."

"BOYS? CAN YOU COME DOWN HERE, PLEASE?"

"Be right there, Mom," Drew said.

Marty grabbed Drew by the collar. "Pull yourself together, Bro. Just say you felt sick and left school early and came straight home."

"Can't do that. Mrs. Dempsey saw me when I came home."

Marty's face crinkled. "Let me think." His face unfolded. "Okay, I've got it. You say you came home sick but went out to buy some medicine."

"They'd remember me at the drugstore, Marty. We need to tell them what *really* happened."

Marty shoved his brother. "Do you want to go to jail?"

Drew shoved him back. "You didn't let me finish. I'm going to say that after I left school I needed to clear my head and took off into the woods. Toward Burroughs."

Marty's eyebrows twitched. "Burroughs? But that's in the opposite direction..."

Drew nodded. "Right. And you went to practice then came straight home. That is what *really* happened, isn't it?" The only real truth now was the one he had just invented. He may turn out to be a good liar after all.

Marty nodded. "Yeah, that's exactly what happened," he said. He raised a clenched fist. "Blood brothers, right?"

"There you are," Alice McCauley said. She shot them freshly sharpened daggers. "These kind officers have been waiting patiently. They're helping to find Scott."

Drew studied the two men. One was old, at least forty. He had mean eyes and an upside-down smile. The younger man was short and muscular, with a squished-in nose and thick eyebrows. A friendly smile rested atop a granite slab of a jaw.

The man with the squished-in nose spoke. "Hello, boys. I'm Detective Hawksworth and this is my partner, Detective Rollins. Rollins, with his upside-down smile, remained seated. The man did not blink as he eyed Drew.

"We'd be glad to help in any way we can," Marty said in his totally convincing boy-next-door tone.

The kinder detective nodded. "Thank you, Martin. Or is it Andrew?"

"I'm Marty, he's Andrew... well, Drew. We're twins."

Detective Rollins laughed, but his mouth remained upside-down. "I think we can see that, son," he said. "I'm surprised your own mother can tell you apart. Mrs. McCauley, may we speak to your boys–in private, please?"

Alice McCauley smiled uncertainly. "Umm... I... I... don't see why not. Can I get anyone coffee?"

Detective Hawksworth said, "No thank you, Ma'am." He turned to Drew and his brother. "Why don't we start with you, Marty. Andrew, if you'll excuse us?"

They want to talk to us separately.

"Alone?" Marty asked. Drew hoped the detectives didn't notice the hint of panic in his brother's voice.

Of course they do. They're trained to look for that sort of thing.

"Is that really necessary, Detective?" Alice said. "My sons have nothing to hide. Scott is their friend."

Just goes to show how clueless you are about my life, Mom.

"Standard procedure, Ma'am," Hawksworth said. "Now if you'll excuse us, please?" He emphasized the last word.

Alice McCauley moved toward the kitchen. "Andrew, are you coming?"

Hammers pounded Drew's ears. What if their stories didn't match? What if someone saw Marty and Scott leave practice together? What if Mrs. Dempsey knew that was blood all over his clothes?

"Andrew?" Alice McCauley frowned.

"Sorry, Mom. Coming." He brushed by Marty, avoided eye contact.

"Mrs. McCauley?" It was the younger detective.

"Yes?"

"About that coffee? I'd love a cup. Cream. Two sugars. Please."

Alice smiled. She loved catering to others. "And you,

Detective Rollins?" The elder detective shook his head. He was all business, ready to do what he did best, catch people in their lies and throw the book at them. Alice nodded politely. "Come help your mother make some coffee, Andrew," she said.

Drew shot a glance at his brother, then watched him disappear behind the swinging door.

"They've been in there forever."

"Well," Alice said, "they have to be thorough, I suppose." She pursed her lips. "Andrew, you haven't touched your lunch."

"Not hungry." What could they be doing in there? Maybe Marty had cracked and confessed. The door opened. Marty emerged, head down, walked right past Drew.

"Andrew, can you come in, please?" Detective Hawksworth said.

Why wouldn't Marty look at him? Had it been that bad? What kinds of questions did they ask? He'd find out soon enough.

Drew sat before the two detectives. The kinder one looked more serious now. *Stay calm.*

"Drew," Detective Hawksworth began. "May I call you Drew?"

"Everyone else does. Except Mom. She calls me Andrew."

"Good. Let's get started." Detective Upside-down Smile scribbled into a notepad. "When was the last time you saw Scott Dempsey?"

"In gym class."

"Tuesday?"

"Yes."

The detective spoke just above a whisper. "I understand you and Mr. Dempsey had an altercation that day."

Did Marty tell him that? "Scott and I weren't exactly buddies."

The detective nodded as if he knew. "Can you tell me what

happened in gym class Tuesday, Drew?"

Drew's cheeks burned. "I'd rather not."

"Drew, we know what happened. Your brother told us."

"Then why do you need me to tell you if you already know?" Drew fought to contain the tears but they spilled out anyway.

"I know this is difficult for you to talk about, Drew," Detective Hawksworth said. "How did what Scott did make you feel?"

Drew swiped at his face. "Angry. Ashamed."

Detective Upside-down Smile spoke. "How mad did he make you?"

"I don't know. Pretty mad, I guess. More embarrassed than mad."

"But you were pretty mad," Detective Rollins said. His upside-down smile turned right side up.

"What are you saying?"

Detective Hawksworth shook his head. "We're not saying anything, Drew. We're just trying to understand what was going through your mind, is all."

Why were they treating him like a criminal? "Detective Hawksworth, were you ever picked on when you were a kid?" Drew asked.

The detective's eyes narrowed, his huge eyebrows became one. "No, can't recall that I was. Why?"

"Didn't think so. Then you have no idea what was going through my mind." Rollins scribbled on his notepad. "What are you writing?" Drew asked.

Rollins stopped scribbling. Detective Hawksworth leaned toward Drew. "Drew, relax. Nobody's accusing you of anything."

"That's what it feels like. I want to talk to my mother."

"One more question," Hawksworth said, "then you can see

your mother. Where did you go after leaving school?"

"I took off into the woods. I wanted to be alone. So I just ran and ran."

"Where?"

"That's two."

"What?"

"You said only one more question. That was two."

"Listen, you little puke," Rollins said, "we'll ask you as many questions as we see fit. Now where did you go?"

"Up toward Burroughs," Drew said. Rollins glanced at his partner. "What, you don't believe me?"

"You sure you headed toward Burroughs, Drew?" Hawksworth said.

"That's what I said."

"Sure you didn't head toward Scarborough?"

"I said I headed toward Burroughs."

Detective Rollins opened his upside-down mouth again. "That's not what your brother told us."

Why would Marty have told them that? They had agreed that Drew was in the forest near Burroughs. Did he forget the story? "Well, Marty gets confused sometimes," Drew said.

"He didn't seem confused at all," Rollins said. "In fact, he seemed pretty sure of himself."

"I don't know what you're talking about, Detective. I really want to see my mom right now."

"Where's the body, Drew?" Detective Rollins said.

"The what?"

The kinder of the two men nodded. "Drew, your brother told us he and Scott met up with you and the three of you went into the forest. Over near Scarborough. We know this to be true because we have a witness who spotted Marty and Scott heading in that direction in their baseball uniforms."

Marty said nobody saw them leave together.

The detective looked down at his notes. "Do you know a Shelby Stack?"

It's She Be Stacked, for your information. "Yes."

The detective nodded. "Miss Stack says she knows all three of you very well, which is why she is absolutely certain of what she saw. And your brother has confirmed Miss Stack's statement to be true."

"What else did he tell you?"

The room spun. His mouth tasted of metal. Detective Hawksworth's voice played over and over in his head.

"He said you killed Scott Dempsey."

CHAPTER THIRTY-NINE

"I believe Drew."

"Why?" Rollins asked.

Jake Hawksworth looked his superior square in the eye. "Just a hunch. I think the brother did it. Something just doesn't seem right with that boy."

"Hunches mean shit, Jake. It's evidence that counts. You're young. You'll learn." Rollins shot Jake his I'm-your-superior-so-I-know-everything look.

Jake's dislike for his partner of seven months grew more intense every time the son-of-a-bitch opened his mouth. "Well, they both say the other one did it. So I guess we'll have to let the evidence do the talking. Who was it found the body?"

"Some guy out walking. The name's Anderson or something like that."

"Walks out here? Talk about off the beaten path," Jake said.

"Yep. Makes it the perfect place to commit a murder now, doesn't it?" Rollins chuckled. Jake found there to be nothing at all funny about a murdered teenager.

Clouds rolled over one another as they made their way through the forest. Three uniformed officers led the way for Jake and his partner. Jake looked to the ominous sky. He still had a lot to learn about crime scene investigation. But one thing he did know. Rain could really mess up a crime scene. And by the look of the clouds overhead, this rain was going to create one serious mess.

"Up here!" Officer Wayne Gibbons, a lumbering hulk of a man, pointed to a clearing. Jake stepped up his pace. Distant thunder sounded its hurry-up-and-get-your-evidence-before-I-wash-it-away warning.

Jake spotted it. A mound of dirt, leaves, and branches. Roughly the length of a teenage boy. A cleated shoe protruded from one end, slightly atilt. "Right where the walker said we'd find him," Jake mumbled. A raindrop pelted his nose.

"Let's get the lab boys here on the double!" Rollins hollered. Jake moved toward the body. "Forget the kid," Rollins said. "He ain't going anywhere. Watch and learn." Rollins walked a circular path, Jake on his heels. Rollins stopped, crouched. "What do you make of these?"

Jake knelt beside his partner. "Footprints."

Rollins scribbled in a small black notebook. "Not just ordinary footprints."

Looking closer, Jake noticed a dimpled pattern within the print. "Cleats."

Rollins stood. "Yep. And something was dragged to the right of the cleat prints."

Jake smiled. "Drew wasn't wearing cleats. Marty was, by his own admission. And there's no other set of footprints."

Rollins nodded and scribbled more notes. "Marty said he took off after the initial blow. I think he has some explaining to do." Another clap of thunder. Closer this time. "Let's get on this before Mother Nature wipes it away," Rollins yelled. The Crime Lab scrambled. The rain moved in for its assault.

"I didn't say I wasn't there," Martin McCauley said, his voice soaked in defiance.

"You said you took off after your brother hit Scott the first time," Rollins said. "So how do you explain your footprints around the body?"

"My footprints?"

"Yes. Cleated footprints. They were along the spot where the body was dragged and in and around where the body was hidden. The prints match your baseball cleats."

Martin McCauley was remarkably composed. Most cold-blooded killers were. Jake recalled once entering the kitchen of a man who had just butchered his wife. While his wife lay mutilated only feet from him, the man feasted on a ham and cheese sandwich. When Jake raised his gun, the man continued to dine, pausing only to ask Jake if he'd like something to eat.

Jake could see the wheels turning inside the teen's head. Martin closed his eyes and smiled slightly. "I did take off," he said at last. "But then I came back."

"Why?"

"Because Drew's my brother. I felt bad about running off on him. He needed my help."

Rollins gave Jake that it's-your-turn-to-ask-questions look. Jake locked in on Martin's unyielding eyes. "What did you do then?"

Martin's steely gaze remained fixed. "I tried to talk Drew into letting me go for help. That's when Scott woke up." Martin's face wrinkled up.

"And?"

"I tried to stop him, but he was out of control. He hit Scott again."

"How many times?"

Martin shook his head. "I'm not sure. I looked away." A tear slid down his face.

Good show, kid. But I'm on to you.

"What did you do next?" Jake asked.

"I wasn't thinking straight. I didn't know what to do. Then Drew said if I didn't help him hide the body, he'd tell everyone

I did it. I was scared. So I helped him."

Rollins interrupted. "So, you and your brother dragged the body then covered it with debris. Is that right?"

Got you now.

Martin shook his head. "No. Only I did."

This kid had it all figured out. He knew only one set of footprints led to the body's resting place. His. "Drew didn't help you?" Jake asked.

"No, he was upset and besides, he's kind of a weakling. I moved the body by myself. Then I tried to cover it up the best I could."

Jake scanned his notes. "Let's go back to the moments before the murder, Martin," he said.

"Jake, we pretty much covered that."

"Humor me, Les."

Martin McCauley sniggered.

"You think my name's funny, tough guy?" Les Rollins barked.

Martin's eyes fell to the floor.

"Just as I thought. Go ahead, Jake."

"Martin." The boy lifted his head, locked gazes with Jake. "You said Scott was walking in front, is that correct?"

"Uh-huh."

"And where were you?"

"Behind Scott."

"And Drew?"

"I already told you all this."

"Tell me again."

Martin groaned. "He was behind me."

"Then what?" Jake asked.

Martin shifted in his chair. The first indication Jake had that the boy might be nervous. "Drew called out to Scott."

"And did Scott turn around?"

Martin grinned. "Well, wouldn't you turn around if someone called to you?"

Jake returned the grin. "Is that a yes?"

"Yeah."

Jake flipped through the small notepad. "Then, according to your statement, your brother swung the bat, striking the victim in the right side of the head. Is that correct?"

"Uh-huh." Martin's eyes shifted to the floor, to Jake, then to the floor again.

Rollins set down a heavy coffee mug. "Jake, do you have anything new here, or are we going to rehash this for the fifth time?" he asked impatiently.

"You got a date, Les?" Jake said. "I just want to be sure we're clear on everything, is all. May I continue?"

Rollins slumped in his chair. "Be my guest."

Jake returned his attention to Martin. Tiny beads of perspiration popped from the boy's forehead. "A little hot in here, isn't it, Martin?" Jake said.

Martin wiped his forehead.

"Sorry, damn air conditioning's broken again. Now, where were we?"

"I don't remember," Martin said, a slight tremor in his voice.

Jake held up the notepad. "Good thing I have this. After Drew hit Scott with the bat, what happened next?"

"Scott fell to the ground," Martin replied. "I saw blood and ran off."

"But you returned."

Martin nodded. "Yes. I wanted to protect my brother, even if what he did was wrong. I thought Scott was dead, what with all that blood and all. But then he..." Martin's voice trailed off. He buried his face in his hands.

Rollins tapped his watch. Obviously thinking about that cold beer waiting for him over at The Dugout. Jake raised an index finger. "Martin. Look at me."

The boy let his hands fall away. "What?"

"Scott wasn't dead, was he?" Jake said.

Martin shook his head.

"What happened next?"

Martin composed himself then said, "I told him we had to get help but he wouldn't listen. He just wouldn't listen." More tears. Like Niagara Fucking Falls.

Jake read from his notes. "You said Drew went at him again with the bat and struck him repeatedly in the head and body. Is that correct?"

Martin rubbed his eyes. "Yes."

"How many times would you say Drew hit him?"

Martin shrugged. "I dunno. Seven, eight."

"How many times in the head?"

"Four or five maybe."

The medical examiner's report indicated that Scott Dempsey had been struck only twice in the head, one on the right side, the second, and fatal, blow connecting with the top of the skull. Superficial bruises on the extremities were not consistent with being stricken. According to the coroner, they were most likely caused from a fall or by being dragged over rough terrain.

"Four or five, huh?" Jake asked. "Sure about that?"

"I can't remember... maybe more... or less..."

Now the kid's adrenaline was pumping. Keep him guessing. "And you just stood there and watched Drew strike Scott repeatedly and didn't try to stop him?"

"I tried to stop him, but–"

"–he overpowered you," Jake finished the sentence. "That's what you said. Isn't it?"

Martin shrugged. "If that's what your notes say."

Jake stood and walked slowly around the table, a panther circling its prey. A disinterested Rollins ran a lazy finger around the rim of his coffee cup. "That's what they say," Jake answered. "What I find interesting is that, according to you, Drew's a weakling. Isn't that what you called him?" Jake moved in for the kill.

Survival instincts kicked in. Martin steadied himself in his seat, as if ready to lunge. "That's what everyone calls him."

Jake inched closer. "Martin, you're a big strapping guy. You look like you lift weights, maybe play a little football." Feeding time. "So tell me, why weren't you able to stop this weakling from finishing off Scott Dempsey?" His eyes were daggers, ripping open Martin's soul.

Martin recoiled. "I don't know..." he stammered. "It all happened so fast–"

Jake pounded the table. Rollins knocked his coffee cup over, spattering the table with lukewarm joe. "Jesus, Jake," he said.

"Enough of this bullshit, Martin," Jake said. "You killed Scott Dempsey and you're trying to pin it on your brother. Isn't that the real truth?"

Martin leapt from his seat. "NO!"

Rollins was on his feet. "Sit down or I'll have to restrain you, son," he said. "For Chrissakes, Jake, what's wrong with you?"

"I want to see my lawyer," Martin said. "I'm not talking anymore until I do."

Heat rose up Jake's neck, spilling into his cheeks. "You do that. But I've got you, you little bastard."

"Jake, that's enough," Rollins said.

Jake put up a hand. "I'm okay, Les." He turned to a shell-shocked Martin McCauley. "Just one more question and then I'll get you your lawyer. Is your brother right-handed?"

Martin put on his confused face, one he used often. "Yeah.

We both are. What about it?"

Jake leaned within inches of the kid's face. The attack had been skillful, the prey a worthy opponent. But it was time to finish him off. "I'm told the initial blow to Scott's head was made from someone batting lefty. I checked around. Your brother bats righty, and not very powerfully I'm told."

Martin's face turned purple. "What does that prove? I bat righty too," he said with a mix of anger and fear.

Jake nodded. "Yes, you do. But I hear you're a switch hitter. In fact, I hear you hit better lefty than righty. So says your coach." Now he had him.

Martin McCauley gazed at Jake, mumbled something.

"What was that, Martin? Speak up."

"I said that I was the one who hit Scott the first time. But Drew did the rest."

Jake looked at his partner. "That's convenient, Les. We tell him the first blow is dealt by a lefty and he fesses up to it now." Jake leaned in close enough to smell fear on Martin's breath. "Anything else in your story you want to change?"

Martin shifted in his seat. "Yeah. I never dragged the body or covered it. I just said that. I left Scott right where he landed."

"Ah," Jake said. "So your cleats came back and cleaned up for you, is that what you want us to believe?"

Martin shifted again. The water was closing in over him now, lapping at his face. He was ready to go under and it showed. "I don't know... maybe Drew... uhhh..."

Jake grabbed Martin by the shirt collar and lifted him out of his seat. Rollins made a move to stop him, then settled back in.

"Maybe Drew what?" Jake said. "You said yourself that Drew wasn't wearing cleats. The dirt taken from the cleats in your closet is consistent with the dirt at the scene. The footprints found at the scene are an identical match to your cleats.

And mysteriously, your baseball uniform and the bat you used on Scott Dempsey are nowhere to be found. Have I missed anything?"

"I'm not talking anymore until I see a lawyer," Martin said. Jake could tell by the determination on his face that he was done.

Jake picked up a metal folding chair and hurled it across the room. It creased the scuffed up drywall and landed hard on the cracked linoleum. Martin, with his eyes on the ceiling, was caught off guard and fell backward, crashing to the floor. Jake moved to the door.

"Get him out of my sight."

CHAPTER FORTY

The media descended on the tiny town of Riverton with a vengeance. Murder trials of this sort are rare. They draw the kind of national attention that can make or break the careers of reporters-on-the-rise who dream of that anchor slot on the six o'clock news.

But these stakes were higher. There was speculation that this kid could be tried as an adult. The physical evidence was overwhelming. And the only witness was his twin brother. There were books to be written, TV movies of the week to be filmed. Jake wondered if anyone would even recall the victim's name after everyone who could profit from this tragedy had filled their deep pockets. Pockets deeper than the scars left on Gretchen and Edward Dempsey.

The McCauley living room window offered a front row seat to The Biggest Show in Town. Vans emblazoned with colorful logos and station identifiers lined Cherry Blossom Lane. Camera crews and perfectly coiffed reporters lurked on the front lawns of both the deceased and the defendant, claws sharpened, ready to pounce.

A long black car inched up the street, sending the vultures scrambling. A blonde woman with high hair and higher heels barked orders to a slight man lugging a camera that Jake guessed outweighed the man. Everyone wanted to be the first to ask the grieving parents how they felt.

They just put their only child in the ground. How the hell do you think they feel?

Edward Dempsey and an unidentified man shielded the

fragile-as-china Gretchen Dempsey as they sliced through the sea of microphones. Mrs. Dempsey stumbled, disappeared into the mob. She popped back up, held a hand to a bloodied forehead. The husky Edward Dempsey swatted at a camera, sent it hurtling into the crowd. It connected with the head of the blonde reporter with the high hair and higher heels. She went limp and fell heavily to the ground.

Funny, Jake thought, *all that hair should have cushioned the blow.*

Two boys in blue rushed into the melee. Jake thought about joining them, then figured he'd probably just end up shooting one of those impossibly attractive reporters. A sound behind him. He turned to a weary Alice McCauley.

"They still at it?" she asked.

Jake nodded. "And they seem to be getting their second wind. How's Drew doing?"

Alice McCauley shrugged her narrow shoulders. "He's confused. I'm confused." She fell in a heap onto a drab green sofa. "Why didn't I see the signs?"

Jake had never been much good at consoling people, most of all mothers of teenaged psychopaths. "Mrs. McCauley, sometimes the signs just aren't there."

"Maybe if Bill was around more to spend time with the boys," she said. "Don't get me wrong. He's a good man and a good father. It's just that he works so damned much."

Come to think of it, Jake had only met the man once. William McCauley was large and brooding, looked to the floor as he grunted what sounded vaguely like *hello.*

Alice McCauley added, "And he just hasn't been the same since the accident."

"Accident?"

Alice McCauley pursed her lips until they became one. "It was a beautiful summer day, as I recall," she said, her voice now oddly upbeat. "Bill was up on a ladder cleaning the gutters out. I'd been after him for months and one day he up and decides to just do it. Probably so as I'd stop nagging him." She let out a small laugh, then frowned. "I told him he'd best be careful up there, but he just laughed and waved me off. Next thing I know, I'm down in the basement doing the wash and Martin comes running down the stairs all out of breath and hollering that his daddy had a fall."

Alice McCauley paused, smoothed her dress. "Well, when I got outside, he was just lying there in the driveway. Funny, he didn't look like he was in bad shape, looked like he may have just laid down there in the middle of the driveway to take himself a breather, but they said it was his insides that were all out of sorts." Tears filled her weary eyes. "But it was his head that never really healed. We thought it was just a concussion..."

A part of Jake wanted to run from the room, from the house, past the swarm of reporters, to the quiet of his one-room apartment. Another part of him wanted to take this tiny woman in his arms and tell her everything would be all right. But that would be a lie. His mouth bypassed his brain. He blurted out, "Drew can't be forced to testify."

Alice McCauley's eyes narrowed. "Why would he?" Her kind face twisted itself up. The transformation was terrifying.

"Well, unless we find the murder weapon, there's a chance that without eyewitness testimony, a jury may not–"

"You want Andrew to throw his brother to the wolves, is that it, Detective?"

"Mrs. McCauley, I'm not saying anything of the sort," Jake said. He was beginning to think he'd fare better with the mob outside. "But let's not lose sight of the fact that a boy died here."

Alice McCauley propelled her tiny body from the sofa. "Lose sight? I don't think a day will go by ever again that I don't think of Gretchen and her boy." She paused to reload. "I want you out of here right now, do you understand?"

Jake gathered up his jacket, headed for the door. He turned to the venomous woman stinging him with her gaze. "If Drew needs to talk to anyone, please have him call me. I'd like to help him."

"You've helped out enough around here. Now you take your shiny badge out of here and leave my family alone. Do I make myself clear, Detective?"

Jake nodded politely. "Yes, Ma'am," he said. "I'm sorry to have upset you. I'll see myself out." Jake hurried down the narrow hallway. Its walls closed in around him. A soft voice stopped him at the door.

"What's going to happen to my brother?"

Andrew McCauley sat midway up a dark thin staircase. Sad blue eyes peered from beneath a shock of hair that fell carelessly across his face.

"I don't know, Drew," Jake whispered. "But if you ever need someone to talk to, you have a friend right here. Remember that."

"Thanks, Detective," Drew McCauley said, his voice rising. "I'll remember." He smiled and said, "Don't worry, I won't tell Mom."

Jake smiled back and, preparing for the onslaught that awaited him, headed out into the balmy May sunshine.

CHAPTER FORTY-ONE

The trial was entering its second week, six months after the murder. Though November was still in its infancy, a blanket of snow covered the region, with more in the forecast. Jake hit the windshield wipers for the umpteenth time. Traffic into the city was at a standstill.

Damn. Of all days to be late.

Today was the day Andrew McCauley, still a boy really, was to take the stand in a murder trial. His twin brother's murder trial.

Jake clicked on the radio. A panel was discussing the big news of the week, the opening of the Berlin Wall. Well, at least it provided a break from the Dempsey case.

Jake had watched on TV as the crowd swarmed the wall, some armed with hammers and picks to chip away at it. Jake, being a history nerd, typically listened to this type of thing over the crap music his friends lived on. Today it only made his head throb. He turned the dial. Two sportscasters were bantering about the Pete Rose scandal, months after Rose was banned from the world of baseball following allegations of gambling. The louder of the two sportscasters argued that the former Reds' star had bet against his own team, while the calmer one questioned how credible the evidence really was. Jake wasn't sure where he stood on the matter. He only knew that "Charlie Hustle" was one hell of a ball player.

He slowed and maneuvered the car in front of the courthouse. That was when he saw her for the first time.

She was pretty. But what caught his eye was the determination on her face as she struggled up the massive granite staircase toting a large cardboard box. He turned off the car, stepped into the bitter air.

"Hey, mister, you can't park there!" A rotund meter maid strode toward him, burnished cheeks puffing as she walked.

"I'm running late for court," Jake replied in his pleasant tone, one he reserved for priests, first dates–and now meter maids. "I'm a detective with the–"

"I don't care if you're the Queen of England," Agnes (proudly stitched on her chest) spouted. "Move your car!" She pulled out a weapon more deadly than Jake's–a ballpoint pen–and pressed it to a pad of parking tickets. "Now do you move the car, or do I start writing?" Agnes's cheeks puffed out, her red face turned redder.

Jake surrendered. "You win." Indeed, the pen was mightier than the sword.

He pulled away from the curb. Agnes watched diligently, chewing on her weapon. He scanned the courthouse steps for the woman. She was gone. *Thanks, Agnes, for blowing what could have been the love of my life.*

The first available parking space was two long blocks away. Jake pulled up his collar and braved the biting wind. Reporters milled about on the courthouse steps, coils of smoke rising in a symphony of anticipation. A woman Jake recognized from the evening news rushed toward him, cameraman in tow.

Lenore or Lenora, whatever her name was, shoved a microphone in Jake's face. "Detective, do you think the McCauley boy will be found guilty?" Lenore or Lenora asked with skilled precision. A puff of air shot ambitiously from her heavily lipsticked mouth.

Jake pushed the microphone away. "No comment. Now get

that thing out of my face before I shove it up your cameraman's ass."

Lenore or Lenora let out an exaggerated gasp. "Did you get that?" she said to her cameraman. He nodded dumbly. "Hey, Detective," she called out. Jake turned. "Look for yourself on the eleven o'clock news."

"I hope you got my best angle," Jake said and hurried up the steps.

The courthouse was bustling. Jake waved to a court officer whose name he couldn't recall. Then he saw her again.

The woman with the determined face. She had shed the heavy outerwear, revealing a figure women surely envied and men surely craved. Her dress was conservative, leaving much to the imagination. And imagine Jake did.

She strode toward him, head down, riffling through a stack of papers. Jake knew his plan was shameless but it was worth a shot. He stepped out in front of her. She looked up in time to say "Oh" but too late to react. Papers fell like confetti. She lost her footing, stumbled. Jake caught her. The plan had worked. They'd be dining at Costello's this evening.

"Clumsy oaf," the woman muttered. She pried herself from Jake's grip. "Look at the mess you've made." She knelt and scooped up an armload of papers.

Not exactly the response Jake had been expecting. *Where have you been all my life?* would have done nicely. He knelt beside her and said, "Sorry."

She frowned. God, she was beautiful. Even with pursed lips and furrowed brow. She stared for a moment, then returned to collecting papers.

Time to turn on the Jake Charm. "How did you know my name?" he asked.

"Beg your pardon?" Her voice resonated the same beauty

as her appearance.

"My name. You knew it. First name Clumsy. Last name Oaf. I know, sounds crazy, but my parents had a great sense of humor." He extended a hand. "Pleased to make your acquaintance, Mrs.–"

"It's Miss," she said. A smile flashed across her face then disappeared quicker than one could say Clumsy Oaf. "I'm sorry I was so rude. It's just that these documents have to be filed right away, and now they're all..." The waterworks started.

"Listen. Let me help you get these things back in order and then, to make it up to you, how about dinner at Costello's tonight?" Smooth as silk.

The future love of Jake's life stood and brushed off her skirt. "Well, aren't we forward?" she said, but Jake sensed she enjoyed the flirtation. "I don't even know your name. Unless it really is Clumsy Oaf."

Jake laughed. "No, I changed it years ago. I now go by Jake. Jake Hawksworth."

"I like that name much better," she said. She extended a hand. "Sheila. Sheila Jamieson. Pleased to meet you, Jake Hawksworth."

Jake shook the delicate hand gently. Also smooth as silk. "Pleased to meet you too, Sheila Jamieson." An overhead clock sent its warning to Jake. He was late. "Listen, Sheila, I'm due in court but I wasn't kidding about that dinner. What do you say?"

Sheila crossed her arms and tapped her high-heeled foot. "I guess that depends."

"On what?"

"On whether or not you're the one on trial." Her smile lit up the dim corridor.

"I'm a police officer. A detective, to be exact." Jake looked at his shoes. Scuffed. This remarkable woman did not date cops, especially cops with bad shoes.

"What time?" she asked.

Jake glanced up. "What time what?"

"Dinner."

"Uh–seven-thirty okay?"

"Perfect. Now run on off to court, Detective."

Jake pointed to the floor. "But this mess..."

"I'm a big girl," Sheila said. "Now run along."

Jake rushed down the hall. As he approached Courtroom One, he turned back to the lovely woman scooping papers from the highly polished floor. "Excuse me, Sheila?"

"Yes?"

"I don't have your number or address."

"Sure you do."

"No, I–"

"Check your pocket."

Jake's hand wrapped around a small square of paper. "How did you–?"

Her answer both shocked and amused Jake. "You aren't the only one who knows how to stage a collision, Clumsy Oaf."

CHAPTER FORTY-TWO

Tension filled the courtroom, oozed from the richly polished mahogany walls, flooded soundlessly down the ludicrously wide aisles. The unnerving silence was shattered by the clack of heels on marble. Prosecuting Attorney Sonia Bowman, dressed to the nines, made her fashionably late entrance.

A heavy door opened and the grossly obese Judge Kevin Hannigan wobbled into the courtroom. All the players were now present in the game called Justice.

Sonia Bowman's eyes swept the courtroom, seared Jake's before quickly moving on. He'd slept with her when she was clawing her way up the ranks. Her newfound prominence left no room for a slouch like Jake. Jake had even heard rumors that she was humping Your Overstuffed Honor. Still, she looked remarkable in her snug-fitting suit and fuck-me heels.

Jake's eyes wandered to the seating area behind Sonia and all illicit thoughts vanished. Gretchen and Edward Dempsey stared straight ahead, their blank faces permanently etched in pain. Equally stoic was Alice McCauley, who refused to glance in Jake's direction.

The jury members looked bored and strangely out of proportion in the massive leather chairs. Seven women, five men. Various races, various walks of life and, Jake sensed, varying degrees of intelligence. None of them looked like they'd be caught dead interacting with one another outside the walls of the courthouse.

No one in the room stood out more prominently than the defense attorney, Mac "Machete" Underwood. Garish orange hair sprouted from a ghoulishly pale and deeply pockmarked face that melded into a long stalk of a neck. His gangling body moved like a puppet across the courtroom. Jake thought if he looked hard enough, he'd see the strings.

Grandstanding was child's play to this bottom-feeding rodent. If twisting the truth was art, then Underwood was a regular Picasso. He'd sell his own mother down the river to get off the likes of child molesters and wife beaters. Or teenage killers.

Beside Underwood, Martin McCauley played the innocent boy-next-door routine, perfectly choreographed right down to the neatly pressed suit and freshly trimmed hair. Martin sat up straight, his solemn eyes begging the jury to acquit.

The words "All rise" reverberated and the Commonwealth of Massachusetts vs. Martin McCauley began.

When all was said and done, justice prevailed. But there were no winners in this game. Martin McCauley, tried and convicted as an adult, would plunge deeper into hell, murdering a prison guard four years into his sentence, then allegedly drowning in an escape attempt decades later. The Dempseys would struggle to move on with their lives, eventually succumbing to their grief in a suicide pact. Alice McCauley would never recover from the understanding that the child she bore was a cold-blooded murderer and within a year would admit herself into a psychiatric institution where she would serve out the remainder of her days. Her husband would be spared his son's sentencing, succumbing to a brain aneurysm.

Others fared better. Sonia Bowman would see her career lifted to celebrity status. "Machete" Underwood would pick himself up by the bootstraps and move on to The Next Big Thing.

Jake decided that Drew McCauley had gotten the rawest

deal of them all. He was left to struggle endlessly with the re-alization that he played a major role in locking away his twin brother, his flesh and blood. His blood brother, a reference Jake recalled Drew using to describe Martin. Marriage, children, and a lucrative writing career would mask the wound, but would never fully heal the scar it left.

Jake would have that dinner with Sheila Jamieson, who would go on to become Mrs. Jake Hawksworth. A child. A re-spectful career. Then tragedy would strike, forever leaving its mark.

But as Jake Hawksworth walked out of the courtroom on that wintry day, he felt only elation. For a legal system that, ev-ery once in a while, actually worked. For the dream date with the intriguing woman he'd only just met. And for a promise that he'd made to himself–to always be there to help a lost young man somehow find his way back from hell.

The media descended upon Andrew McCauley. He looked more forlorn than usual. Jake nodded, threw him a wave. Drew managed a smile and was lost in a flurry of cameras. Jake would not see him again for more than a quarter of a century.

The promise would remain.

PART THREE

The Old Dinosaur in the Sky

Fall

CHAPTER FORTY-THREE

She places the scorched turkey on a beautifully appointed table. Her husband sits to her left, her daughter to her right. Everything is perfect. On her command, her family attacks the blackened bird. They work feverishly, stabbing at the turkey. A gold taper topples over, igniting the freshly ironed tablecloth. She rescues a bowl of sweet potatoes from the conflagration. A boy huddles in the corner, bound, gagged, shivering spasmodically.

She turns to him and says, "I made your favorite, Ben. Eat up or you'll starve to death."

Paige's eyes snapped open. The ceiling stared back at her. Fingernails clicked against the window. The room was cold. She hugged her body and moved to the window.

Thanksgiving had brought the season's first snowfall. Mutant flakes ricocheted off the glass. Somewhere beyond this blur of white was her son. Did he even know it was Thanksgiving?

Jake rose early and attacked the holiday with a vengeance. He got the turkey in the oven, showered, shaved, and dressed in a crisp shirt and pants Sheila would have approved of. He considered a tie, then decided to hell with it.

He checked his watch. They should be here any minute. He took one last look around. Turkey. Check. Broccoli. Check. Peas. Check. Bottle of Merlot and two wine glasses. Check and check.

The snow was picking up. Maybe he should call Nikki and cancel. The front door opened. Too late. His daughter's voice rode in on a gust of wind.

"Dad, we're here!" Nikki hollered, never one to make a graceful entrance.

Before Jake could make his way to the living room, Nikki bounded into the kitchen. Her outstretched arms wrapped themselves around his body, making him aware of his recent weight gain. Snow dissolved into Nikki's head and parka. She turned to the young man standing in the doorway. "This is Chip."

So that's what a Chip looks like.

Jake extended a hand. Chip took it. Firm handshake. Starting off on the right foot. But the day was still young. So this was the guy who caused Nikki to go weak whenever she mentioned his name. Chip was handsome in a bland sort of way, neatly pressed and barbered. Two large pools for eyes didn't stray from Jake's bloodshot set. He looked intelligent, but not bookish. The tie was a little much. Two points off.

"Interesting name, Chip," Jake said. "Is there an interesting story that goes with it?"

Chip laughed. "Not really, Mr. Hawksworth. My real name's Bob, but when I was ten my little brother caught me in the mouth with a hockey stick and chipped my two front teeth. The name kind of stuck after that."

Nikki cringed. "Well I think that's a pretty interesting story," she said. "Gross, but interesting."

"So, how was the driving?" Jake asked.

"A little slow going, Sir," Chip answered in a much-too-polite voice.

"My partner calls me that sometimes," Jake said. "Makes me feel older than I already am. Call me Jake." *You're trying too hard, Chip. Two more points off for ass-kissing.*

An uncomfortable silence floated around them. The first of many, Jake suspected. At last, Nikki shook her head and giggled.

"What?" Jake's eyes followed her pointing finger to his chest. An apron emblazoned with the words *Kiss the Cook* wrapped his torso. "You mean you didn't tell Chip what a fashion maven I am?"

Their laughter broke the tension. "What can we do to help with dinner, Dad?" Nikki asked.

"How about setting the table?" Nikki complied and ushered a grateful-to-be-out-of-the-spotlight Chip toward the dining room. "Use the best dishes," Jake added.

Nikki stopped. "You sure?" A hint of sadness gathered in the edges of her voice.

"I'm sure," Jake said. Since Sheila's death, the dishes remained untouched in the china cabinet, as if dusting them off and enjoying them again would wipe away all memory of the woman they both loved.

Jake turned off the oven, discarded his apron and made his way to the dining room. Nikki hummed as she folded napkins. "Where's Chip?" Jake asked.

"Miss him already?"

Jake scowled.

"He went to the bathroom. If that's allowed."

It was Jake's turn to get his jabs in. "You mean Mr. Perfect shits like the rest of us?"

"Quiet, Dad. He's going to hear you."

"You really like this guy, huh?"

"Yep. But don't be jealous. You're still my number one guy."

"Speaking of number one, that better be all he's doing in there."

"Dad!" Nikki was appalled, embarrassed and amused at the same time.

"Okay, the old man will try not to make too much of a fool of himself."

Nikki gestured toward the living room. "Could you get me the candlesticks on the mantel?" she said.

Jake nodded.

"Oh, one more thing."

"What is it, Nik?"

That you're-not-going-to-like-what-I'm-about-to-say-but-I'm-going-to-say-it-anyway look washed across her face. "I saw the wine on the counter. Chip and I can drink something else."

"Don't be ridiculous. I'm fine."

"You sure?"

"Never been better," Jake said. "My problem shouldn't be yours. It's Thanksgiving. Enjoy."

You old liar. You're not fine. You're holding on by a thread too thin to sew a button on with. Even your own daughter can see it. If you're so fine, why is there a bottle of vodka tucked away on reserves?

Jake moved into the living room. Chip stood before a side table brimming with framed photographs, his back to Jake.

"Beautiful, isn't she?"

Chip spun around. Blood spilled into his cheeks. "Sorry, Sir," he said in a near whisper. "I was... I didn't... I was just looking at these pictures."

Jake laughed. "That's what they're there for. I didn't mean to startle you."

Chip relaxed. "You're right."

"Come again?"

"She is beautiful."

"That she is, but if we don't get in there for dinner, she may get ugly awfully fast."

"I was talking about that picture," Chip said. He raised a tentative finger at a photo of Sheila, sun-kissed hair blowing in the breeze, a fog-shrouded ocean behind her.

Heat rose up the back of Jake's neck. "Oh, right. She sure was. Well, we'd better get back in there before Nikki eats up all the turkey." Chip grinned but the tension was so thick, Jake could have cut it with the carving knife.

Dinner went off without a hitch. Nikki shared endless stories about school, most involving Chip. Jake's assumption that her new beau attended school with her was wrong. They'd met at a frat party. Something about a friend of a friend. Nikki rambled on. When she got excited, it was all Jake could do just to keep up with the words spilling from her mouth, much less process them.

"So, do you go to school, Chip?" Jake finally asked.

Nikki groaned. "Here it comes. Interrogation time. Dad, he's not one of your collars."

"I'm not interrogating him, Nik. I'm asking him a simple question."

Nikki opened her mouth to protest, but Chip put up a hand. "It's okay." He took a generous gulp of wine. "I dropped out."

Jake's eyes remained fixed on the young man seated across from him. Chip stared down his glass of wine. Lose eye contact, lose their trust. Chip's fingers drummed the table. Fidgeting. Another fatal character flaw. "Mind if I ask why?" Jake said.

Nikki pushed away from the table. "This interrogation is over. Obviously, Chip doesn't feel comfortable talking about it. Who wants dessert?"

Jake eased back in his chair. "Sorry. Force of habit. Excuse my manners, won't you, Chip?"

Chip's eyes met Jake's. This time they didn't wander. "I'll tell you why if you really want to know, Mr. Hawksworth," he said. "I can understand. You want to know if I'm good enough for your daughter. Well, I'm not sure if I am or I'm not. But I do know one thing. I, nor anybody else for that matter, will ever be good enough. Am I right?" His intense gaze locked on Jake, a wild animal daring its prey to make a move.

The kid had balls, Jake would give him that. "Down, boy. It was a simple question, is all."

"It felt more like a judgment."

"It wasn't intended to be," Jake said. Then he added: "But you are right about one thing. Nobody will ever be good enough for my daughter. Not because there's a damn thing wrong with you." Jake leaned forward. "Because I'm her father and she's my little girl. Maybe someday when you have a daughter of your own, you'll understand that."

They ate dessert in silence. The snow had subsided, but Nikki used the weather to her advantage. Besides being a good icebreaker, it also made the perfect excuse for a quick getaway from a sticky situation.

Jake saw them to the door. "It was a pleasure meeting you, Chip. I hope I didn't offend you in any way."

Nikki, wearing her anger on her sleeve, said: "Must've been the water talking."

Low blow. Except, that wasn't water, my dear. "I guess I deserve that."

Chip extended an arm. "Everything's cool, Mr. Hawksworth. No hard feelings."

Nikki gave Jake a halfhearted embrace, then hurried down the slick steps. Her spirited wave was absent as the car pulled away. Jake lingered in the chilly air. A bulging-at-the-seams moon hung overhead. Jake could have sworn it frowned at him.

Good going, Jakey ol' boy. You ruined your daughter's first

Thanksgiving without her mother. You've alienated her boyfriend. And you sipped vodka right in front of her.

Jake's reflection looked on in disgust. "Now you know what rock bottom looks like," he said to the sleet-streaked window.

CHAPTER FORTY-FOUR

Blake Redmond sat on the rumpled cot, hugged his knees tightly to his chest. His right foot throbbed. He removed his sock. A bandage covered his five toes. Funny, it didn't look like five toes. Must all be squeezed together. He unwound the bandage. Red spots stained the white gauze. He unwound faster. The bandage fell away. Blake screamed.

He rewrapped the foot, as if covering it would bring back the missing digit. He sobbed loudly, rocked back and forth. A memory of his mother wiggling his toes popped into his head.

This little piggy went to market, this little piggy stayed home, this little piggy had roast beef, this little piggy had none, and this little piggy cried...

"My piggy," Blake cried. "What have you done with my piggy?"

Ben tried to ignore the throbbing in his right foot. No big deal, he rationalized. It's just a baby toe. Probably the most useless part of the body.

You still have nine more.

He raised his hands to his eyes, tried to push back in the tears that spilled out. Dad always said it was okay to cry. But he felt silly crying over a stupid useless toe. Then he got mad. Mad at the kidnappers. Mad at Dad for not protecting him. Mad at himself for sitting here crying like a little girl.

Ben hoped Dad had gotten his hint about their vacation. Maybe he'd figured it out and was on his way here now. Right. And maybe that toe would grow back too.

He slipped the handcuff through the split joint, hoisted himself onto the creaky bed frame. His foot screamed. He was too mad to care. He reached for the crank on the window, turned it. The window resisted, then slid open. Fresh air rushed in, mixing with the stale thousand-year-old air. He gripped the window ledge and pulled himself up.

GETY FROGGY.

Those familiar curly green letters came into view. Snow spotted the roofline. He pulled himself up, stuck his head out. The cold air felt good. He looked down. A ten, maybe fifteen foot drop. The snow should soften the blow. And if he rolled into the slope, he might be able to avoid breaking anything like, say, a neck.

He took a gulp of clean air, then lowered himself down. Tonight. Escaping in daylight would be suicide. The kidnappers had fallen into a routine. They checked on him constantly during the day, but usually only once or twice in the evening.

Ben slipped the cuffs back through the rusty frame and settled back. Tonight he'd be sleeping in his own bed. Or he'd die trying.

CHAPTER FORTY-FIVE

Jake loaded the last of the dishes into the dishwasher. The phone offered him a break. Geoffreys. "How was your Thanksgiving, Frank?" Jake said.

"Let's skip the formalities, Jake." Frank sounded serious. Then again, Frank always sounded serious. "Alan said you're hindering the case."

"Listen, Frank, things got a little heated, but–"

"Spare me the song and dance," Geoffreys said. "I told you, Alan runs the show. You don't like it, you're out."

"Frank, McCauley said he wanted me alone at the drop. Said he'd kill the kid if I'm not. And I believe he will."

Frank cleared his throat. "Do you really believe that, Jake? He kills the kid, he loses his edge. And the money."

"I'm not sure money is his main motivator."

"Money is always the main motivator," Frank said and cleared his throat, louder this time. "Besides," Frank added, "these guys are pros. He'll never even know they're there."

Jake shook his head. "He'll know, Frank. I say I go alone. Let the tracking device in the bag lead us to him, and the boy. We'll just have to pray he's still alive when we find him."

No more throat clearing. Only silence. A good sign. It meant Frank was thinking about it. Finally, he said: "Sorry, Jake. No can do. We're talking about a mall filled with innocent civilians. If something goes wrong, I need to know we did everything we could to ensure the public's safety."

"What about Ben McCauley's safety?"

"Trust me, Jake. Our men will be so inconspicuous, I'd

challenge *you* to spot them." The frog hopped back into his throat. "That's where we stand. Are you in or out?"

"Do I have a choice?"

"No."

"And if I refuse?"

"Then Gil Burrows will make the drop."

"Burrows? That jackass could play all Three Stooges at the same time. You send him out, you may as well start digging a hole for the McCauley kid."

"Then I guess you'd better be there," Frank said. "I'll touch base with you in the morning. Hope you had a nice Thanksgiving." *Click.*

"You too, Frank," Jake said to dead air. He hung up the phone, plodded up the stairs. He stripped down to his boxers and fell heavily onto the bed. It winced beneath him, cursed him for the extra pounds he'd put on. He stared at the ceiling for a long time.

He thought about something he had said to Frank. About money not being the motivator. His gut told him he was right. Martin McCauley had one mission. To destroy his brother's life by destroying all that he held dear. His wife. His kids. His friends.

If it was only about the money, why let them know his true identity? Why not just play the role of random kidnapper, collect his cash, and run off to the Virgin Islands?

No. This was not about the money at all. And that thought scared the hell out of Jake. It meant Ben McCauley was as good as dead.

The old mahogany clock Sheila had purchased on her final antiquing jaunt chimed. Jake instinctively counted the number of chimes to see if just once the old ticker missed a beat. On the tenth chime–*right again*–the room fell silent. Jake scrolled through his cell, found his partner's name, and pressed on it.

"Hello?"

"Kyle, it's me. I need you to meet me in twenty minutes."

"Jake, it's Thanksgiving. Gimme a break."

"You stuffed your face. You fell asleep watching football. You did your part. Thanksgiving's over, partner."

A woman's voice, too faint to make out. "Jake, I have company," Kyle whispered.

"Well, lover boy, if she cares about you, she'll wait. This is important. I need to check out a hunch on the McCauley kid and I need backup."

Groaning, followed by heavy breathing. "You and your hunches. Jake, this isn't your case," Kyle said, clearly fighting off the attacking lips of his latest conquest.

One more notch in that bedpost and you'll be sleeping on the floor.

"What does Weeks think of this?" Kyle said.

This time it was Jake who groaned. "Weeks doesn't know."

"What? Jake, Geoffreys will string you up by your–babe, gimme a second–by your balls if he knows you're sneaking behind Weeks's back."

Geoffreys would do more than that. When he was finished, he'd serve them up to Jake with a big fat helping of desk duty. But first, it was time to serve his partner up a big fat helping of guilt. "Kyle, if you don't want to help, I'll go it alone. Just a kid's life at stake. No big deal. Go back to your Flavor of the Month."

"Hey, watch it, Jake–"

"What did he call me–?"

"Nothing babe–Jake, I'm not falling for your–no, babe, he wasn't talking about you–Jake, you can kiss my ass–"

Time to finish him off. "Okay, partner. Thanks for nothing. Gotta go."

Three... two... one...

Kyle groaned again. "Where and when?"

CHAPTER FORTY-SIX

Bud grabbed another beer from the fridge and sank into the musty sofa. Moans slipped under a closed door. They'd been going at it for hours. He turned up the television.

There had been nothing on the news about the kidnapping. How the hell had it been kept from the press? The reception on the set was for shit. Not even a goddamn remote. All the conveniences of home. Someone spun the Wheel of Fortune as the studio audience cheered. At least it drowned out Lynette's squeals of pleasure.

Bud was still reeling from the moment when Chance had walked through the door looking just like the McCauley guy. How the fuck could someone do this to his own brother? Or, worse, his own nephew?

The needle was just a sedative to keep the boy comfortable, Chance had explained. Even when the knife emerged, Bud thought nothing of it. And when Chance sliced the toe off, he was sure he was dreaming. It was his own screaming that assured him it was no dream.

On more than one occasion, he'd thought about releasing the boy. He'd had plenty of opportunity. Hell, he could do it right now if he wanted to. He could take off too. Chance would never find him. Nice plan. Only one problem. He had nowhere to go. And no money even if he did.

Tomorrow it would be over and he'd be on a plane headed to somewhere warm. He didn't even have a destination. Anywhere with beaches and bikinis would be just fine. Tomorrow. No more of this hellhole. He'd get a small place with a square of sand for a backyard. No more lousy television. He'd buy one of those fancy flat-screen numbers with the works. And, the best part, no more of The Pig With Orange Hair. Blonde and tanned would do just fine, thank you very much.

The door flung open and The Pig With Orange Hair stumbled out, sheet draped carelessly around her ghost-white torso. "Hope you didn't drink all the beer," she said. She pointed at the television and the sheet slipped, revealing a surprisingly shapely breast. "Ooh, I love this show," she crowed. "Buy a vowel, you dumb-ass!"

The contestant seemed to hear her crowing and bought the letter U. Lynette frowned. "He goes and buys the most useless vowel. Dumb-ass." She waved a hand at the TV in disgust and dragged her sheeted body to the fridge.

Bud hated striking up any conversation with the beady-eyed bird, but he had no choice. "Did he say who's collecting the package?"

Lynette surveyed the contents of the fridge. "Hasn't decided yet. Said he'll tell us in the morning."

"Why not tonight?"

Lynette pulled two beer cans from the fridge, slammed the door hard. "He said in the morning. And that's all you need to know." She dragged herself back toward the bedroom. "Chance wants you to check on the kid one more time."

"I checked on him a couple of hours ago. He ain't going anywhere. He's cuffed to a goddamn bed."

Lynette's face turned red, clashing with her hair. "You can either do it, or I can report back that you won't." Her smile taunted him, dared him to say no.

Though Bud acted the tough guy, the truth was Chance scared the shit out of him. Any guy who could cut off a kid's toe and smile while doing it, well, they just weren't right in the head. Bud sighed. "I'll check on the goddamn kid. Now run along and play."

With that, Lynette exposed both breasts and said, "Eat your heart out." Then she and her somewhat remarkable breasts disappeared behind the chipped door.

Bud watched the dumb-ass who had bought the letter U enter the bonus round. Maybe not so dumb after all. A shiny black BMW sent the audience gasping. The puzzle was a long one. The man looked all shiny and clean like the car he was playing for. He probably already had a car just like this one sitting in his driveway in his nice suburban neighborhood where well-scrubbed kids played catch on perfect green lawns while their nipped-and-tucked moms sipped tea from fancy china in fancy dining rooms.

The man picked that damn U again. Most useless vowel, according to Lynette. Funny, Bud always figured all the vowels to be pretty important. After all, there were only five of them. It was the Q, the X and the Z that he thought mankind could do just fine without.

The selected letters were revealed. Bud had no clue. Maybe Mr. College Degree could figure it out.

UN – – RESEEN – – R – U – ST – N – ES

Time ran out. Maybe Mr. College Degree was a dumb-ass after all. Maybe the letter U was the most useless vowel.

UNFORESEEN CIRCUMSTANCES

The audience groaned. Mr. College Degree slapped his knee as if he should have known the answer. Bud smiled, a rush of satisfaction knowing that Mr. College Degree was going home without that shiny black car.

He clicked off the TV and plodded down the hall, past the moaning, toward the boy's prison. He paused at the door.

That damned bonus round puzzle popped into his head.

UNFORESEEN CIRCUMSTANCES

He jammed the key into the lock. He thought about tomorrow. And of all that could go wrong.

CHAPTER FORTY-SEVEN

An angry mob of snowflakes pelted the windshield as the car sliced through the blackness. An old Waylon Jennings song droned from the radio. Kyle slumped against the passenger door, pouting like a six-year-old who's been sent to bed without TV. Jake hummed along to Waylon, just to piss his partner off even more.

"Where we going?"

"He speaks," Jake said. "Sorry to take you away from the future Mrs. Kyle."

"Screw you, Jake."

"Ouch. Really, thanks for helping me out here," Jake said.

Kyle grumbled, pulled his jacket collar over his ears. "So you gonna tell me where we're going while a beautiful woman lies naked in my bed?"

"Clearview."

"What's in Clearview?"

"A campground."

"A campground. In the winter. In a snowstorm. Sounds like a hoot. Shoulda brought my harmonica and marshmallows."

"First, it's not officially winter yet. And second, we're not actually going camping. I told you Drew talked to Ben yesterday, right?"

"Yeah? And, let me guess, he told you he wanted you to drag your about-to-be-laid partner out into the cold on a not-officially-winter night to go to a campground, but not to actually camp. Does that about sum it up?"

"You are a cranky sonuvabitch tonight, my friend." The

snow picked up. The right windshield blade squeaked with every sweep. One more thing for Kyle to bitch about. "Anyway, when Drew spoke to Ben, Ben asked him about going back on a camping trip they took two summers ago. The thing is, Drew said it was the worst vacation they ever had. Doesn't that strike you as odd?"

"No odder than two grown men driving out to a campground in the middle of the night on Thanksgiving," Kyle said. The Everly Brothers drifted through the car's stuffy interior. "Mind if I turn this off?" Kyle asked, but clicked it off before Jake could respond. "You don't think we're going to actually find the McCauley kid out there, do you?"

Jake shrugged. "No–maybe–I don't know. But I think the kid was trying to tell us something and–I don't know–do you ever get a gut feeling about something?"

"Yeah, I have a gut feeling that I'll be going home to an empty bed tonight," Kyle said and pulled the collar back up over his ears.

The snow lost its steam and died out. The moon emerged from a shroud of clouds. Then Jake spotted it. The giant dinosaur stood lonely and majestic against the backdrop of night. The moon smiled on the weary old skeleton. Jake hit his partner in the arm. "Wake up, Sleeping Beauty."

Kyle groaned. "What? We there?"

"Almost. Just wanted to show you something. To your right."

Kyle massaged his eyes. "What is that?"

"That, my friend, is the end of an era. Clearview Amusement Park. Closed a couple of years ago, before you moved up here." Jake pointed at the dinosaur. "And that is pretty much all that's still standing. The Colossal. One of the tallest wooden roller coasters in the world. That big drop right there, almost vertical.

Scared the shit out of generations of kids, including me."

Kyle's eyebrows did that funny high-arching thing they did when something intrigued him. "*You* rode *that* when you were a kid?"

"Damn straight I did."

Kyle laughed. "In addition to being the tallest, it must be the oldest too."

"Okay, smart guy, but I'll bet you wouldn't have had the balls to ride it."

Kyle flashed his pearly whites. "I get all the action I can handle right here at ground level."

Jake didn't doubt that. The man should put a revolving door on his apartment with a sign that reads NEXT. "Anyway, my old man used to call that thing The Old Dinosaur in the Sky. Said it stood as proud as one. And as graceful."

"Why'd they close the place?"

"About ten years ago, it started attracting a rough crowd. That crowd kept getting rougher until folks just kept their kids away from it. Last I heard, they were going to tear down the old dinosaur and throw up some condos. Looks like he ain't gone extinct just yet."

The impressive structure seemed to span the horizon for miles. The dinosaur and its home had been one of the few constants in Jake's life. He could hear the circus music, smell the popcorn and fresh-roasted peanuts, see the flashing lights on the Matterhorn. His fondest memory was of Pop carrying him up on his massive shoulders as they shared the biggest wad of cotton candy imaginable. He'd gotten his first kiss here too, in the haunted house. Henrietta Gillis. A pretty girl with striking auburn hair. A girl too pretty to be burdened for life with a name like Henrietta.

Clearview was a memory to share with generation after

generation. Nikki loved the place. Jake and his girls would stroll hand in hand through the midway, neon lights bouncing off Sheila's cheeks, shrieks of delight as Nikki tugged them from one attraction to the next. He'd watch as his girls came into view, mounted atop garishly painted horses. They'd slip away, then reappear, waving wildly to him. Just before the carousel swept them out of view, Sheila would spin her head and blow Jake a kiss. She turned away, hair dancing in the breeze.

And she was gone.

CHAPTER FORTY-EIGHT

Blake stared at the door. Usually when The Big Man in Dark Sunglasses slammed the door, Blake would hear a loud click. Not this time. Maybe it was a test. To see if he would try to escape. Maybe when he opened the door, he'd find The Big Man in Dark Sunglasses standing there waiting with a big old axe.

He gulped in some air. He really needed his Puff-Puff. He had to try. Maybe when everyone at school heard how brave he'd been escaping from The Big Man in Dark Sunglasses, they wouldn't pull his sweater over his head or kick him in the butt or send his books flying across the corridor. Maybe they'd invite him to sit with them at lunch or leave someone else standing alone on that white line when siding up for basketball. Just once he didn't want to be picked last. Just once.

Anger drove him toward the door. He touched the knob with one finger, as if it had teeth. It was cold. He wrapped his hand around it and turned it. Slowly.

He opened the door.

Ben moved through the snow as though it were tripped with land mines. The jump from the window to the snow bank had been longer than he figured. His right side burned. The cold air snapped at his arms and legs. And without his cleats, he'd be lucky to come out of this with his remaining nine toes.

Pure terror propelled him forward. He could stand the pain. And the cold. He was free! If he could just find help before he froze to death. The moon looked on from above, offering him enough light to make out shadows and outlines. The falling-down building he had left behind got smaller, the tree line ahead grew larger.

Where was the road? Where were the people? Why couldn't he hear a sound, not even an owl or an airplane? There had to be a road somewhere around here. And that would lead to people. Maybe someone was at Camp Tomahawk. He knew that was just up the road. But who camped in this weather? He looked back one more time at the building behind him, now a tiny black square on the dull gray sky. How long did he have before they realized he was gone?

A glint of light caught his eye. From what seemed like miles away. The speck of light grew to a circle. Another circle appeared beside it. The two circles moved across the horizon. Headlights! A car! There was a road after all. Ben forgot about the pain in his right side. In his elbow. Where his toe used to be. He broke out into a sprint.

CHAPTER FORTY-NINE

The Old Dinosaur in the Sky slid behind a dense wall of trees. Jake was overcome by loneliness, the kind that sticks to your clothes and buries itself in your hair and up your nostrils, so that no matter how hard you scrub, you just can't shake the smell. His partner's voice brought him back to Earth.

"How much longer?"

Jake pushed all thoughts of his wife into the back corridor of his brain, behind the door labeled *Memories of Sheila*. But all the pushing in the world wouldn't get that door to stay shut. Too many damn memories.

"Should be just up the road a bit, if I remember correctly," Jake said. "Called Tomahawk Campground."

Kyle stretched. "This place bring you back to Memory Lane too?"

"Naw," Jake said, "I only came here a few times with the Boy Scouts. No earth-shattering memories. Ah, there it is."

TOMAHAWK CAMPGROUND
The Family-Friendly Vacation Spot!
Campsites • Cabins • Swimming • Activities

The headlights splashed across the weather-beaten brown sign, its letters formed from childish looking yellow logs. Jake killed the lights. "So, partner, what are you up for first, archery or canoeing?"

It took a moment for it to register. The kid was gone. Bud stared at the bed frame, his eyes followed the sweeping curves of the rusty metal, stopped at the gap in the joints. The kid was gone. His eyes moved up the wall, flecks of pitted drywall hanging listlessly, decades-old paint holding the whole goddamn mess together. Cold air rushed through the open transom, slapped him in the face.

The kid is gone.

His first thought was to get Chance and The Pig with Orange Hair. Bad idea. No telling how Chance would react. Hell, the guy was crazy enough to kill Bud, the pig, and the kid. And then sleep like a baby. Bud snatched up a coat, flashlight, and his hunting knife and slipped out into the night.

Tomahawk Campground was everything a good old-fashioned campground should be. The upper level was ideal for the wealthier, less adventurous camper. A neat row of tiny log cabins stood at attention, silently awaiting the return of summer, when the John Q. Campers with their miserable, suntanned wives and pale, chubby kids would awaken them from their slumber. Down the hill from the cabins was the place to be for the no-frills, outdoorsy types, the Jake Hawksworths of the world. Squared off plots equipped with fire pits, electrical outlets, and nothing else except room for a tent that, if strategically placed, might avoid the outcropping of tree roots and jutting rocks. All the comforts of home.

Jake and his partner moved slowly past the small cabins, watched by slick-black windowpanes that hid whatever horrors lurked on the other side. Jake moved to a cabin labeled 5 and pulled on the doorknob. Locked. He could try every one, but he was sure he'd find them all as sealed up as Cabin 5. If he were going to hole up here with a kidnapped kid, he wouldn't lock him up in one of these cold, cramped cabins. But where? The boathouse? No. Somewhere more comfortable. Like the Tomahawk Lodge.

Jake signaled his partner. They sidestepped it down a steep hill, using the moon's eyes to avoid the tangle of roots and boulders. No wonder the rich folk stayed on the upper level. The lake came into view, white and yellow flecks dotting its smooth surface. The A-line roof of the Tomahawk Lodge carved a pie-slice silhouette into the watery backdrop.

He stood at the face of the lodge, gazed up at the dramatically pitched roof. As a child, he had marveled at its height, like one of Egypt's ancient pyramids. It looked smaller now, old and tattered, like most of his childhood memories. He moved to the massive wood door, flanked on either side by large, cartoonish tomahawks. He turned the ridiculously oversized knob. Like Cabin 5, locked. "Let's see if there's a back way in," he whispered to Kyle, now looking totally alert and ready for action.

The moonlight didn't follow them as they went around back. There was a thud, followed by his partner cursing. Jake clicked on a small flashlight. "I was hoping I wouldn't have to use this," he whispered, "but if I don't, you may end up in the ER."

"Cute, Jake," Kyle said. "This is crazy. There's nobody here. Are you satisfied?"

"Not yet." Jake pointed at a narrow door. "We're here. Might as well check it out."

Kyle groaned. "Should I bother making plans for Christmas, or do you have a master plan to ruin that holiday too?"

"That's what I love about you, partner. Never lose that sense of hu–"

"Don't move."

Something hard pressed into the small of Jake's back. Something that felt an awful lot like the tip of a rifle.

Bud waved the flashlight across the blanketed ground, scanned for footprints. The kid couldn't have gotten too far without shoes. For all Bud cared, the little shit could freeze to death. He stopped, listened to the wind. Footsteps. His ears were playing tricks on him, the way they used to when he was a boy.

He'd lie in bed at night and, with one ear pressed into his pillow, listen to the crunching of footsteps outside his window. Many restful nights were lost to the phantom that roamed his backyard. Bud (Gerry back then) even gave his stalker a name. The Cruncher.

The Cruncher haunted his childhood years, and though Gerry waited every night for The Cruncher to crash through his window and drag him off into the night, it never happened. Many years later, an adult Gerard (now known as Bud, due to his affection for the drink of the same name) heard The Cruncher again. Only now he knew there was no man outside his window. The sound he heard was his own pulse, magnified in his pillow. All those sleepless nights. So goddamn many of them.

The flashlight sliced back and forth through the darkness. To the left. To the right. *Wait!* Back to the left. *Bingo!* In the snow, a small freshly stamped footprint.

"I said don't move." The voice was gravelly, peppered with traces of nicotine and booze. Hints of an accent that Jake couldn't quite place.

The gun pressed deeper into Jake's spine. One slip of the finger and Jake would be sipping his dinner from a straw for the rest of his days. "Take it easy," he said, noting the tremor in his voice. "We're–"

"Tryin' to rob me blind, ain't ya?" The gun burrowed further into Jake's back with every word. "I ain't done nuthin' to nobody. I mind me own beeswax, don't I?"

Jake relaxed (as relaxed as one can be with a shotgun sticking into his back) as he realized this was no kidnapper, no murderer. Probably a vagrant seeking shelter for the winter. "I'm sure you do mind your business, sir," Jake began, "and I promise you we meant no disrespect. We're police officers. So, if you would be so kind as to remove the gun from my back, I'd be much obliged."

The gun held firm, then slowly disconnected itself from Jake. "If you's really the police, then where's you badges?" The man stammered on the last word.

Kyle flashed his light on the man. The man recoiled, threw an arm across his eyes. Jake drew his gun. "FREEZE!" The man dropped the rifle and raised his arms high.

"I was just blockin' me eyes, Officer," he said, fear etched into the haggard face. He was a sorry old thing, with a beard ZZ Top would be proud of. Layers of tattered clothes covered a body Jake suspected was not unlike the skeleton that hung in Chief Medical Examiner "Chilly" Lin's House of Horrors.

Kyle moved in beside Jake, gun drawn. "Get down on your knees and lock your hands behind your back," Jake ordered. The man stood there with his hands high over his head. "I said on your knees." This time Jake's tone must have meant business. The man lowered himself, his knees disappearing into the cold white stuff.

"I ain't no criminal," the man spit out. "I is the caretaker."

"You're the–this place has a caretaker?"

The man nodded and then shivered. "Every year get lots of damage from kids. You know, partyin' and, you know, doin' the sex thing." The man giggled like a ten-year-old sneaking a peek at a girlie magazine.

Jake grabbed the man's arm, thickly padded with layers of rags, and hauled him to his feet. He pointed to the Tomahawk Lodge. "You live in there?"

"Uh-huh. I make sure there ain't no trouble, they give me place to live. Good deal, no?" He smiled. His heavily stained teeth went in every direction.

"Yeah, good deal. What's your name?"

"Eddie. Eddie Gomes. But yous can call me Eddie. Sorry about the gun, Officer."

"Hey, just doing your job, right?" Jake said.

"Yeah," Kyle added, "we could have been kids doing the sex thing." He chuckled and Jake hated him for a moment.

Jake picked up Eddie's rifle. It was a plastic faux wood thing like the one he owned when he was eight. A cap gun. He almost laughed but, unlike his partner, he had respect for the less fortunate. He handed the gun to the old man and said, "Better keep this handy in case those kids come around." Eddie flashed his not-so-pearly whites. "Mr. Gomes, I do have a question for you. Have you seen any unusual activity in the area lately?"

"Uh-uh. Just me. And Killer."

"Killer?" Kyle said in his I-have-no-patience-for-lowlifes-like-you tone.

"My hamster. You like to see?"

"Not right now, Mr. Gomes," Jake said politely. "So you haven't seen or heard anything out of the ordinary?"

Eddie Gomes shook his unkempt head. His ZZ Top beard sported tiny icicles. "No. All quiet until yous gentlemen come along."

A shiver up his spine made Jake aware of how cold he was. He pulled out a card, placed it in Eddie Gomes's rag-wrapped hand. "This is my name and number. You do have a phone, is that right?"

"Uh-huh. Ya wanna see?"

"No, I believe you," Jake said.

Kyle chuckled.

For such a good kid, Kyle could be an insensitive bastard. "Anyway, if you see anything, anything at all, you be sure to call me right away," Jake said.

Eddie smiled his Julia Roberts smile again. "The party kids with the radio and the sex, yeah?"

Jake smiled back. "Yes, Mr. Gomes, you let me know if they come back."

They hurried back to the car. "What'd you make fun of the guy for?" Jake said, not bothering to mask the disgust in his voice. "Can't you see he has problems?"

Kyle pulled his collar around his perfect face. "I just hate people who live off the system is all," he said matter-of-factly.

"You think Eddie Gomes is living off the system, pal?" He turned and looked back at the raggedy old man, holding his cap gun in one hand, waving furiously with the other. "The guy lives in a rundown camp with a hamster named Killer, probably the only friend he has. Lucky to know his own name, even luckier to know how to spell it. I wouldn't say he's living large."

Kyle shrugged. "I'm just saying. He should get a real job. And some deodorant while he's at it." He chuckled and Jake saw a side of his partner that he always suspected might be there, rearing its ugly head from behind the impossibly handsome one he showed off to the world.

They reached the car. As his partner slid in beside him, Jake said, "You know, I think I'll go solo on the next holiday jaunt, partner."

CHAPTER FIFTY

Blake Redmond gazed at the world on the other side of the door. It was as dismal as the world he'd just stepped out of. A long hallway with dark walls and darker floors went on forever. Three doorways were carved out of the left side of the wall, two on the right wall. At the end of the narrow hallway, another door beckoned him. His freedom lay beyond one of these six doors. And behind any of them could lurk The Big Man in Dark Sunglasses.

He stood there for a long time. Staring at the six doors. At the dark walls, stained with something that looked like ketchup. Or blood. At the black wood floors that may as well be a pit of lava. Because Blake knew he wasn't going to take one step forward.

There would be no welcome-back celebration at school. No kids cheering his escape from The Big Man in Dark Sunglasses. But there'd be plenty more kicks in the butt, books flying across the corridor. And that white line on the shiny gym floor with only one pair of sneakers left standing on it.

IN OUR BLOOD

Blake backed up and quietly closed the door, retreating to the safety of his prison. To a room that had no white lines on its floor.

Halfway up the hill, Ben realized it wasn't the cakewalk he'd sized it up to be. The road was at the top, he was sure of it. His toes tingled. He'd watched enough of The Discovery Channel to know what frostbite was. And what it could do to you. Maybe he could go back and try again tomorrow. No. There was no tomorrow. Even if he went back, he'd never be able to go back in the way he'd gone out. This was the only way. He grabbed at a tree root protruding conveniently from the slope and pulled himself higher up the hill.

He wondered if Anna missed him. Hell, he never thought the day would come when he'd miss her. But right now, there was nothing he wanted more than to be right smack dab in the middle of one of her tantrums. If he got out of this mess alive, cross his heart and hope to die, he was going to be a better big brother to her.

And maybe Dad would be more of a dad.

It was always something. A business trip. A book tour. Or another stupid book to write. He knew Mom wasn't happy. Hadn't been for a long time. He'd heard the late-night sobbing coming from the bedroom. And the fights. Mom was always saying, "Keep it down or the kids will hear you." If only she knew the kids were standing right there on the other side of that locked door.

Maybe this whole thing would bring them back together. He'd heard about these kinds of situations bringing families closer to one another. What if he didn't make it out of here? What was already bad between his parents would only get worse. And

God help Anna then.

Another jutting branch reached out to him, as if it knew a kid in a soccer uniform would one day need to climb his way up from hell. Almost to the top now. His uncleated feet slipped and, if not for his friend the jutting branch, he'd be crumpled in a heap thirty feet down. The branch was strong. He held on tight with his right arm, grasped for the top with his left. His hand patted a flat surface. He'd made it.

Swinging from branches was Ben's specialty. He and Donnie Myers used to see how many trees they could swing to. Ben still held the record (seven), even if it meant half a dozen trips to the emergency room and a couple of weeks in various casts or slings.

He used what strength he had and launched his body upward. His first two attempts failed. The third almost did him in. On the fourth, he landed hard. On pavement. Back from hell.

Bud stopped. The footprints ended where he stood, as if a giant hawk had swooped down and snatched the kid up from this very spot. Was the kid covering his tracks? No, he'd be too damn cold to bother. What, then? A gust of wind slapped him in the face. Swirls of white dust danced around his feet. Damn. There was no giant hawk, no kid. Just good old Mother Nature making his life more miserable than it already was.

He surveyed the area with his flashlight. Almost-impossible-to-penetrate thicket to his right. A steep incline to the left. Using the light as eyes, he studied the slope. It'd be tough for the kid to negotiate. He turned away from the slope, started back. His brain grabbed hold of his ears, turned his head back to the slope. He shined the light on it once more. This time he saw it clear as day. A disturbance in the perfect landscape of snow.

As if someone had just scaled it.

Ben moved slowly down the highway. His feet screamed with every step, his body trembled uncontrollably. Where were all the cars? Maybe it was the middle of the night. Still, even an occasional trucker or cop was sure to pass by. He had to keep moving. To get as far away as he could. To keep from freezing to death.

Bud struggled up the final feet of the incline. He hefted himself onto the roadway. Splayed out, legs jelly, heart ricocheting off his ribs. If a semi came barreling down the road right now, he'd just let it roll right over him. If he ever decided to go the kidnapping route again, he'd sure as hell get his ass in shape first.

His heart nestled back into its cavity. He propped himself up on one elbow. Snow danced around his face like those annoying little gnats that used to reside on the porch of the halfway house he'd called home for close to a decade. He squinted, focused on the line running down the sleet-slick, moon-bathed highway.

The kid staggered along the white line. The way his body jerked and dragged itself, catching him would be easier than catching a social disease from Lynette. A flicker of light beyond the kid.

Headlights.

Headlights.

Just like the ones Ben had seen before. Only these were a lot closer. Ben tried to run. His right leg wouldn't cooperate. He waved his arms. The headlights were close. But not close enough to see him.

Stand right here. Let them come to you. And just hope they don't run you over.

The headlights closed in, two circles melding into one blinding blob.

You're free.

His face hit the icy road hard, ruining the orthodontic work Doctor Samuels had been so proud of. His shoulder was on fire. A swarm of bees swam in his head. He was moving backward, his face sliding through the slush-ice that blanketed the roadway. The headlights swept across the ground before him, highlighted the streak of red his shattered mouth left in its wake. The car whizzed by, spit chunks of ice at his face. So close he could've reached out and touched the tread on the tires.

He felt the vises grip tighter around his ankles, and he knew it was the hulk with the leathery face from those old spaghetti westerns. His face bumped over something hard and sharp. He watched the car's taillights fade until they were gone. Gone. Like any hope he had of escaping again.

CHAPTER FIFTY-ONE

Jake picked at the remnants of the turkey, its skeletal frame as hollow as his life. He'd really made a mess of things with Nikki this time.

Every time she tries to get closer to you, you push her away.

He glanced at his wrist. 11:52. Too late to call. Tomorrow he'd set things right.

Except tomorrow his dance card was filled.

He peeled a healthy slab of dark meat off a brittle bone, shoved it into his mouth. It was cotton in his big fat trap. He picked the turkey up, platter and all, and tossed it in the trash. It was going to be one hell of a Christmas.

He clicked off the lights, padded down the hall. The wind beat its fists against the house. Windowpanes shuddered. Two-by-fours whimpered. But nothing short of a direct hit from a missile would fell this place. Of this, Jake was certain. Because he'd worked right alongside the builders, learning their trade through every nail hammered and wall erected.

It was a modest place; the only way Sheila would have it. Let others show off their square footage, she'd say. She'd rather show off her family. Still, the house was as beautiful as the two-times-the-size atrocities that surrounded it. Sheila always said the Cape Cod style looked as though it had been plucked directly off Nantucket, weathered shingles, arbors, beach roses and all, and dropped right smack dab in the middle of Live Beyond Your Means Land.

Sheila had been the sociable one, organizing block parties and Fourth of July parades and Halloween bashes. With Sheila gone and Nikki grown, Jake saw no reason to bother with any of his neighbors, most of whom he detested anyhow.

He supposed he'd eventually sell the old place. That was sure to put a smile on the neighborhood. But not yet. Sheila was still everywhere. In the dining room wallpaper. In the mural of a little girl kneeling beside a garden that adorned Nikki's bedroom. In the barely visible crack in the patio slider, a casualty of a Sunday morning lovemaking session that also sacrificed a fragile side table and the even more fragile (and expensive) antique vase it displayed.

The phone buzzed. Its shrill cry crawled up Jake's arms and legs and spine and through his hair. It buzzed a second time, echoed through the halls, bounced off the walls and the windows. Maybe this house could be felled after all.

Nikki. Something had happened to Nikki. Or Ben McCauley. They'd found the body, tossed carelessly in a field or a parking lot, like so many others Jake had stored in a room in the dark corridors of his mind, a room labeled *Unsolved Murders*.

Halfway through the third ring, he snatched up the cell and braced himself for the news.

Silence. But he could feel the hot breath licking at his ear. "Who is this?"

It was no hospital with news of an accident. Or Frank Geoffreys telling him to get his ass over to the Fellsway Park to secure a scene. It was The Devil Himself calling.

"What do you want, Martin?"

A muffled laugh, probably followed by a smirk. "Sorry to wake you so late, Jake." The tone was soft, almost sincere.

"I wasn't sleeping. I won't until I see you in hell."

Another laugh, this time more sinister. "Your daughter isn't sleeping either."

The room spun. Jake caught hold of a wall, steadied himself. *Nikki.*

"Did you hear wh–?"

"You go near my daughter and you'll find out what real hurt is, you sorry sonuvaBITCH!"

"Such a pretty girl."

Jake spewed a string of profanities, then realized he was wasting them on silence. Trembling fingers fumbled for Nikki's number on the too-small keypad. It went straight to voicemail.

He dialed up Kyle on his way to the car.

"Jake, what the–"

"Shut up and listen to me. He's after Nikki. Get backup over to the dorm. Kyle, he's got my baby!"

The Kyle that Jake respected and trusted was on his side tonight. Probably with his latest conquest beside him. But this time the conquest would wait. "I'm on it," his partner said.

Jake tore down the street, right out of Live Beyond Your Means Land, headed for a date with The Devil.

The car lurched as it hit the curb. Jake threw it into Park and was pounding pavement when the car emblazoned with the words CAMPUS SECURITY pulled up alongside him. A fat man with a mop of curly black hair signaled him to stop.

Jake slowed to a trot. The security car breathed a sigh of relief as the hefty guard stepped out. His uniform was three sizes too small for his body. As was his head. "You Hawksworth?" he said authoritatively.

"Yeah," Jake said, further distancing himself from the guard. Jake pointed at the brick and stucco building looming before him. "I'm going in. Wait here for backup."

The man took a step forward, then back. "What should I do?"

"Room 823. When assistance gets here, tell them room 823. Got it?"

"Got it," the guard replied, looking pleased with himself. He started to say something else but Jake was already through the door and up the stairs.

Jake dragged himself up the last flight of stairs. His chest heaved. Sweat slicked his face. The words *heart attack* briefly entered his mind. He steadied himself, entered the hallway.

A large number 8 was crudely painted on a wall that had seen a lot of abuse. Beer cans and candy wrappers decorated the carpeting. The hall was dim, most of the light bulbs shattered. Must have been one hell of a pre-holiday party.

An eerie silence enveloped him. The majority of the students had left for the holiday weekend. Any who remained were either sleeping or screwing at this hour. He drew his gun and moved slowly toward his daughter's room.

A stick-on whiteboard adorned Nikki's door. A marker-on-a-string hung from the board. The board was jammed with messages in a variety of hands.

Jake studied the door. Looked accessible enough. Muffled sounds behind the door. Someone cried out. Nikki.

The door was easily accessible all right. It splintered against his weight. Split in two like a movie prop.

His daughter in silhouette on the bed. A figure on top of her. Jake raised his gun, cocked it. "FREEZE or I'll blow your damn head off!"

The world stopped for a moment. Or an eternity. The silhouette of Nikki was still, a mural on the moon-bathed wall. Her attacker also appeared to have been painted on the backdrop. Jake was aware of his own breathing, low and shallow. His finger massaged the trigger.

The Nikki silhouette came alive. "Dad?" A groan from the attacker silhouette. Jake leveled the gun at it. The Nikki silhouette spoke again. The words were slow to reach Jake's brain.

Daddy... don't... please... it's... Chip

Jake felt blood rushing full-force into his face. His shirt was damp. His meaty legs were two breakable toothpicks. He lowered the gun. His arm trembled. "I'll be outside," he said at last, barely audible to himself. He backed out of the room. The toothpicks snapped.

The elevator opened. Kyle Henderson stepped out, gun steady, eyes steadier. "Jake? Jake, you okay? Are you hurt?"

"I'm fine," he said, knowing his partner didn't buy it. "False alarm. Go on home."

"Jake, what happen–?"

Jake lifted his eyes. The shattered doorway framed his daughter. Tears streaked her face. A sweep of hair plastered itself to her cheek. She hugged her body, draped in a short robe. Her eyes evaded Jake.

"Kyle, I said go home."

Kyle's mouth snapped shut. His eyes volleyed between Jake and Nikki. At last, a light bulb clicked on in his head. "Yeah, sure." He stepped into the waiting elevator. "Call if you need anything." The doors silently swallowed him up.

Chip slipped past Nikki. He tucked his shirt in with one hand, smoothed his hair with the other. He whispered something to a motionless Nikki and, sparing himself the discomfort of having to wait for the elevator, opted for the stairs. The metal door thundered as it swung back. Neither Jake nor his daughter moved.

They remained that way for a very long time.

CHAPTER FIFTY-TWO

The wind knocked at the window, serenading Drew. He strained to listen. Paige's rhythmic breathing interfered. The clock read 1:59. He blinked. 2:00. Last call for the Sleepytrain.

He was a boy again, too young to ride a bike, never mind sleep beside a beautiful woman. His father's voice wrapped him in comfort with the tale of the Sleepytrain. It was a story Drew had heard countless times, yet each rendition varied just enough to keep it interesting. But the basic gist was the same. Climb on the mystical Sleepytrain and it will take you to Dreamland, the most magical place in the universe.

"All aboard the Sleepytrain," Dad would say in his best conductor's voice. "If you don't hurry, the train will leave without you."

Of course, the story was no more than a clever ploy to get your kid to go to sleep, but it worked like a charm every time. Until the night Drew asked his father to tell him about the Sleepytrain and his father's face melted into a frown. "Grow up, Andrew. That story's for babies. Go to sleep." And just like that, the Sleepytrain never again returned to his bedroom.

Drew slipped soundlessly from bed, fumbled his way to the bathroom. The light sent shockwaves through his body. He avoided the mirror, sparing himself the train wreck and attacked a bottle of ibuprofen. He gobbled up more than the recommended dosage, relieved himself, then crept past the stranger in his bed. Moonlight splashed across the hallway, painting an eerily abstract glow.

He peeked in at the heap of pastel bedding that was Anna and, when he was certain the heap was rising and falling, made his way down the staircase.

An image of his son wrapped itself around his eye sockets. Even with his eyes squeezed shut, it remained. Alone and cold in some dank basement or, worse, in a coffin-like box that Drew had plotted out in his head only–*Thank God!*–for an upcoming story that even Thora didn't know about yet.

He always feared that one day Pandora's Box would throw itself open, spilling out all the secrets he'd neatly stuffed away so many years ago. Some secrets are just too big. Not a carton of milk running across the floor. Not that unintended insult made to the pregnant woman who isn't really pregnant. No, this mess was one that could not be mopped up or slinked away from.

Some secrets are just too damn big.

He stared out at the black night for a long time. He had to stop the approaching storm before it destroyed everyone in its path. Because he knew the aftermath would be devastating.

He pushed his face closer to the window and searched the blackness for a light. A light that signaled the Sleepytrain's arrival. A light that would whisk him away to a magical, mystical world. And clenched in his fist, a one-way ticket.

PART FOUR

A Beautiful Death

Friday

CHAPTER FIFTY-THREE

The instructions were simple. Put the money in a white pillowcase. Then put the pillowcase into a large Macy's shopping bag. This would make concealing a tracking device difficult. That was fine with Jake.

He was the tracking device.

Martin's other instructions lacked creativity. Sit by the fountain in the center of the mall and wait for one of the antiquated pay phones to ring. Talk about clichéd. Hell, why didn't someone with a similar looking shopping bag distract him and switch bags when he wasn't looking? Oldest trick in the book.

Jake figured Martin for the more imaginative type. After all, he'd masterminded a prison break, and had been the only survivor of a nearly-impossible-to-survive accident. He'd managed to somehow gain access to the McCauleys' personal information. He'd even gotten hold of a manuscript Drew's own wife hadn't seen yet.

A scuba diver popping out of the fountain he was seated by– now that would be creative. The diver snatching the bag and disappearing through a trap door at the bottom of the fountain. That would be creative. Absurd. But creative.

Jake's eyes scanned the countless pennies mixed with the occasional silver coin on the fountain's floor. Each one signified a wish. Jake wondered if any of them had come true, and if the higher denominations increased their chances.

As he suspected, no trap door. To hell with creativity.

A phone rang. Not one of the four with the scratched-to-hell

Plexiglas privacy panels twenty feet to his right. The one in his shirt pocket.

"Yeah."

"Good morning, Jake."

"Thought the plan was a pay phone."

"You pay for this phone don't you, Jake?"

"Through the nose. How'd you get my num–never mind. Let's do this."

A muffled laugh. "I like efficiency, Jake. That's why I chose you for this job. You always get the job done, don't you?"

"I always get my man."

"We'll see about that, won't we? And don't get any ideas about trying to trace the cell I'm on. You'll find it belongs to a Nora Cummings. Poor woman had her hands full with three little rug rats. Probably hasn't even noticed her purse or her phone missing yet."

"So, you're here."

"Aah, efficient *and* smart. The coat is nice–Sears? Shoes have seen better days, if you don't mind my saying so."

Jake scanned the crowd for a man with a cell phone and an ass ready to be kicked.

"Jake," Martin said, "is that old lady with the bad dye job and fake fur coat at three o'clock one of your men?"

The lady was easy to spot in the sea of shoppers. The purplish hair was a dead giveaway. The coat, on the other hand, Jake would've guessed was real. But then, he was the same guy who was wearing a coat bought on clearance at Sears and shoes a homeless person would turn his nose up to.

"How'd you guess? She's my lead sharpshooter."

"Never lose that sense of humor, Jake."

"Enough foreplay, Martin. Let's skip to the good part. The part where I take you down."

No laughing this time. Jake had touched a nerve. Playtime was over. Martin said, "You're going to leave this mall with that money and nothing else in tow or I'll mail the rest of the kid's foot special delivery–to you. Now get off your fat ass and head toward the food court."

Jake rose on shaky legs and pushed past the old lady with the purple hair. She frowned at him. Maybe she was one of Weeks's men after all.

CHAPTER FIFTY-FOUR

Paige busied herself, fetching coffee for the odd assortment of federal agents stretched out across her furniture or smoking cigarettes on her deck. This was not her beautiful life. This was not her beautiful house. This was not her nightmare.

But it was.

"How are you holding up, Mrs. McCauley?" Gil Burrows. A man she did not know, and already did not like.

"I'm fine," she said. "I usually like to spend my holiday weekend with my family but, what the hell, the more the merrier, eh?"

Special Agent Burrows frowned the way a parent frowns at a disobedient child. "We're just doing our job, Mrs. McCauley."

Paige got up into his face. It reeked of cheap cologne. "And what exactly is your job, Agent Burrows? Besides lounging around my house?"

Burrows pushed the sleeves up on his wrinkled white shirt. Dark half moons soaked the underarms. His impish face puckered into itself. "I'll have you know that this is the finest team of agents I've ever worked with," he said. "You're damned lucky to have them. Now, if you'll excuse me, I have some lounging around to do." He spun on one leg and left the room, his cheap cologne a step behind.

Anna's distant laugh called out to Paige, carried her across the foyer. It was furnished more expensively than most people furnish their entire home, and larger than most of those homes. She felt sickened. Not by the outlandish cost. But by the exhilaration she remembered experiencing when she had completed the finishing touches. Looking at the hallway through a new, wider set of eyes, it seemed overdone, bordering on gaudy. The whole damned place could burn down and she wouldn't shed a tear.

Anna's laugh grew closer. Paige exited the pretentious foyer and entered the equally pretentious family room.

Drew rolled Anna onto her back, gently tickled her. Anna's laugh was one part cloying, two parts wonderful. Paige longed to join her husband in giving their daughter a tickle sandwich. Duty pressed its cold fingers on her shoulders, reminding her of her role in this family, keeping her at arm's length from anything that remotely resembled fun.

Playing the part of The Fun Parent, the Oscar always went to Drew. This was the same man who would lock himself away for days at a time behind that door with the clever (so he called it) sign that read:

HELP! I'M BEING HELD PRISONER
BY THE CHARACTERS IN MY BOOK–
SEND IN THE CAVALRY!

The Fun Parent would then whirl through like a tornado, laying waste to any rules Paige had set, any punishments she'd doled out, tossing her into a corner alongside her code of ethics. The children would dance in the eye of the storm, shrieking with delight, ignoring the arm their mother stretched out to them.

When the storm subsided, and the door with the clever sign was shut tight once again, Paige would sift through the rubble, dusting off Responsibility and Tolerance and putting them neatly back up on the shelf labeled Parenting.

"Hi, Mommy."

"Hi, Anna Banana."

Her family–what was left of it–gazed lovingly at her. She forced her lips up into a half smile, tilted her head in that reassuring way a mother and wife does to let her family know everything is okay.

But everything was not okay. This family was not okay. She was not okay.

"Hey," Drew said.

Anna leapt from the floor as only a five-year-old can do and rocketed herself into her mother's body. Paige wrapped her arms around her child, pressed Anna's fleshy body to hers. Paige hoped her daughter would shed the baby fat soon. She knew how utterly ruthless and unforgiving little girls could be.

"You okay?" Drew asked. He kissed her neck lightly.

"I'm fine," she said. "I wish everybody would stop asking me that. Do I look like a head case?"

Her husband, the man she'd fallen head over heels for so many years ago, the man she'd fallen out of love with somewhere over the past year, smiled his reassuring smile and said, "You look beautiful." He kissed her cheek this time.

When had the touch of her husband not made her skin crawl? She couldn't remember, and that realization frightened her. Regardless of the outcome with Ben, she knew it was over. They were long past reconciliation. Hell, it was like putting a Band-Aid on a shotgun wound.

"Mommy, why are you crying?"

"Am I?" Paige brushed a hand across her cheek. "Well, what do you know?"

Drew brushed the other cheek. "What's wrong?" he asked with overly exaggerated brow-furrowing concern. There were times when she saw a glimpse of the old Drew. And she hated him for that.

"Nothing. I was just thinking–about how nice it will be to

have the whole family together again."

Anna rocketed into her again. "Can we go to Disney World when Ben comes home? Can we, can we? Pleeeease?"

The Fun Parent chimed in. "Of course we can, Angel! Where do you want to go first–The Magic Kingdom–Cinderella's Castle?"

Anna jumped up and down. "Cindyrella's Castle! Yay!"

Drew jumped with her. "Cindyrella's Castle it is!"

Paige wondered what they would do if she jumped with them. High-five her? Have her committed?

"Can we, Mommy?" Anna wrapped herself around Paige's legs and squeezed.

"If Daddy says so," Paige said. She'd mastered the screw-you-Drew tone so that it sounded perfectly loving to her daughter's ears.

Anna squeezed tighter. "Yay! Daddy, do you think they'll have a Fidgety Froggy at Disney World?"

Drew laughed. "No honey, I don't thi–" His expression froze.

"What is it?" Paige said, concern not yet giving way to panic.

"My god," he muttered. "That's what he was trying to tell me."

Concern turned the corner and ran smack-dab into Panic. "Who? What?" Paige said. "You're scaring me. Is this about Ben?"

Drew nodded. "I think I know where he is."

CHAPTER FIFTY-FIVE

The tall man in the UPS uniform gave Jake a slight nod. After that smooth move, the agent would be wise to hold on to that uniform.

Martin's voice crawled inside Jake's ear. "A friend of yours, Jake?"

He was close. Damn close. "Come again?" Jake scanned the crowd for anyone talking on a cell. That meant roughly ninety-nine percent of them.

"Don't play me for a fool," Martin said. "Is that blonde bitch to your left one of your guys, too?"

Jake instantly recognized the woman under the blonde wig. Agent Leslie Turnbull. Six years with Alan's team. Not a natural blonde. But she looked pretty damn good as one.

Unlike UPS Man, Leslie played her part well. That of the attractive, somewhat privileged, shopper on a mission. Neiman-Marcus and Macy's bags mixed with Gap and J Crew bags. Something for everyone on her Christmas list.

"You got me," Jake said, knowing his bluff was futile. "I hand picked that one myself."

"Bet you did more than hand pick her, you old dog. Listen hotshot, it seems we have a problem."

"What's that?"

"This place seems to be swarming with your pals. Which means we need to get out of here. Pronto."

Bud cracked another beer.

"You ain't gonna be much use to us drunk as a skunk," The Pig With Orange Hair said.

"So, shoot me," Bud said and raised the beer can as if about to toast some happy couple. Instead he took a healthy gulp. What happy couples did he know?

The Pig With Orange Hair breezed by him. Bud took another swig. Maybe he'd pass out and wake up a millionaire. He stared through the smeared glass at the cold world. A world that was about to get a lot sunnier.

If Chance didn't screw things up.

The whole solo thing made no sense. They didn't need two of them watching the kid. Especially now that the kid was wrapped up nice and tight. Unless Chance was planning on skipping out on them.

Hell, he'd be tempted himself. What did Chance have to come back to? That chain-smoking whore in the other room? That'd get any guy on the next train home.

Bud's heart danced.

Movement outside.

A man. Holding a gun. No more than twenty feet away. With nothing but one inch of iced-up, grime-stained glass between them.

CHAPTER FIFTY-SIX

"Move like you're heading toward the men's room." Martin's voice was relaxed and deliberate, as if it had been scripted. "Good. Now stop. See the staircase for the commuter rail?"

"I see it."

"There's a train due in–oh, let's see–about forty-five seconds. Miss it and the kid is history."

Jake pushed his way past a tired young couple toting two tired kids. The father cursed about having to spend a much-needed day off from work fighting pushy shoppers. Jake brushed his shoulder. The straw that broke the camel's back.

"Hey, pal, want to watch where you're going?" The man shoved Jake hard.

"Thirty-five seconds, Jake."

"I'm not looking for trouble," Jake replied. "I just want to catch my train." Jake bounded for the staircase. A hand wrenched him back.

"And I just want to be sitting on my couch with a beer watching my sixty-inch flat screen," the man said.

"Let go," Jake said. He didn't want to kick the asshole's ass (was that a contradiction of terms?) in front of his kids, but it was probably nothing they hadn't seen before.

"Twenty-two seconds."

"Who's gonna make me?" The guy held tight. His wife's I-sure-hope-nobody-from-the-country-club-is-here eyes nervously scanned the gathering crowd.

"I'm going to say it one more time. Let go."

"All aboard! Train's getting ready to leave."

The dickhead with the sixty-inch flat screen was sprawled out across the marble floor holding a bleeding and broken nose, screaming about his lawyer and taking Jake for every last penny. Good luck with that. Jake was already halfway down the stairs.

The train loomed before him, a sea of commuters–some with purpose in their step, others out for a Sunday drive–deciding the fate of Ben McCauley.

"Too late, Jake. A valiant effort, though."

Jake propelled his hefty frame forward, leaving a hapless young hipster scattered on the platform. The doors snagged the Macy's bag. He pulled it free, almost lost his footing as the train lurched forward.

"Nice job," Martin said. Only this time the voice did not come from the phone that was melted to Jake's hand.

It was directly behind him.

Jake turned. Martin McCauley looked eerily like his brother. He grinned. Jake's instinct was to attack.

"Don't be stupid," Martin said. Jake's eyes followed Martin's down the length of Martin's arm. It disappeared into his coat pocket. The outline of a gun strained against the felt material. A pregnant woman stood directly in its path.

Jake lifted the bag. "Here it is. Take it. There's no one here to stop you. Just one thing," Jake added.

"What's that?" Martin asked.

"Give me the boy."

A smile consumed half of Martin's face. "In due time."

"When?"

"When I'm free and clear."

"Not good enough."

Martin's eyes fell to his pocket. "I'd say you're in no position to make demands, Jakey Boy."

The train slowed. The pregnant woman stumbled. Martin caught her. He smiled at her.

She returned the smile. "Thank you," she said.

"My pleasure," Martin replied. With his new makeover, he looked like the guy men envy, women dream of. "Why is a pretty lady in your condition standing?"

"Oh, it's okay," the woman said. "I find that most people would sooner part with their wallet than with their seat. Really, I'm fine." The pretty woman looked to the opening doors. "Besides, this is my stop anyway."

"Ours too," Martin said. He cleared the way for the woman, motioned for Jake to follow.

The train pulled away. The woman waved and said, "Nice to meet you." She turned to leave.

"Miss," Martin said, "may I trouble you for a tissue?" He touched his nose. "Sinuses."

The woman showed her infectious smile again. "Of course. I'm sure I have one in here somewhere." She rummaged through her bag.

"What are you up to, Martin?"

"Where's the tracking device?"

"What? There's no tr-"

"You have exactly five seconds to tell me or that pretty little lady isn't going to have to worry about labor pains."

Jake wondered if he'd really shoot a pregnant woman. Then he remembered the toe. The platform was nearly empty now. Just the three of them and a small elderly man Jake prayed was one of Alan's men. Fat chance.

Maybe he could take Martin down before anyone got hurt. Maybe if his reflexes were twenty years younger. Maybe wasn't good enough.

"Time's up, Jake."

"It's sewn into the pillowcase."

"Wrong answer." He pulled the .357 from his pocket. "Say goodbye to our friend." Martin leveled the gun at the woman. She was so immersed in the contents of her bag, she didn't realize her life and the life of her unborn child were one flex of a finger away from becoming a blip on tonight's local newscast.

And Jake had no doubt in his mind that the man who had killed as a teenager would not hesitate to take out the woman, the old man, and Yours Truly.

"It's on me."

Martin lowered the .357. "That's more like it."

The woman pulled her arm out of The Grand Canyon. "Here we go," she said. "Sorry, I feel like I have to carry my life in this silly thing."

Martin politely thanked the woman. She walked away without ever knowing how close she had come to a reservation for a table at Chilly's House of Horrors.

A dozen or so more people entered the platform, including three children. Any attempt at retrieving the gun was out of the question.

"Move." Martin directed him to an exit. Jake stood firm. "To the stairwell. Now."

The stairwell was empty. A perfect opportunity to take Martin on. Except for one minor detail.

He had a .357 in his back.

A phone rang. Martin pulled a cell phone from his pocket. "Shit." He tossed Nora What's-Her-Name's cell away, pulled out a second phone.

"Slow down. There's what? Where? Okay, remember Plan B? Yes, that's right. Yes. It's time for Plan B. Yes, you can. You can do it. Okay. Love you too." Martin snapped the phone shut. "Stupid sorry little bitch." Panic seeped from his eyes.

"Everything okay, Martin?"

"Get on your knees. NOW!"

Jake stood stock-still. "Martin, you want to kill me, do it. I don't bow down to scum like–" Fire erupted in his brain. He groped for the yellow metal railing in front of him. He grabbed air instead and landed the way any overweight, out-of-shape man would. Hard.

The cement was cold on his cheek. The five-alarm blaze in his head roared on. He knew he was about to die. Alone. In a dirty stairwell that smelled like piss. Not quite the way he'd envisioned it. Then again, what is?

Martin whispered something into his ear. And Jake knew he was not dying. Not yet anyway.

CHAPTER FIFTY-SEVEN

Blake was awakened by a noise. The Big Man in Dark Sunglasses. And he sounded angry. Blake pressed an ear to the door. The voice faded in and out.

—useless piece of—have to do everything myself—out of my way—

The impact of the splintering door lifted Blake off the floor. He hit the wall hard. The room spun.

The Big Man in Dark Sunglasses towered over him. Something glimmered in his hand. He raised the gun and said, "This is it, kid."

This is it.
Ben knew it because he'd heard the lady with the orange hair yelling at the hulk to kill him.

This is it.

He was crying and he didn't care. He had pissed his pants and he didn't care. It didn't matter anymore. Because he was going to die.

He'd never learn how to drive a car. Or kiss Sandra Simmons.

Someone fidgeted with the lock. He strained against the ropes, but it was no use. The Hulk had made sure there'd be no repeat of the last escape.

The door opened.

This is it.

CHAPTER FIFTY-EIGHT

I need you for the final act.

That's what Martin said before he disappeared. That's how Jake knew he wasn't dying.

He hefted himself up from the cold floor, groped for the railing. The word EXIT was barely visible on the chipped and abused steel door that danced before him. He reached for the doorknob, missed. *Better wait until you can see just one of them.*

I need you for the final act.

What did that mean? It meant he was not going to die today. It meant, as Jake had suspected, that money had never been the main motivator. It was merely payment for a job well done.

The upbeat tempo the door had been keeping slowed to a lull. Jake attacked the knob, made his way back to the platform.

Commuters backed away, cut a path for what to them was another crack-smoking, wine-guzzling homeless person looking to take some of their hard-earned money.

Jake frisked himself in search of his phone and his gun. He had neither. A terrified young mother pulled her son close to protect him from the horrible man staggering toward them.

The woman said something. Jake couldn't hear her over the army of ringing bells in his head. He fell to one knee, reached into his pocket, groped for his badge.

The mother backed away, dragged her child with her. A kind-faced elderly man, whom Jake decided looked like a college history professor, stood over him. The man said something, but the ringing in Jake's ears had moved from obnoxious to deafening. Jake managed to flip his badge open. The man's concerned face told Jake he understood.

The darkness scooped him up once again.

Bud knew the dream was over.

There'd be no tropical beaches. No blonde beauties telling him they loved him. He knew the man outside was a fed. He could tell by the way the man moved. By the way he held his gun. By the determined look in his eyes.

And Bud knew the man wasn't alone.

When The Pig With Orange Hair waved the gun in front of him he should have taken it from her. But there were a lot of things he should have done, could have done.

He should have enlisted in the Navy with his cousin Ronny, now a highly decorated officer with a pretty little wife and two pretty little rug rats, instead of knocking off that 7-Eleven with the Hicks brothers.

He could have listened when Lisa begged him to clean up his act. Maybe they could have had a couple of rug rats of their own. Officer Ronny could have invited them down to his tidy little government-financed home. He and Ronny could have sat in the hot sun with their cold Budweisers talking about the good old days while their four little rug rats ran through the lawn sprinkler and their pretty little wives swapped cooking recipes.

That's how it should have been.

"Kill the kid." The Pig With Orange Hair said it so matter-of-factly and with such conviction, Bud knew it had been her intention all along.

He should have said something. He could have taken the gun.

"Chance said you wouldn't have the balls," The Pig With

Orange Hair said. "He also said you weren't worth the price of this bullet."

She leveled the gun at his face.

A moment's hesitation was all Bud needed. He swatted the gun away, took The Pig down with a blow to the face.

The Pig With Orange Hair crashed into the bed. Inches from the gun.

And Bud knew it was over.

The Pig raised an unsteady hand, cocked the gun. The first shot, intended for Bud's head, tore through his left thigh. He'd been shot two times before, once in the shoulder, the other in the abdomen. Neither of those compared to the pain that screamed in his leg.

The Pig leveled the gun at his head again, her hands steadier now. Bud squeezed his eyes shut. He waited for his life to flash before his eyes. Definitely not worth the price of admission.

A muffled moan. Metal hitting floor.

He opened his eyes.

The Pig With Orange Hair was on the floor. The kid's manacled legs hung over the edge of the bed. *Thanks, kid.* The gun rested in the pool of blood beneath Bud's wounded leg.

The Pig scrambled across the floor, groped for the gun.

"Game's over, Sweetheart," Bud said. His leg was an inferno. But it was nice to be on the other end of the gun.

The Pig fingered a bloody lip. "You're gonna just give it all up after all we've been through?" she asked.

"The only place we've been is to hell." He was so tired. "And there ain't no place lower to go than that."

The Pig nodded as if in agreement. Then she was upon him.

Bud remembered a struggle. Claws swiping his face. A flash of light. A hollow pop. The Pig's weight pressing down on him.

He pushed her lifeless body off. Pain tore up his left side, exited through his head. The boy looked at him with wide-eyed horror. His mouth moved beneath the duct tape.

Bud staggered over to the bed. The boy recoiled. Bud removed the tape as gently as he could.

"Thanks for saving my life, kid." The kid opened his mouth to speak. Terror crept back into his eyes.

"FREEZE!"

The command was deep, urgent, right behind him.

"DROP THE GUN AND STEP AWAY FROM THE BOY."

The gun dangled from his hand. He stood motionless, rested for a bit.

"I SAID DROP THE GUN AND STEP AWAY. NOW!"

He almost did.

"Mister, don't," the boy said, anticipating his plan.

Bud pivoted on his good leg, raised the gun. He was jerked back by the initial shot. The second threw him onto the bed beside the boy.

This time his life did flash before his eyes. But instead of passing by quickly, he was able to slow down the good parts and speed up the bad.

Most of it was bad. But not all.

He watched himself playing catch with his father on the old ball field behind the library. He could see bruises on his own neck and arms. But this was his movie, and he imagined them away.

He fast-forwarded through his teen years, slowed briefly to see his cousin Ronny, his only real friend in life, then sped up the film again until...

Lisa.

He went into freeze-frame mode. He lingered on her face. The soft curve of her nose. The light creases formed when her mouth turned up into a smile.

Hers was a quiet beauty, the kind that goes unnoticed in a crowded room until you got up real close. He zoomed in, traveled up and down the contours of her face, her body.

His life had been shit except for the final reel. Lisa.

The screen flickered, but he could still see her. She was foggy now, her blonde hair blurred into her peach complexion. She called out to him, offered him one more chance to get it right.

He was in blackness now but could feel her beside him, swimming through the dark, her hand lightly brushing his.

A pinpoint of light broke the darkness. The light grew, engulfed them. He turned his head. Lisa smiled at him.

It was a beautiful death.

CHAPTER FIFTY-NINE

Alex Marsh dumped out the jumbo box of Crayola crayons, a birthday gift from Nina, his favorite teacher at the Woodbrine Center for the Deaf. They all still looked so pointy and new. He pushed the pile around, searched for the right shade of blue. He snatched up a crayon called Navy Blue and drew the outline of a car. He colored in the car, careful to stay in the lines. Next he found the shiny black crayon and made the tires.

He sat back and studied his blue car. One tire was smaller than the other and looked kind of flat. But the car came out pretty good. Movement to his right.

Raindrops splattered against his window and drizzled down. He wondered what rain sounded like. Was it softer or louder than snow? Snow looked bigger so he decided rain must be quieter. But how quiet?

Quieter than the noise that blue car made when it ran over that fancy lady?

He returned to his drawing. He found the flesh-colored crayon and drew the lady's head in front of the car. He put XX in for eyes, drew an upside-down smile. He finished the body then looked for the reddest red he could find. He scribbled a little on the lady's head, made drops falling from her head to a puddle below it.

He drew himself and his mother standing on the curb. His mother's mouth was a big "O". Tears ran down her face. He drew some other people standing behind them but didn't bother to give them faces.

Alex studied his drawing. He frowned. Something was missing. He found the black crayon again, its pointy end already gone, and drew lines on the front of the car. It didn't look much like a dent, but it would have to do. Then he added a rectangle coming out of the back of the car and carefully wrote the six-digit license plate number in the box.

The red light flashed on the Fisher-Price monitor in front of him. Dinnertime.

He neatly folded the drawing and put it away in the bottom right drawer of his desk. The smell of spaghetti sauce drifted up the stairs. He closed the drawer and ran downstairs for spaghetti and meatballs. His favorite.

Into the Storm

December

CHAPTER SIXTY

Jake pushed through the herd of last-minute shoppers, angry that they'd all waited so long. It wasn't as if a new holiday had been suddenly sprung upon them. The herd came to a dead stop. Damn.

He spotted an opening in the pack and decided to throw all caution to the wind. He zigged and zagged his way past the old, the young, the perpetually grumpy and the annoyingly cheerful. An obese woman and a skeleton of a man blocked his path. If he could just manage to squeeze between Jack Sprat and his wife, he'd be free and clear.

What's your excuse for waiting until the eleventh hour, Jack? Did you just recover from a severe concussion like Yours Truly? Doubtful. If you're shopping for the wife, just remember to avoid anything lean.

He squeezed between the Sprats and popped out to freedom on the other side. Free from the crushing herd, Jake headed toward a less congested area. He scanned festively decorated storefronts, hoping the right gift would magically appear.

Jake wandered on autopilot into a jewelry store and gazed with disinterest at the ostentatious displays of shimmering diamonds and rubies and pearls. A brilliant necklace beckoned from behind the glass. An elegantly handwritten placard beside it read:

This Christmas, give her the gift she wouldn't dream of returning.

"May I help you?" The woman, all makeup and no substance, moved in with viper-like skill. "Looking for something for that special lady, sir?"

Now that was original. Almost as clever as diamonds being a girl's best friend. "No, thank you," Jake said curtly.

Viper Lady was not about to hand over her commission so easily. "May I show you something in ruby? Or perhaps diamonds? After all"–

–Don't say it–

–"diamonds are a girl's best friend."

"Really, I'm just looking."

"Surely your lady friend deserves something special."

"Like I said, I'm all set."

"But, sir, if you'll just tell me a little bit about your wife's style, I can help you pick out the perfect gift."

At first glance, the woman had appeared to be attractive, if a tad underweight. Upon close inspection, her features were cartoonish, eyeballs busting out of their sockets, brightly lipsticked mouth turned up in a permanent smile. Not for long.

Jake stared into the bulbous eyes and said, "My wife is in a wooden box, six feet under the ground. You got anything that goes with that?"

The permanent smile flipped over. Cartoon features morphed into a twisted, horror-movie expression. The woman's reed-like body, which seemed too frail to support a head so large, trembled. She tried to speak, nothing came out. Tears formed in the giant orbs that dominated half her face. She turned on high heels and scurried away.

Jake exited the store, made his way through the herd again. To hell with this, he thought. Online shopping was sounding awfully good. No rude shoppers, no cloying saleswomen–he could even shop buck-naked if he felt like it.

Suddenly his thoughts turned to Martin. And to what he'd said that night in the dark stairwell.

I need you for the final act.

Did it mean Martin was still here, waiting, watching? Geoffreys, Weeks–hell, even his partner–they'd all scoffed when Jake had suggested this. Long gone, they said. Probably enjoying his newfound wealth on some tropical island. Without having to worry about a three-way split.

Jake knew better. He knew Martin.

I need you for the final act.

Martin McCauley never made threats he didn't intend to carry out. It had never been about the money. Jake knew this. He suspected Drew knew this as well. There was still work to be done.

Jake had convinced Frank Geoffreys to assign protection to the McCauleys as a precaution. Geoffreys agreed, but only through the holidays. With budget cuts strangling him, he couldn't afford to waste invaluable manpower on one of Jake's hunches.

Except Jake's hunches were almost always right.

He passed by another jewelry store. A saleswoman guarded the entry, ready to pounce. Behind her, another brutish saleswoman fawned over a middle-aged couple. The man rested a hand on the beaming woman's shoulder as she studied a dazzling necklace. She was the happiest woman in the world.

Jake was the loneliest man on Earth.

Sheila adored Christmas. She loved the hustle and bustle–even loved Jake's grumbling. Sheila wasn't like the other last-minute shoppers. Most of them were procrastinators, poor planners, or just plain lazy. Not Sheila.

She thrived on the mayhem, said it energized her. All it gave Jake was a headache.

Last year, he and Sheila had walked through this same mall, her arm tucked safely into his, fighting the same mob Jake now found himself trying to escape. He could still hear her voice, the way it rose above the roar of the crowd, the way it made Jake feel like the most important person in the world.

"I'll know it when I see it," she said, dragging Jake by the arm into yet another jewelry store. "It has to be perfect."

"Nikki doesn't need expensive jewelry," Jake remembered saying. "She's still a kid."

Sheila released her delicate hand from his big fat meat hook. "A kid? Jacob Francis Hawksworth, it's about time you accept the fact that your little girl is all grown up."

Jake hated when Sheila used his full name. Especially when she threw in the middle name he'd kept secret to all but the chosen few. What he hated even more was accepting that Nikki was no longer that pigtailed tomboy he used to play catch with down at Stevens Field on Sunday mornings before all the teenagers came and claimed it as theirs.

"Let's try this one," Sheila sang. She pulled him into a store with an expensive façade of marble and brass.

Jake was invisible to the perky saleswoman. She and Sheila were kids in a candy store, scanning case after case of earrings, necklaces and bracelets–all with price tags that laughed at Jake's paycheck.

At last, Sheila said, "This is the one."

The ecstatic saleswoman clasped the ruby and diamond tennis bracelet onto Sheila's wrist. It was something, all right. So was the price.

"We can't afford it," Jake said.

Sheila deflated, her Christmas joy tossed into a dirty snow bank by her very own personal Scrooge.

"But, Jake, can't we just this once..." Her voice swallowed itself up. She knew Scrooge was right.

The saleswoman arched her back. Jake was sure her

dagger-like fingernails grew another inch. He was ruining everyone's Christmas spirit. "We have a payment plan," the woman said in a last-ditch attempt to salvage her sizeable commission.

Sheila smiled weakly at the woman. "No, my husband is right. Maybe next year." She turned and walked out, leaving Jake awash in a sea of guilt. Guilt for not being able to give his family the finer things in life. Guilt for ruining his wife's holiday. And in this sea a shark circled. In the form of a very angry saleswoman with very long fingernails.

Jake paused at the exit to the parking garage. A short, roundish woman toting armloads of shopping bags warned Jake to "move it or lose it." He stepped out into the cold air.

Maybe next year.

His stride had purpose as he moved through the mob, oblivious to the shoves and mumbled curses. He walked into the store, ignored a stick-figure salesman with a womanish walk and headed toward the cartoonish saleswoman. Her colossal eyes averted his attention.

"Excuse me, Miss."

The woman turned slowly, fearfully, like a wallflower that has just been asked to dance by the star quarterback. "Sir, I'm very sorry abou–"

Jake's hand stopped her. "I'm the one who should apologize. I had no right to do that to you."

The woman's features softened. "Thank you," she whispered.

Jake nodded. "If you're not too busy, I'd like to see what you have in the way of ruby and diamond tennis bracelets."

CHAPTER SIXTY-ONE

While Jake Hawksworth was doling out some serious cash for a tennis bracelet, Paige McCauley was putting the finishing touches on the wreath that adorned her stately front door. She shuffled down the icy walkway and turned to admire her handiwork.

The façade boasted twelve windows, each framing a wreath, each wreath donning a red bow. Three spotlights bathed it all in a warm glow.

"Perfect," she whispered. Perfect. And normal. That is what this holiday season was going to be at the McCauley residence. Perfectly normal. She caught a glimpse of the police cruiser idling in the driveway.

Almost normal.

A surprise gust sent swirls of snow dancing about her feet. The wreaths scratched at the windows. Paige hugged her coat to her throat and half-walked, half-skated to the house.

She slammed the door, punched the code on the alarm pad, removed her coat and boots, and hurried into the living room. A blast of heat from the fireplace welcomed her. Aside from the occasional crackle of wood or wind gust slapping the shingles, the house was silent. Too silent.

Not a creature was stirring...

Paige wished she had decided to join Drew and the kids in their quest for the perfect Christmas tree. She glanced out the window. The sight of the police cruiser was comforting.

She took in the grandness surrounding her. The house was bedecked in holiday elegance that would make Martha Stewart's mouth water. All it lacked was the piece de résistance, the fifteen-foot-plus tree.

Drew would struggle to set it up, struggle with the lights. As a family, they would trim the tree. Ben, it had been decided, would put the star on top. Then they would all sit by the roaring fire and play board games until late into the evening.

For the very last time.

This realization hit Paige hard. She and Drew had discussed it at length two nights ago. They would play happy family right up to Christmas. On the day after Christmas, the family would leave on the two-week cruise Drew had booked almost a year ago. Jake had tried to convince them to move the trip up, but Drew insisted on spending Christmas at home.

When they returned, all tanned and rested and with ten extra pounds to their frames, they would break the news to the kids. Ben, Paige feared, would take it the hardest. And it was for him that she wept the most.

She glanced out at the cruiser again. Puffs of smoke from the exhaust mixed with gusts of white powder. The officer on duty was invisible behind fogged up glass. *He must be cold,* she thought. She could use a cup of tea anyway. Why not make enough to go around?

She entered the kitchen. A chill seized her. The moon bathed the backyard in an eerie light, playing off the blanket of snow, filtering through the triple sliders, ending in a pool of yellowish glow at her feet.

Paige padded across the highly polished floor in stocking feet. She picked up the kettle and shook it, force of habit. Almost empty. She placed it under the faucet, turned on the water. She gazed out at the row of hedges, soldiers standing guard along the patio's edge, confetti falling all around them.

A flicker of light to the right.

Movement.

A shape. Sliced neatly from the moonlit backdrop.

The shape of a man.

Paige had always heard that sheer terror was paralyzing. She'd heard wrong.

By the time the kettle connected with the sink, she was halfway across the floor. She bolted down the hallway. The front door grew nearer. Beyond it the protection of an armed officer.

Shaky fingers fumbled with the deadbolt. A blast of cold air slammed her as the door flew open. The alarm was deafening. Eyes focused on the cruiser, she hit the walkway running.

She lost her footing, went down hard. Her head connected with a granite step. The cruiser went to soft focus. The alarm continued its dutiful cry. She turned her neck. The pounding in her head took a back seat to something worse. Total and utter horror.

The shape. Coming closer. Coming fast.

Drew heard the wail of the alarm as he maneuvered the Range Rover down the driveway, the weight of the massive car crushing ice into dust. He floored it.

"What's that noise, Daddy?" Anna asked with sleepy disinterest.

Drew caught his son's eyes in the rearview mirror. They registered the same terror they'd revealed in that horrific Polaroid Drew had found on The Day Life Became a Living Hell.

The house came into view. It looked magnificent. Once again, Paige had outdone herself.

The blare of the alarm and the crunching ice created a symphony of horror, rattling Drew to the core.

Paige made no effort to move, knew it was in vain. *This is what it's like to be paralyzed by fear.* The black shape sailed toward her. The screech of the alarm pulsated in her head, but the noise was distant now, miles away.

The crunch of footsteps was on her. Rapid-fire questions raced through her mind.

–Why didn't I go with them?–

–Why didn't we listen to Jake and leave for that damned trip?–

–Who's going to teach Anna how to grow into a woman?–

–How is Drew going to raise them on his own?–

–Why isn't that bastard here to protect me?–

Something cold brushed her cheek. A voice faded in and out. A kind voice. A concerned voice. The voice was not Martin McCauley's.

"Mrs. McCauley, are you okay?" The almost-young-enough-to-be-her-son police officer knelt beside her. Another voice, farther away.

Drew.

Her husband's face appeared next to the kid playing cop. Though Drew's forehead was creased with worry, he still looked remarkably youthful.

"What happened?" Drew demanded.

The officer shook his head. "I don't know, Mr. McCauley. I was doing my rounds out back when the alarm went off. I came back around front and found your wife right here."

Drew instructed the officer on how to turn off the alarm, then turned to face Paige. "Paige, can you hear me?"

Paige managed a nod. This sent a whole new set of spikes jamming into her brain. "I thou... I thought..." The words slipped off her tongue like honey off a spoon, slowly, deliberately. "... it was your brother."

Drew stroked her hair. "My brother is long gone."

The alarm silenced. The wind whipped around them. The soft crunch of footsteps.

"Mommy!" Anna threw herself onto her mother, sending daggers through Paige's body.

Drew gently lifted Anna's tiny body off and pulled it close to his. Ben stood behind his father, body trembling. The officer appeared again and said, "Ambulance is on the way. Hang tight, Mrs. McCauley."

The faces of her family floated above her, their lips moving, their eyes caverns of sadness. They came in and out of focus, danced in and out of her field of vision. She rotated her head, tried to keep up with them as they bobbed around.

And then he was there.

Behind the police cruiser. Smiling.

She tried to cry out, but nothing came out.

Drew put a gloved finger to her lips. "Try not to move."

The faces of her family and the police officer danced around again. Her eyes searched for Martin. Maybe she'd imagined it after all. He reappeared.

Martin no longer smiled. His face was pure hatred. He blew her a kiss. Then he was gone.

She no longer felt cold. Her head no longer ached. She desired only one thing. To sleep.

CHAPTER SIXTY-TWO

"I know what I saw," Paige McCauley demanded. She was stretched out on an overstuffed sectional.

"You hit your head hard," Drew said. "The mind can play tricks."

"I saw him," she said, turning her icy gaze to Jake. "Jake, I saw him."

Jake circled around the sofa, rested a hand on her shoulder. "I believe you."

Paige looked incredulous. "You do?"

Jake nodded. A sincere nod. Because he honestly did believe her. "Yes."

"Wait a minute, Jake," Drew said. "Everyone said Martin's long gone."

"Everyone except me."

Drew shook his head. A shock of healthy hair fell out of place. "He got the money. Lots of money. Why would he risk getting caught?"

"Because it's not the money he wants," Jake said.

"Then what does he want?" Drew asked.

"You. Your family. And me, I suspect."

Drew brushed thick hair off his forehead, exposing creases Jake had not noticed before. "You're wrong, Jake," he said. "He got what he wanted and that's that. You're scaring my wife."

Paige put a milky hand to her head. "Drew, I've been nothing but scared since this whole thing started."

Time to take charge. "I think it's time you and your family take that vacation," Jake said matter-of-factly.

Drew's face reddened, the creases in his forehead rivers of worry. "I am not going to be driven out of my home like a scared rat!"

"So, tough guy," Jake said, "you'd rather put your children in harm's way?"

Drew came at Jake, guns blazing, barrels cocked. "Are you insinuating that I–"

"STOP!"

Ben McCauley looked small in the massive doorway. He didn't have to say another word. His face said it all: *I'm the kid here, I'm the one missing a toe, I'm the one who was stuck in a prison, I'm the only one acting like an adult here!*

Paige broke into a million pieces. Drew deflated, his shoulders crumpling into his chest. Jake looked at the boy, a tower of strength. It was then he realized who had held this family together for this long.

CHAPTER SIXTY-THREE

It was the dark he feared most. Not the moonlit kind of dark or the movie theater kind of dark. The can't-see-your-hand-in-front-of-your-face kind of dark. That's what really got under his skin.

As a kid, he loved the dark, loved not knowing what lurked around the next corner. The cave had been like that. Crawling through the cave now, he felt none of that childhood exhilaration. Only loneliness.

Loneliness seemed to follow him wherever he went. It tagged along on his first night at Cedar Junction, cramming itself into that postage stamp of a cell right alongside him, overstaying its welcome by about twenty years, give or take.

Then there was Solitary. No place lonelier. Not even the bottom of a dried up old well.

He'd spent his share in Solitary, a place where minutes become hours, hours become days. Days become endless, rolling over one another, a sea of blackness. The worst part about Solitary was leaving it. Reentry into daylight was like being Dracula stuck in traffic with dawn barreling up over the horizon.

He knew Solitary was not to blame for his fear of the dark, however. November 6, 1992. There was the guilty party.

It was a run-of-the-mill day at The Junction. KP duty in the morning. Some poor fuck taking a shiv in the gut during a basketball game in the yard. A lame-ass movie shown on a lame-ass projector. Same shit, different day.

Then everything changed.

He'd been alone in the shower when the lights went out. He heard the whispers. And the darkness became his enemy.

He never saw their faces. But the voices seared into his memory. This memory would serve him well later when he enacted his revenge.

He remembered his cheek pressing into the cold tiles, the sound of sizzling steak as the water pounded the floor around him. His arms, rendered useless under the crushing weight, splayed out to either side. His legs forced apart, they too, useless.

His screams drowned out the sizzling steak until a bar of soap silenced the screams. He lost track of how many times they went at him, all sense of reality blurred by shame, anger, and loss.

November 6, 1992. The night he lost everything.

He sucked in damp, musty air and burrowed deeper into the cave. He thought of the story of Winnie the Pooh, one of the few books he'd actually read on his own as a kid. Drew was always the bookworm in the family, tearing through book after book, most of the pages filled only with words, no pictures, and too many damn words at that.

In the Pooh book, a book with lots of pictures and just enough words, the dumb old bear gets himself wedged in the doorway of that annoying rabbit's cave. Too much damn honey. Served him right.

Right now, walls of dirt pressing on him from all sides, he felt an awful lot like that stupid bear. Except for one major difference.

He had no one to pull him out if he got stuck.

He dragged himself by his elbows. The flashlight flapped awkwardly in his left hand, like a bird's broken wing.

Then the unthinkable happened.

The flashlight went out. And his whole world was dipped in ink.

The blackness was suffocating, as if he'd been dropped head-first into a vat of coal. He feared the pounding in his heart would loosen the dirt, turning his childhood fort into a tomb.

But, no, that would not happen. He had too many loose ends to tie up. In one big bloody Christmas bow.

His elbows found new purpose. He propelled his body through the tunnel. Then he saw it.

It was only a speck of light, but it reminded him he had not gone blind, that he was not in hell just yet. The sliver of light crept into the fissures of the stone-mixed-with-dirt ceiling. He focused on the light beam, got his bearings. The room was right around the corner.

He felt the walls push out, away from his shoulders, his chest, his back. And he knew he was in the room. The room provided no light, the opening in the ceiling sealed long ago by a tangle of vines and branches. The sliver of light lingered around the corner, offering no assistance, instead whispering, *I'll wait out here for you.*

He flipped himself over, relieved the pressure on his elbows, now home to thousands of pins and needles. *Get what you came for and get out. It has to be here somewhere.*

Groping fingers brushed cold metal. The toolbox. If he had a little light, he'd take five and get reacquainted with his old girlfriends, their ageless bodies still smooth and tight, though probably dulled and yellowed.

A few feet to the right of the toolbox, he began to dig. Jagged stones nicked fingertips, frozen dirt rubbed them raw. His forearms screamed. His fingers, though he could not see them, bled. Shit. He'd imagined the ground to be softer, insulated from the elements.

Maybe he was digging in the wrong place. He found a new spot and dug in.

It has to be here.

His fingers grazed something hard.

He worked furiously now, digging out around it. It took some work to free it from its grave, but then it was out, and with it secrets thought forever buried. Secrets as dark as the hole he had just crawled into.

CHAPTER SIXTY-FOUR

Lydia Marsh watched the bad news unfold on her television set. The stout, balding man standing before the computerized map of the state had just said the magic word. Nor' Easter. His animated arm gestures and childlike grin told Lydia it was going to be a whopper.

She let out a heavy sigh. A laundry basket idled on her hip. As if things weren't already tough enough, now Our God and Savior had to toss a snowstorm into the mix.

Alex flashed a smile from the kitchen table where he scribbled furiously, and for a moment Worry slid off Lydia's shoulders. She managed a smile, then moved down the hallway, Worry climbing its way back up onto its perch.

She set the laundry basket on Alex's unmade bed, plunked down beside it. The room was like a typical seven-year-old's. LeBron James and Tom Brady flashed their multi-million dollar smiles from their prime spots on the worn blue plaid wallpaper. Books on sports and science and animals spilled from a red plastic bookcase. This morning's pajamas lay in a heap by the bed, having missed the hamper by a mile.

In fact, aside from the Special Olympics ribbons tacked with pride to the cork board, one would never know there to be anything out of the ordinary.

Lydia reached for the solitary photograph on the nightstand. Though the frame was made of wood, she handled it as though it were the Hope Diamond.

It was more valuable.

The photograph was Alex's last memory of his father.

Sunlight bounced off the gleaming faces, Alex in his favorite baseball cap, Wayne in his ridiculous fishing hat. Dangling in front of them were two tiny fish, insignificant in size but sure to grow each time Wayne relayed the story.

Lydia pulled the photo close enough for her breath to fog the glass. She searched the crevices in Wayne's face for any hints of illness. There were none. And, still, two weeks later she'd find herself a stranger in her own home, people carrying casseroles and telling her how unfair life could be.

"We just have to accept the hand God deals us," Wayne's Uncle Danny had said as he shoveled Gwen Livingston's home-made meat lasagna into his mouth.

"If this is the hand meant for me, then get me a new dealer," Lydia had replied. She had laughed hysterically at her joke, was still laughing when she was admitted into the place with stark white walls and no laughter, only hushed whispers in the corridors.

Lydia returned the photograph, positioned it to stand watch over her little man. She hummed a tune she couldn't place as she neatly put tee shirts and sweaters and jeans in their right place, noting that they looked more like the wardrobe of a five-year-old.

She arranged the eruption of books. She snatched up the pajamas with a weary hand and tossed them into the hamper. Passing by the window, she paused.

A woman peered in at her. The woman was much older, with hollowed cheeks and hair that didn't know which way to go. The woman wore the same tired blouse and when Lydia frowned, the woman frowned back.

Turning to leave, she gave the room a once-over. Something seemed out of place. Then she spotted it. A pie-shaped piece of drawing paper protruding from one of the desk drawers. She opened the drawer and the creased sheet of paper slid silently inside. On the sheet was a colorful rainbow, a pot of gold at one end, a dancing leprechaun at the other.

Lydia pulled up a spot on the carpet and settled in. She lifted the stack of drawings onto her lap. The rainbow. A lion sitting atop a hill. An adult Alex dressed in a policeman's uniform. Another rainbow. Alex and Wayne fishing, the fish larger than the boat. She smiled and flipped to the next masterpiece.

Her smile fell apart. The paper trembled in her hands. The word came out in a single puff of breath.

"Omigod."

CHAPTER SIXTY-FIVE

The campus was abuzz with students rushing to finals or departing for the holiday break. Jeeps and SUVs lined the ice-slicked roads, trunks and hatches agape, ready to devour laptops and bags of laundry.

Jake moved slowly, in no hurry to get where he was going. His mind replayed the shame and embarrassment etched into Nikki's eyes. They'd spoken on the phone a few times since, mostly small talk mixed with long awkward pauses. He could handle the pauses. As long as he didn't have to look into those eyes.

What had Nikki read in *his* eyes that night? Anger? Disappointment? Disbelief?

There'd have been a little of each, he was sure of that. But if she had looked a little more closely, she would have seen something else.

Fear. And relief.

Fear that he had lost the only two people he'd ever really cared about. And relief that one of them was still with him.

A couple not a whole lot different from Nikki and Chip hurried by, locked in an embrace that told the world they were taken, that they'd found their soul mate.

What happened when your soul mate was taken from you? Were you given a consolation prize, someone who could make you forget the other existed, until those dead hours when the world slept–all except for you–because you knew that the bump in the covers beside you would never measure up?

And what if Nikki had found her true soul mate? Should Jake

rob her of that gift the way he was robbed of his? So what if the kid had eyes that couldn't be trusted. Or that his education level was probably on a par with Jake's. If it were good enough for Nikki, well then, goddammit, it would have to be good enough for him.

The late morning sun skipped across the tired brick building, scoffing at the weatherman's forecast. Jake gazed up at the neat rows of windows, slick gray squares secreting the potential that hid behind them. He counted up and across to Nikki's window. It stared coldly at him. He clenched his fingers around the beautifully gift wrapped bracelet and wondered if his daughter was staring at him too.

CHAPTER SIXTY-SIX

The snow galloped into town, on a mission. Tiny orange dots glowered in the blur of white, the only indication that the house was still there. It was risky, but he had to get closer.

He stopped at the forest's edge. A perfect blanket of white stretched from his feet to the house. He took a step forward. At the rate the snow was falling, his footfalls would be veiled in a matter of minutes. He stopped. He'd come too far to get sloppy.

Twin lights blinded him. Instinctively, he fell to the ground. The lights melted away into the storm. Car doors. Muffled voices.

It was him.

The gang's all here. Still trying to save the day, Jake? And you've brought your trusty sidekick, Tonto. Maybe I should have put you out of your misery. But then, that would spoil the surprise.

The two Supercops skated up the driveway. The house swallowed them up.

He stood and brushed himself off. The impulse to go right on in there and finish this up Charlie Manson style was overwhelming. He needed to get out of these wet clothes. To soak in a warm tub. To feel her body against his for one last time.

Relax. Too much company. The one in the patrol car. The fat one inside. And now Tonto.

The Okie in the patrol car was a no-brainer. The fat one could be a problem.

Been here all goddamn day. Probably eating Baby Brother out of house and home.

Movement in an upstairs window.

The snow-streaked glass distorted her features. But he knew

them intimately. The silky hair brushing his neck. The eyes that searched desperately for the love they'd lost. The pinched up nose expressing its dislike for tattoos. The pouty lips whispering his name over and over.

–Drew, Drew, it's been so long... how long has it been... I'm so sorry... Drew, tell me everything will be okay–

He'd touch those lips, that hair one more time. And those eyes, those desperate eyes, would beg him to stop the pain, to make it end. To show some mercy.

–Drew, tell me everything will be okay–

–everything will be okay–

–promise?–

–promise–

–Drew, I love you, I've always loved you–

–show me–

–I don't know how anymore–

–show me–

–I'll try–

The blurred silhouette in the window came into focus, then evaporated.

He whispered two words. Words that were swept up by the ever-increasing storm.

"Show me."

CHAPTER SIXTY-SEVEN

With a body that perfectly suited his last name, one would think that Officer Lenny Tubbs's nickname was Tubby. One would think.

"How's it hanging, Tiny?" Jake said. The warmth of the McCauley home wrapped itself around him.

"Can't complain, Jake," Tiny said, chewing on something. Tiny was always chewing on something. "Storm's getting bad."

Snow melted into Jake's coat. "Yep. Channel 5 says it's going to be a whopper. Better hit the road before you end up snowbound with this schmuck." Jake slapped his partner on the back. Kyle grunted.

Tiny stopped chewing. Jake wondered if the endless eating machine's body would shut down and die on the spot. "Thanks for getting me the overtime, Jake," Tiny said. "It'll sure come in handy this Christmas."

"No problem, Tiny. And take Federman with you. He must be freezing his ass off out there."

Jake's cell buzzed in his pocket. "Hold on a sec, Tiny," he said. "Hawksworth here."

"Jake, it's Hassleback. I'm over at the lab." Bruce Hassleback always sounded glum. Tonight his voice was downright somber. "We have a lead on Sheila's case."

The words slammed into Jake, each one a bullet to his gut. "Wha–who?"

"Lydia Marsh came by the station this afternoon."

Lydia Marsh? Who is Lydia Marsh? The deaf boy. The deaf boy's mother.

"I don't get it," Jake said. "I spoke to her half a dozen times and she said she didn't remember anything."

"She doesn't. Her kid does."

Jake's legs went weak. He tasted metal. "The kid?" he said incredulously. "But he's deaf."

"He may be deaf, but he isn't blind. He got the license plate number."

"He got the–why the hell didn't he tell us this before?"

Bruce cleared his throat. "I asked Mrs. Marsh the same question."

"And?"

"She said when she asked Alex that, he said nobody ever asked him."

"Nobody ever asked him?"

"That's what he said." Bruce cleared his throat again. "Nobody ever asked him."

Nobody ever asked him. I never asked him. All this time.

"Who–what do you know, Bruce?"

"We're running the plate as we speak, Jake."

"It's him."

"Who?"

"Martin. Martin McCauley. I know it."

"We're working on it. As soon as I know anything, I'll–"

"–I'm on my way." Before Bruce could respond, Jake was halfway to the door. "Tiny, can you do me a favor?"

"Sure, Jake," Tiny said. He was chewing on something again.

"I need to head back to the station. I hate to ask you this, but can you or Federman hang in here a while longer?"

Tiny stopped chewing. "Federman's got a wife and kids. Me, well, all I've got is a fridge and remote waiting for me."

"What's going on, Jake?" Kyle Henderson appeared genuinely concerned.

"Sheila. We got him. Take care of the McCauleys for me, will you?"

Kyle was already pushing him toward the door. "Go."

Jake's heart was two steps ahead as he pushed through the wall of cold that pressed against him. Bruce Hassleback's deep hushed voice rose up through the biting wind.

Nobody ever asked him.

How could I have been so stupid? I never asked him. Never leave a stone unturned. That's what I'm always telling Kyle. Why didn't I ask him? Because he was seven? Or because he was deaf?

It was really quite simple, if you thought about it. Ask a seven-year-old a question, he'll answer it. Usually quite candidly. Don't ask, and he'll smile and go about his business, without so much as a second thought.

You never asked.

He watched The Lone Ranger get into his car and drive off. Where was he going? And why wasn't his trusty sidekick Tonto with him?

This was not part of The Master Plan. Hawksworth was supposed to be here. Not some fat piece of shit rent-a-cop and the pretty boy.

Pins and needles tickled his cheeks. His feet throbbed. He'd just have to improvise, is all. He could catch Jake up to speed later.

He moved in for the kill.

CHAPTER SIXTY-EIGHT

It was whiteout conditions when Jake reached the station. Shirley Morris, a curvaceous woman with cocoa-colored skin and a sense of humor bigger than her bra size, was on desk duty. Shirley was loud, obnoxious, a bit overbearing at times. And one of the most lovable people Jake knew.

"Well, I'll be damned," Shirley said through a smile that could swallow up Texas. "If it ain't the man of my dreams. Jake, when are you gonna take me away from all this?"

"Shirley, I told you, I'm nothing but trouble," Jake said. He laughed. Inside he was screaming. "You need to find yourself a man who'll treat you like the queen you are."

Shirley raised her arms to the heavens. "Amen to that." Shirley pointed toward a long corridor. "They're waitin' for you out back, Jake. I sure hope you get the answers you been lookin' for."

Jake sent a silent kiss Shirley's way and moved down the hallway. His insides knotted up. He expected to see Lydia Marsh and her son sitting in the row of hard plastic chairs. They were as empty as his heart.

The lab was a sauna. Bruce Hassleback waved Jake over to a corner crammed with computer equipment and more wires than there could possibly be outlets for. A lab technician who looked no older than Nikki pounded away on a keyboard.

"Long time no see, Bruce."

"Good to see you too, Jake." Bruce Hassleback held out a brittle arm.

Jake resisted his usual firm handshake, afraid he'd break every bone in the man's hand.

"We have a name," Bruce said. "Ready to take a look?"

After all the hours, all the dead-end leads, they actually had a name. "Sure. Who's our guy? Or is it a gal?" *Or is it Martin McCauley?*

Bruce's head pivoted back and forth on a skeletal neck. His Adam's apple pulsated. No wonder the guy couldn't get a date. "It's a guy." His eyes fell to a sheet of paper. "A Robert Garrity."

"Sounds like a middle-aged accountant from the suburbs," Jake said. "So, what do we have on this Robert Garrity?"

"Let's see," Bruce said, his Adam's apple now moving under his skin like a Mexican jumping bean. "Twenty-five years old, a carpenter who works on and off for various companies. Arrested on a DUI six years ago, got community service and a slap on the wrist. Been clean since."

"Twenty-five? I liked my middle-aged accountant theory better," Jake said. The lab technician turned her head and muffled a laugh.

Bruce rested a veiny hand on the girl's shoulder. Jake found it disturbing that she didn't flinch. "Becca, can you print me out a picture of our Mr. Garrity, please?" Bruce said.

Becca nodded and clicked through a series of boxes. An image popped up on the screen. Robert Garrity stared at them.

Jake took two steps back. His head was a balloon.

I am not seeing this.

Bruce's voice called to him from miles away.

This is not happening.

"Jake, are you okay?" Bruce Hassleback's voice floated around him.

Jake's eyes remained locked on the face peeking over Becca's shoulder.

"It can't be."

CHAPTER SIXTY-NINE

Paige packed for a trip she knew she'd never take. Even if they could fly out tomorrow, all the problems they left behind would be waiting for them, snowed in on the couch with arms crossed and feet tapping, as if to say, *What took you so long?*

She tossed a stack of tank tops into the suitcase and fell onto the bed. Who was she kidding? They'd be lucky to get to the end of the driveway, much less the airport. She was now literally trapped in this home she'd felt trapped in for years. From the imported draperies and carpets right down to the hand-cut Italian tile. This was her prison. This was her hell.

A rap at the door startled her. "Come in."

Kyle Henderson entered. The temperature clicked up a notch. His stride was confident, maybe too confident. When you're as attractive as Kyle Henderson, everything comes just a little easier. He said, "Mrs. McCauley, I just wanted to make sure you're okay."

Paige smiled, wondered if he could tell she'd been crying, if he sensed the sudden urge she had to ravage him. "I'm fine. Thank you."

Kyle smiled back and Paige was overwhelmed with guilt. Guilt for thinking of seducing a man almost young enough to be her son. In her bedroom. With her family one floor below. "Will that be all, Officer?" The words came out harsher than she meant for them to.

Kyle's smile drizzled away to nothing. "Yes, ma'am, sorry to have bothered you." He turned to leave. "One more thing."

"Yes?" Electricity rippled through her body.

"Ben and Anna were wondering if it would be okay to play in the snow for a while before things get too bad. Officer Tubbs or I would be right there with them at all times. Your husband said to ask you."

Ask me? Is he incapable of making a decision regarding our children? Or is he trying to save what can no longer be saved?

"Okay," Paige said. "I suppose that would be okay, as long as you're going to be with them." Kyle Henderson nodded and pulled the door shut behind him. His scent lingered in the heavy air. Paige suddenly regretted casting him off.

She moved to the window, lost herself in the rush of snow. Snowflakes bombarded the window soundlessly. An overstuffed moon bathed the blanketed lawn below in an iridescent glow that was at once eerie and breathtaking. If she didn't know better, she would have sworn it was mid afternoon.

Movement disrupted the Hallmark moment. A brightly wrapped Anna plowed through the perfect white carpet, ruining it in typical Anna fashion. She plunked herself down on her back and flapped her arms and legs furiously. When she stood, the snow collapsed in around her perfect snow angel.

I want to make snow angels too! Paige screamed from silent lips.

Ben entered the Hallmark painting. Drew crept up from behind and tackled him. Anna joined the pig pile. Officer Tubbs cast a generous shadow across the shimmery blanket.

Paige considered joining them. Instead she watched from her window, a safe haven from a man she loved but was no longer in love with. She imagined Kyle Henderson downstairs alone. She imagined herself downstairs with him, making love to him while her family frolicked only steps away.

A snowball fight erupted below, Officer Tubbs the easy target. Paige watched the silhouettes bob and weave against the snowy backdrop. Her eyes wandered. To the trees. Their branches strained under the weight of the snow. Another silhouette cut itself from the landscape. Was it a dog? A fox?

Paige wiped a sleeve across the fogged glass. A blur of white made it difficult to see. Still, there was something there. Just beyond the tree line.

She pressed her face into the glass. The slick cold bit into her cheek. She scanned the tree line. The dark shape was gone. It had never been there. She had imagined it, just as she had imagined Kyle Henderson coming up behind her, pushing his firm body against hers.

There it is again! The snowflakes seemed to clear a path, allowing her a better look. Something was there, not fifty feet from her snow-spotted family.

She pulled her face from the glass. Her eyes ping-ponged from the shape in the trees to her family and back to the shape again.

It was no dog. Or fox. Her scream was silenced as it made its way through her windpipe. She could not move. All she could do was stare at the man who stared at her family.

Martin McCauley had come back.

CHAPTER SEVENTY

Interesting name, Chip. Is there an interesting story that goes with it?

Not really, Mr. Hawksworth. My real name's Bob.

Jake gazed at the face on the screen.

My real name's Bob.

Bob. Robert.

Robert Garrity.

"Jake, what's wrong?" Bruce Hassleback asked. Becca's manicured fingers rested on the keyboard, taking a breather.

Jake wished his hunch had been right. He wished it had been Martin McCauley. He could have handled that. Christ, if it had been the Pope he could have handled it better.

Bruce Hassleback's voice was there again. But it was very far away. "Jake, you look like you've seen a ghost."

Chip. The kid who shared his Thanksgiving table. The kid who shared his daughter's bed.

Becca, sensing what was about to happen, leapt from her chair. She gasped. Just as Nikki had gasped the night Jake kicked in her door.

Jake gripped the vacant chair and vomited, releasing all the pent up pain of not knowing, and the greater pain that came with knowing.

CHAPTER SEVENTY-ONE

Snowflakes the size of boulders tumbled around him. He watched his family, his flesh and blood, as they danced around, so close he could see the fine lines on his brother's face, the snow licking at the children's faces.

He could take them all out right now if he wanted to, splashing red across the virgin snow. He'd take out the fat rent-a-cop first, then the young ones, forcing his baby brother to take it all in. Tonto would come to the rescue but not even his good looks could save him. Then when they were all out of the way, he'd give his brother one final gift. His wife's lifeless body. But not before squeezing all the life out of it first.

The girl's shrill laugh shook him back to where he was, feet two blocks of ice, body headed for hypothermia. Movement to his left. Tonto.

"We really should all come inside now, Mr. McCauley," he heard Tonto yell over the strengthening gale.

The two brats groaned. "Can't we stay out just a little longer, Daddy?" the shrill little girl whined. "Pleeeez." She held out her hands as if in deep prayer. Her brother joined her. Smart ploy. Outnumber the parent. The weak parent.

Drew McCauley said, "If Officer Henderson thinks we should go inside, maybe we should."

Spineless. Like you've been your whole life. Take a stand for once in your life, Baby Brother.

Ben McCauley said, "Officer Henderson is just afraid we'll kill him in a snowball fight."

Tonto smiled that Dentyne smile of his and said, "Oh, is that so?" He bent over and balled up some snow. His delivery of the ball was Minor League quality at best. It slammed into the kid's heavily padded chest.

What followed was an all-out war, giving Martin the break he needed. He scooped up the bag, made his way to the side of the house. He reached for the door that led into the garage. Locked. A window. Worth a shot. It slid open. He tossed the bag through and climbed in.

When Paige last saw the intruder in her backyard, she had acted quickly. Why was it that now she could not move? The storm clawed at the windows, pounded on the walls. The room waited for Paige to make her move.

This fear that now paralyzed her had occurred only two other times in her life. The time she'd lost Anna in a Target for five minutes that may as well have been five years. And the time she found her son's crumpled bike in her driveway. She knew then that something horrific had happened.

Just as she knew now that something horrific was about to happen.

Unless you pull yourself together. Now.

She focused on the door. *One step at a time. Get to the door.* She padded soundlessly across the lushly carpeted floor, another extravagance that seemed so trite now. The doorknob. *Turn it. Don't think about what's on the other side.*

The door creaked open. She stepped into the hallway. Nothing there. Just the side table that had once belonged to Betsy Ross. And the Andrew Wyeth original that Drew had given her for one of her twenty-ninth birthdays, a painting she hated almost as much as the horn-tooting that had gone along with it.

The hallway stretched a good fifteen feet before turning sharply to the main hallway that ran the length of the house. The main hallway housed a number of doors leading to a number of rooms on one side, and opened to a soaring foyer and magnificent staircase that made Paige feel like Cinderella arriving at the ball every time she walked down it.

She moved, catlike, hugged the wall. She reached the corner. Her heart shifted in her chest. She took a breath, stepped into the main hallway. The highly buffed cherry floor felt harder than usual. Paige suddenly longed for the security of her bedroom carpet. Moonlight flooded through the foyer's massive windows, cutting daggers of light into the walls. The rush of snow projected onto these walls, creating a dizzying sense of silent chaos.

"Officer Henderson." Her faint voice was swept up in the moving walls. She repeated his name again, louder. Nothing. Sheer terror shoved her toward the staircase. She called out again. "Kyle."

Where was he? Wasn't he supposed to be protecting her? Maybe Martin had slaughtered them all and now waited below, dipped in blood and melting ice, leaving a trail all over her Persian rugs.

She searched for a weapon. Perhaps a Medieval décor would have made more sense. Something rested against Ben's bedroom door.

A Christmas present.

Wrapped in shiny red paper and topped with a large gold bow, the cheap peel-and-stick kind. The gift was long and slender, almost tube-like. A tag hung below the bow. Something was scrawled in black pen.

Paige studied the odd package. The paper shimmered as

slivers of light danced across it. She read the hastily written message.

To Ben–The Next Generation McCauley
Merry Xmas ... The Blood Brothers

Paige tore feverishly at the pretty paper.

CHAPTER SEVENTY-TWO

The storm raged. Snow piled up on the windshield as quickly as the wipers could sweep it away. If he sat there long enough, maybe the storm would entomb him.

It beat having to face Nikki.

How does one tell his daughter that he has found the person responsible for her mother's death, and that this person is the man she thinks is her Prince Charming? Being buried alive looked more and more appealing.

Jake's fingers searched under the seat, force of habit he supposed. He knew they'd find nothing, except maybe a few nickels or, on a good day, a quarter. Those weren't going to help him get through this. Not like his old friend Jack could.

Enough procrastinating. He tugged on the door handle. The door fell open. Mother Nature wasted no time climbing on in beside Jake, bringing with her an onslaught of numbing wind and a pile of the white stuff.

He stood before the dorm. Rows of glowing orange squares and the occasional string of Christmas lights beckoned him. He lingered outside the entrance, until the biting wind pressed hard against his back, prodded him to get on with the task at hand.

Sheets of paper decorated the lobby's stark white walls, some bearing frat names, others advertising tutors and study groups. Clusters of orange couches and chairs formed random seating areas. Drab gray industrial carpeting was marred by well-worn traffic areas and muddied footprints.

For what I'm paying, this place ought to look like The Ritz.

An elevator door pinged, slid open, and discharged two

students. The couple laughed and stumbled and spilled their beers all over the lovely carpeting. The girl, who looked like she'd be nursing a hangover tomorrow, fell onto one of the orange couches. The contents of her cup dissolved into the carpet. The man, who looked like he'd be more at home on a beach with a surfboard tucked under one arm, joined his lady friend.

The couple fondled and groped and tore at each other, oblivious to the storm rattling the floor-to-ceiling windows, oblivious to the man watching them like a voyeur. Jake felt his face flush. Still, he didn't move. One more excuse to avoid the unavoidable.

The girl, unbuttoned blouse exposing a black lace bra, at last noticed Jake. She pushed away a persistent Surfer Dude and whispered, "Someone's here."

In typical Surfer Dude fashion, it took a few moments for him to grasp what his friend was trying to say.

"Omigod, it's Nikki's dad," the girl said. "He's a cop."

The last word took no time to register in Surfer Dude's half-baked brain. He bee-lined it for the elevator before you could say *Surf's up*. His untucked girlfriend poured herself into the elevator, disappeared behind this week's plaything.

Surfer Dude smiled at Jake. "Going up?"

Jake resisted the urge to bust a gut. He could peg someone from a mile away. Just like he'd pegged Martin McCauley all those years ago. So why hadn't he pegged Bob? Or was it Chip?

"Like, are you coming?" Surfer Dude asked. He stood patiently, held the door. No cares. No worries.

"I think I'll take the stairs."

"Whatever, Grampa." The door wiped Surfer Dude away.

Jake labored up the eight flights of steps, wishing he'd accepted Surfer Dude's invitation. The final flight nearly did him in. The hallway was vacant. Not even the usual remnants of a party. No empty beer cans for Jake to kick as he made his way to his daughter's room. Not even a cigarette butt.

Cheerful holiday messages filled the memo board. Damn, she was one popular kid. Got that from her mother. Jake knocked softly on the door.

He didn't notice the tears streaming down his face.

CHAPTER SEVENTY-THREE

He watched her from the shadows. A robe hung loosely around her body, doing it a great disservice. Moonlight streaked her hair, splashed across her face, making it more radiant than ever. She studied the bat, turned it in her hands, as if it held the secret to the Holy Grail.

Martin stepped out of the shadows. "I took you as more the tennis type."

Paige turned and raised a wobbly bat. Even in her terrified state, she was as beautiful as the night they went at it like wild dogs in that fleabag motel.

I love you. I always have.

Show me.

Just for fun he said, "Didn't your mother tell you it isn't polite to open someone else's presents?"

The bitch tightened her grip on the bat, opened her stance. "Stay away from me!"

He raised his hands in mock surrender. "Put the bat down, Wendy," he said in his best Jack Nicholson. He was sure Stephen King would've given his imitation a big thumbs up.

Her eyes widened, a potent mix of hatred and terror. They darted back and forth, searched for help that wasn't there. "Stay where you are." It sounded more like a pathetic plea than a demand. She sidestepped to her left, toward the staircase.

Playtime was over. He lunged, underestimated her. The bat connected with his right hand, sent shockwaves up his arm. Before he could react to the first blow, she took a swipe at his head. She got the next best thing. His left shoulder.

He crashed into the wall. She hightailed it for the stairs. This time she underestimated him. He tackled her. They came down hard. He flipped her over, straddled her. "Just like old times, darling." *Show me.* "What say we have a little fun?"

Voices. Laughing. A door opening.

"Kids are home, honey," Martin said. He pulled himself up. The hand hurt. The shoulder hurt worse. "Get up."

Paige struggled to her feet. Her children's voices danced below. Then she saw it. And panic set in.

A gun. Tucked into his side. Maybe if she pretended she didn't see it. Too late.

He rested a hand on the gun and said, "You didn't really think all I brought was that old baseball bat, do you?" He smiled. A smile stolen from her husband. He retrieved the bat, held it out. "Take it."

Paige obeyed. "What do you want me to do with it?"

"Give it to your son."

"Why?"

Anna's voice, a slightly out-of-key melody, floated up the staircase. "Mommy, I made snow angels! Mommy, where are you?"

"Please don't hurt my children," Paige whispered.

"Move. Now."

Paige reached the landing and spotted Anna twenty feet below. From here, she looked very small. Anna looked up. Her crooked smile opened up. Her burnished cheeks were a healthy shade of crimson. Crystallized ice clung to the ends of her hair.

"Mommy, did you see me–" Her tiny scream ricocheted around the cavernous foyer.

Paige felt the gun in her back. If only she could have one

more shot with the bat. Just one more shot. She'd hit one right out of the park.

Kyle Henderson came into view, gun drawn, followed by Tiny, still fumbling to release his gun. Then Drew. Then Ben. All eyes looked up at Paige. Kyle leveled his gun at Martin. Realizing it was futile, he let it drop to his side.

Martin was the puppeteer and, as long as the gun stayed trained on Paige, he could pull any strings he wanted. He ordered his marionettes to the family room, directed them where to sit. Ben and Anna buried themselves in their mother's chest. Kyle sat stoic. Tiny looked like he'd just been asked to skip dessert.

The wind shook the house. The lights flickered. A power outage would sure come in handy right about now, Paige decided. No such luck.

"Give it to him," Martin demanded.

"Give who what?" Paige said, her voice edged in anger.

"Your son. Give him his present."

Paige looked down at the bat. Funny, she'd forgotten all about it. It felt weightless in her grip. She lifted it.

Her husband gasped. It was a strong reaction, doused in surprise and fear and utter dread. "Paige, where did you get that?"

Martin's laugh rattled Paige's bones. "Bet you never thought you'd see that again, Baby Brother, did you? Found it right where you buried it."

Paige said, "Drew, what is he talking about?" She held the bat like it had been dipped in a plague. "What is this?"

"Tell her," Martin said. "No, wait." He did a little dance, waving the gun in the air. "We're missing one key player." He leveled the gun on Kyle Henderson. "Tonto over here is going to get him for us."

CHAPTER SEVENTY-FOUR

Jake was still picking up the pieces of his daughter when his phone rang. "Hawksworth," he said.

"Hey, Jake."

Henderson. "Kyle–what's up?"

Silence. Then: "I need you back out here at the McCauleys."

Jake glanced up at his daughter. Throw a frame around her face and you had yourself the ultimate portrait in grief. "I can't leave Nikki right now," Jake said softly. If Nikki heard him, her eyes didn't show it. She was lost in a sea of anguish, without a life jacket, not even a goddamn piece of driftwood. "You and Tiny are going to have to hold down the fort for a while."

"Tiny left. He was... uhhh... sick."

Why the stuttering, pal? "You okay, partner?"

"I'm fine, Jake," Kyle said. He didn't sound fine.

"Okay–then have backup sent for Tubbs." More silence. "Not too quick on the uptake tonight, partner."

"Already tried that," his partner said. He sounded put out. "Merrill says there's no one to spare, with the storm and all."

Merrill? Who the hell is Merrill? "Kyle, what are you–"

"–gotta go, Jake," Kyle said abruptly. "Just get back here as soon as you can." *Click.*

"What the..." Jake stared at the cell phone as if it might tell him what the hell had just happened. *Merrill. Who is Merrill? What are you trying to tell me, partner?*

And Tubbs sick? The guy had never taken a sick day that Jake could remember. Hell, he was the guy who usually filled in when someone else was sick.

Who is Merrill?

"Daddy, what's wrong?" The Sea of Anguish had carried Nikki in on its wake, carelessly tossing her ashore, yet capable of pulling her right back into its churning abyss in a heartbeat.

Jake touched her hand. The absurdly expensive tennis bracelet spilled carelessly across it. He looked into his daughter's eyes and decided it was worth every damn penny. "It's okay, baby. Nothing's wrong. I'm here for you." He was her driftwood.

Nikki threw herself into his arms, the way that pigtailed little girl used to whenever he came home after working a double shift. He held her so tightly, he feared he might burst her like a balloon. They hugged and cried together, a cathartic bonding between father and child.

Merrill.

The answer came, nearly cut him off at the ankles. The Name the Crime Game. Merrill was a name Kyle had used in The Name the Crime Game only a few weeks ago. Jake had gotten it, as usual.

So, why the hell can't I remember it now? Think. Was Merrill a guy from Kyle's childhood? High school? The academy?

"Who is he?" Jake said.

Nikki pulled back, met her father's gaze. "Who's who, Daddy?"

"Merrill," Jake mumbled.

"Who's Merrill?" his daughter asked. He'd plucked her from the Sea of Anguish and thrown her headfirst into the Sea of Confusion. Right beside her Dear Old Dad.

"I don't know," Jake said, not so much speaking to his daughter, more just talking things out. "Something Kyle said. Mentioned a guy named Merrill down at the station. Funny thing is, there is no guy by that name on the force."

"Are you sure Merrill is a guy?" his daughter asked.

Bingo. He kissed Nikki. "You're a genius." Jake dialed up headquarters. "Martha–Jake Hawksworth–yes, I'm fine–yes, it's been a long time–listen I need you to send a dispatch out to the McCauleys–no one?–but it's an emergency–get Geoffreys's ass out of bed if you have to–yes, you heard me right–okay, Martha–happy holidays to you too."

Jake cradled his daughter's face in his hands. "Nikki, I have to go. Kyle's in trouble."

Nikki smiled. "I understand, Daddy. I'll be okay."

Jake kissed his daughter and headed toward the door.

"Daddy?" He loved hearing her call him that again.

"What is it, baby?"

The Sea of Anguish spilled back into his daughter's eyes. "Please be careful. If anything were to happen to you–"

"Nothing's going to happen."

Nikki's reply was a one-two to Jake's brain. "When Mom died, I was lost. I wasn't sure I'd ever find my way back. But you pulled me back from the edge. If I lose you, there's no one left to keep me from falling off."

"I'm not going anywhere. I promise." Jake closed the door gently, as if that would somehow make his exit easier on his daughter. He'd been making a lot of promises lately. Promises he wasn't sure he could keep.

Especially this one.

CHAPTER SEVENTY-FIVE

Frank Geoffreys had never been happy about the shortage of manpower. He'd pissed and moaned along with everyone else when the cuts came, publicly rebuking the Commonwealth of Massachusetts, the President of the United States, even God Himself. When you're Head Honcho, you do this for your team as a show of support. And yet, for all the sorries expressed to the team and their families affected by the cutbacks, the layoffs had never personally burdened Frank Geoffreys.

Until now.

It was because of those damn cutbacks that he, instead of some still-wet-behind-the-ears, straight-from-the-academy new-bie, was plowing through a raging snowstorm in a tin box instead of relaxing by a fire in his well-insulated den. And, to add insult to injury, it was all because of another one of Jake Hawksworth's damn hunches.

Frank clicked open the armrest. He reached inside the compartment, fumbled around, pulled out a CD from his secret stash. A stash that, if discovered by the guys down at the station, would shatter his reputation as the fearless hardass who eats nails for breakfast and pisses them out without so much as flinching.

And the winner is... *The Very Best of Linda Ronstadt*. Could just as well have been Celine or The Bee Gees. Not exactly names most people would guess Frank Geoffreys to be a fan of. Hell, they wouldn't even make it in anyone's top 100 guesses.

What was wrong with them anyway? They were all great talents. Most importantly, they made him forget about the rapists and child molesters and countless other degenerates that filled his days. That said, he'd take a bullet to the gut before letting anyone other than Trish in on his dirty little secret.

He hummed along to *When Will I Be Loved?*, arguably one of pop music's catchiest tunes. Right up there with The Beatles' *Yellow Submarine* and Elvis's *Hound Dog*. Okay, not as good as The King. But pretty damn close.

The snow outside seemed to churn rather than fall, making him feel as though he were inside the world's largest snow globe, shaken vigorously again and again by a hyperactive child bouncing on a trampoline.

The headlights sliced through an endless wall of white that was Route I-86. Frank drum rolled the steering wheel and sang along to the beat.

A dark spot in the sea of white. Closer. Right in front of him.

The dark spot slammed the windshield. Glass exploded into thousands of intricate fractures, sagging against the weight of the dark spot, miraculously remaining intact. The airbag snapped Frank back. He had the sensation of falling. He seemed to fall forever. Linda, the consummate professional, never missed a beat. Without warning, he was jerked forward, smothered by the airbag.

Poor, Poor Pitiful Me blasted from the CD player. Frank found the timing almost too perfect to be a coincidence, as if Ms. Ronstadt had secretly choreographed it herself. Wait'll word got out to the guys what was playing in Frank the Crank's CD player when they found his frozen body come springtime.

CHAPTER SEVENTY-SIX

Had it not been for an itch, Jake would have missed it. He'd been thinking about Merrill. Merrill wasn't one of Kyle's college buddies. Or academy mates. Merrill was another in the long list of Kyle's conquests.

In the Name the Crime Game, Merrill referred to a hostage situation, due to one young lady's penchant for handcuffs. According to Kyle, this Merrill chick had handcuffed him to a motel bed and left him there in all his glory. The next morning, he was discovered by a housekeeper named Tamara (also inducted into the Name the Crime Game by association).

Traveling down I-86 in this blizzard was like being on a giant treadmill. Going nowhere fast. The road blurred in and out of focus. Jake's fingers became one with the steering wheel.

The back of his neck itched. Damn wool. He cocked his head downward to the left, raked his fingers across his neck. A red smudge disturbed the white panorama. A siren. A police siren.

Jake eased the car to a stop. He pulled his jacket collar up, tugged his hat down and exited the vehicle. Even for a big old fat guy, it was nearly impossible to maintain his footing as Mother Nature pelted him with her arsenal. He positioned himself in the direction of the flashing light and prepared for a long journey.

The beacon took him down an incline that, when snow-free, was probably a lot steeper than it now appeared. The snow spilled over his knees. His legs screamed in protest as he pressed forward.

The car was buried up to its door handles. Even under all that white stuff, Jake recognized the car.

Frank.

A shattered windshield sagged beneath the weight of a large deer carcass. Its vacant eyes gazed up at the heavens.

Jake tugged on the door handle. Nothing. A translucent fog glazed the windows, erased whatever lay behind them. A woman's familiar voice drifted along on the wind. The back door of the sedan offered easier access. Jake wrapped a gloved finger around the ice-encrusted handle and gave it his all. The door groaned. It snapped open.

A blast of warm air slapped Jake in the face. Linda Ronstadt crooned *Blue Bayou* to anyone who would listen. CD jackets littered the floor like carelessly dealt cards. Frank Geoffreys slumped forward, dissolved into a deployed airbag.

Jake clicked off the radio, silencing Ms. Ronstadt. He touched a gloved hand to the burly chief's shoulder. *He's dead.* "Frank? Frank, can you hear me?" *Dead.*

Frank shot up, wild eyes softened as they connected with Jake's. "Jake," he said in his trademark monotone. "What brings you out on a night like this?"

Frank Geoffreys had cracked a joke. There was a first for everything. "Frank, can you move?"

Frank shook his huge head. "Think my legs are broken."

"Let's get you out of here."

"I'm okay," he said. "Your partner and that family, I suspect, are not. It'll take three days to drag me up that hill."

Point well taken. "I'll radio in your position."

"I'd appreciate that," Frank said. "Now get the hell out of here."

"Hang in there, Chief." Frank gripped Jake's arm. "What is it, Frank? You okay?"

Frank released his iron grip. "I'm fine. I just wanted to say good luck to you. I hope everyone's okay."

"So do I, Frank."

"I don't just mean the McCauleys." Frank's hard expression softened. "I mean you... and Nikki. I heard they caught the guy. Whatever you need–"

"I appreciate that," Jake replied. "Let's just get through tonight in one piece." He stepped out into the storm. "Stay warm."

"You too," Frank said. "Jake, one favor before you go?"

"Anything."

"Mind checking that my exhaust is clear? Trish would kill me if I went ahead and asphyxiated myself."

"I'll do that." Jake turned.

"One more thing."

"What's that?" *I'm freezing my ass off here and Mr. Serious decides to grow a personality.*

"About my music. You know–" He pointed to the faces peering up at them through tiny plastic windows. Cher. Celine. Andy Gibb. Frank's pained face said it all.

"Don't worry, Frank," Jake said, "your secret's safe with me." Before he slammed the door, he winked and said, "Aren't I about due for a raise?"

CHAPTER SEVENTY-SEVEN

The house loomed before Jake, a towering monster cloaked in a white death shroud. No lights. No movement. No sign of life. That scared the shit out of Jake.

I need you for the final act.

He surged forward. Crushing gales pressed their iron thumbs on his shoulders. Each step was a victory. Each step brought him closer to whatever horrors awaited him behind the doors of 66 Cliffside Drive.

Jake hugged the tree line, suddenly wishing his navy parka was white. He circled around to the back of the house and cut a sharp path for the garage, the most unlikely place Martin would be waiting. Or so Jake hoped.

The window took some effort; he chipped at the ice until, at last, it slid open, exhaling a breath of warm air. It occurred to Jake that he might actually be too big to fit through the opening. Too many burgers and fries–and let's not forget the milk shakes to wash them down–could result in the deaths of six people. Wouldn't that beat all?

He removed the bulky parka, entered the opening headfirst. Halfway through, he got stuck. His body seesawed. He groped with his arms and kicked his legs. He imagined how comical he must look–coming or going. He reached in the darkness, desperate for anything to grab hold of. His fingers brushed something cold and smooth. A car! He stretched until he thought his arm would burst right open, spewing sinew and tissue all over the cement floor. His hand glided along the sleek surface. A crack. He'd found a door. His fingers groped for the door handle. He used everything he had and pulled.

He was inside.

Paige hugged her children close to her body. She was not about to lose one of them again. She studied the faces of the men seated around her, penetrating their eyes, swimming around in their heads, and discovered four very different sensations.

Officer Tubbs was the epitome of fear. Sweat-slicked face. Shifting eyes. If the situation took a turn for the worse, Tubbs would crumble like the cookies he was so fond of.

Kyle was a time bomb waiting to blow. His left knee spasmed involuntarily, quickened with his pulse rate. His dark eyes had the steely determination and unnerving trepidation of a soldier treading into unknown territory.

Shame and remorse wrapped their massive arms around her husband's frame, which now seemed more fragile than the imported crystal vase centered on the mantel. He had put his family in jeopardy; and he was powerless to protect them.

Most unsettling was the composed, almost dormant, rage she sensed swelling inside Martin. For reasons unknown to her, he needed Jake in order to unleash whatever horrors he had planned.

In the end she knew each of these men, save for the latter, would do anything within his power to save the children. But none more readily than their mother.

Jake tucked himself into the shadows of the kitchen. A moonbeam made its two-hundred-thousand-plus-mile journey, slashing through the storm, slicing through the room, bouncing off an overhead rack of stainless pots, skating across the sleek granite countertops and burrowing into the wall. The storm unleashed its fury in a violent blur beyond the windows, shadows dancing frenetically in the slash of light.

Where are they? Maybe they're already dead.

Then he remembered those words. *I need you for the final act.* And he knew that wasn't true.

He leveled his gun, stepped out of the chaotic action of the kitchen into the staid hallway that led to the great room. He had a hunch that was where he'd find them. And his hunches were almost always dead on.

He decided he should have taken out Tonto and his big blue friend an hour ago. They were superfluous, after all; and Tonto looked like he was ready to take on an entire army of trouble rather than wait for the cavalry to ride into town. But killing them now would only set the two brats into fits of screaming. Besides, he enjoyed the soothing rumble the storm made as it thrashed the house.

His eyes unleashed their wrath on his captive audience. They skimmed over the fat guy and kids, lingered on Paige. Sweet wonderful Paige. Even painted in ten shades of terror, she was a captivating sight. As his eyes drank up her full lips, his brain tugged annoyingly on his eyelids, forced their line of vision on the little girl brat.

Fear dissolved from her face. Replaced by something else. Something not quite happy, not quite hopeful. More a mix of the two.

Her gaze was fixed on the black smudge that was the doorway. Her eyes widened. Her lips curled up slowly. "Daddy, look," her breakable voice whispered, "it's Mr. Jake."

CHAPTER SEVENTY-EIGHT

Jake had tried to warn Anna. But she was five. That was like trying to warn a puppy not to follow a bouncing ball into the path of a freight train.

Everything happened in a split second. It's amazing how many things your brain can process in that time. Jake's told him that the hostages, at least some of them anyway, were still alive. It also acknowledged that Martin was close by and was now aware of Jake's presence. The last thing Jake's brain told him to do before he stormed the room was to kick his ass into high gear.

Paige's protective instincts shot from the gate. She positioned her body between Martin and her children. Officer Tubbs scooped the children up in arms roughly the size of steam shovels and moved, rather quickly Paige noted, toward the hallway. Paige sensed the gun rise to her left. She threw her body at Martin. They crashed to the floor in a tangle of arms and legs.

She remembered seeing her husband's face, then Kyle's, then Jake's. Each one exhibited the same emotion. Desperation. Maybe it had something to do with the gun pressed into her cheek.

Jake was fast. But not fast enough. Before he could train the gun on his target, Martin had secured his hostage.

"Drop it," Martin said, his smug tone announcing that, once again, he'd gotten the upper hand. The gun made a dull thud as it hit the carpeting at Jake's feet.

"Kick it over here."

Taking Martin out no longer an option, Jake complied. Martin tucked the gun into his back. Back to square one.

Martin rose, bringing a horrified Paige with him. "Somebody get those rug rats," he said.

"No," Paige whispered.

Kyle said, "I'll go." He took a step backward.

Martin pressed the gun deeper into Paige's face. "Sit your ass down, Tonto. You think I'm stupid? Never mind. They're not going anywhere. I'll deal with them later. Everyone sit. Now."

Dread crept into Jake's body, dispersed itself in large doses through his extremities. The situation couldn't be worse. He and the other Two Stooges were lined up like target practice. And the closest help was stuck in a car listening to Linda Ronstadt.

"Let her go," Drew said. "This has nothing to do with her."

Martin laughed. "Actually, it has nothing to do with your friend." He leveled the gun at Jake.

Jake squeezed his eyes shut and did a lifetime of thinking in that split second. The summers on his granddaddy's farm. His first kiss. His stint in the Air Force. Most of that split second was reserved for Sheila; his mind flipped leisurely through the pages of their life together. The last thought he had before the gun went off was of what Nikki had said before he left her.

If I lose you, there's no one left to keep me from falling.

CHAPTER SEVENTY-NINE

There was no pain that followed the bang. He thought, *well hell, dying's not so tough. What have you been so afraid of all these years?* Then he heard the moans. His eyes snapped open.

Kyle had the surprised look of someone who has just opened his door to find The Prize Patrol standing right there on the porch, toting one giant-sized check. His hands were pressed against his stomach, trying to prevent the blood from seeping out. He was going to need a bigger set of hands. He tried to speak, fell face-first, hit the floor with a dull thud.

Jake moved to assist his partner, but a gun pointed dead center on his face had other plans.

Martin grinned and said, "Tonto was expendable. This game is reserved for four players."

"What game?" Jake asked, not even trying to mask the anger building inside.

"It's a surprise."

"What surprise?"

"Why don't I let Baby Brother do the honors?"

All eyes turned to Drew. "I don't know what you're talking about," Drew said.

"Oh, I think you do."

"Drew, just do what he wants," Paige pleaded.

"Tell them," Martin said, his voice riding on a wave of urgency.

"I said I don't know what he's–"

"–TELL THEM!"

The room shuddered. Jake wasn't sure if it was from the

raging storm outside or the one snuggled right up beside them.

"I don't know–"

Martin yanked Paige back by the hair, centered the cold hard steel square between her eyes. "TELL THEM OR SHE DIES!"

Jake fought the urge to lunge, knowing Martin would take both he and Paige out before he took two steps. Jake's gaze went from Martin to Drew to Paige. Utter rage consumed one. Utter horror the other two. Martin cocked the gun.

Tell him what he wants to know.

A silent scream twisted Paige's face.

Tell him, goddammit.

Martin pressed the end of the gun firmly to Paige's head.

He's going to do it. TELL HIM!

A wave of nausea washed over Jake as Drew uttered the four words.

CHAPTER EIGHTY

"I killed Scott Dempsey."

The room went in and out of focus. Jake heard the words, his brain processed them, deciphered them, spit them out. Still, he could not accept them. "Martin killed Scott Dempsey," he heard himself say.

The spinning room slowed, stopped on Drew. "No, Jake."

Martin relaxed his grip on Paige, moved the gun down to her chest. "Don't that beat all. Been waiting a long fucking time to hear that," Martin said.

Jake tried to sort out the questions that flew in and out of his head. The left-handed batter. Martin's cleats beside the body. "Drew, the evidence showed conclusively that Scott was struck by somebody batting lefty."

Drew nodded slowly, drinking in each word. "And he was. Marty did strike him. The first time."

Paige looked on in stunned silence. Drew continued, his voice steady and deliberate, as if relieved of this lifelong burden. "After Marty hit him, I thought he was dead. I mean, that was one hell of a swing." Martin grinned proudly. "But then Scott woke up. And attacked me."

Paige whispered, "Why did he attack you? You said Marty hit him."

"That's what I tried telling Scott," Drew said. His delivery was detached, as if he were acting out a scene in a local play. "But he came at me and said he was going to kill me. The bat was right there at my fingertips. And Scott was coming. Coming, with murder in his eyes. So I..."

Paige folded up into herself, as if the events were taking place before her.

"Drew, it was self-defense," Jake said.

"Who would have believed that?"

"I would have," Jake said. "I mean, after what you had been through–"

"I knew what I was doing." The words stabbed Jake. Paige let out a loud gasp. Drew looked directly at Jake and said, "I meant to do it."

The realization that he had been duped hit Jake hard. He'd fallen for Drew's story, hook, line and sinker. And convinced everyone else of it too. He wanted to wash away the guilt that seeped into his pores. But there were more answers to be had.

"What about the cleats?" Jake didn't pretend to mask the betrayal in his voice.

Drew appeared calm, as though the world had been hoisted right off his shoulders and tossed in the trash. He was cleansing himself. Jake was the one in need of a shower.

Martin spoke. Jake had almost forgotten he was there, pointed gun and all. "Yeah, Baby Brother, tell him about the cleats."

Drew squeezed his eyes shut. An audible breath shot from his mouth. "Marty came home," Drew began. "Said Scott was definitely dead this time. He said we had to get rid of our clothes. So we did. Buried them out in the woods behind our house." Drew opened his eyes. "Except for the cleats."

"Why not the cleats?" Jake asked.

"Marty said they were his lucky cleats and there was no way he was going to bury them. Figured he just had to wipe off any blood, I suppose."

"Guess that was my first mistake, Baby Brother." Martin spit fire as he spoke. "Trusting you was my second."

Drew lunged, then retreated as his eyes met the gun. "You want to talk about trust? I was going to cover for you and you said you'd do the same for me. Blood brothers, remember?"

The events of three decades ago were becoming clear to Jake. "So Drew," he said, "you went back to the scene wearing Marty's cleats, is that right?"

Drew nodded. Sadness crawled out from under his eyelids and settled in his eyes. "The next day."

Jake shook his head. "But if you were covering for each other, why would you do that?"

"Insurance," Drew said matter-of-factly.

"How's that?" Jake said.

"I never really trusted my brother," Drew replied. "I mean, he always went back on his word. Ever since we were little kids. So I thought, just in case..."

"Is that why you buried the bat?" Martin tightened his grip on Paige. She appeared catatonic. Jake suspected shock was setting in.

Drew smiled at his brother. Not the best time for a pissing contest, Jake thought.

"Yes," Drew said. "When I went back, the bat was just sitting there in plain sight."

Martin snickered. "My other mistake."

"I knew I had to get rid of it. So I buried it."

Martin let out a hearty laugh. "You got me there, Bro. And of all places." He picked up the bat with his free hand and swung it like a golf club. Paige recoiled. "Can't believe I never thought to look in there for it before now," Martin said. "Right under my nose the whole time."

Jake raised a hand, force of habit from all those years in Catholic school. Martin toting a gun was almost as terrifying as those nuns. "So, Drew, it was you who dragged the body and covered it." He turned to Martin. "Then Martin, why did you first tell us you moved the body, then said you didn't move it?"

Martin swung the bat wider, faster. Paige put a hand to her face. "You and your shit-for-brains partner had me tried and hung from day one. I told you whatever you wanted to hear."

Heat rose up in Jake's neck. Martin was right. He'd never given Martin the benefit of a single doubt.

"And then," Martin continued, "I got myself so deep in lies that I didn't know what was up or down anymore. Nothing would have convinced you." He held up the bat. "Except maybe this."

Paige found her voice and said, "Drew, how could you do what you did and then let your brother take the blame? Don't you have a conscience?"

Drew was visibly shaken to the core. "Of course," he said with how-dare-you acid in his tone. "Not a day has gone by that I haven't thought about it. But I knew we were both going to fry for what we did. And I had a future to think about."

Martin exploded. He grabbed Paige by the hair, pressed the gun to her cheek. *She's dead,* Jake thought. And her husband had only himself to blame. Then, without warning, Martin flung her to the side and went full throttle at his brother.

"What about MY future? I get it–the one with the brighter future gets to skip out on the murder rap, is that it?" Martin was upon his brother. "Old Marty wouldn't have amounted to anything anyway, so let's just throw him to the wolves!"

Jake knew this was going to go from bad to worse in a matter of seconds. If he could just get Paige to the door...

"DON'T MOVE!" Martin screamed. Jake froze. Martin's lips curled up into the biggest, most insane smile. "Jake, you can't leave before the verdict and sentencing." With that, he turned to Drew. "Baby Brother, I hereby find you guilty of all charges and sentence you to death." He raised the gun to his brother's face.

The gunshot was deafening. Then the room fell silent, disturbed only by the lull of the storm as it thrashed the world outside.

CHAPTER EIGHTY-ONE

Officer Lenny "Tiny" Tubbs cut a massive silhouette in the doorway. His right arm stood at attention, gun steady in his hand.

Martin's face crinkled up like the face of a man crying. But there were no tears. Jake wondered if this monster was capable of producing them. Not even a stint in an onion factory would do the trick. Martin stumbled backward. The fresh wound darkened across his midsection; he pressed a shaky hand to the dark hole. The gun waggled in his other hand.

Paige lay a few feet to his left, on her side like a swimsuit model posing for *Sports Illustrated.* Drew was fixated on the hole in his brother's stomach. Jake moved toward Paige. Martin staggered, the gun hanging on by a thread.

Just die, you son of a bitch.

"Get up," Jake whispered to Paige. She scrambled to right herself.

"Drop the gun, Mr. McCauley," Tiny said with authority.

What was with the formalities? Still, Jake was impressed. He'd always pegged Tiny as the type of guy who'd run for cover before engaging the enemy. With a stash of donuts in his foxhole. Tiny kept the gun trained on Martin.

Martin did not seem to hear him. Life was slowly leaking from his body; pretty soon, shock would set in. Martin fell hard against a wall. The gun remained in his grip.

"I said drop the gun, Motherfucker," Tiny said with a Dirty Harry coolness to his voice. So much for formalities.

The lights flickered. Just for a moment. But a lot can happen in a moment.

Before Tiny could react, Martin hoisted the gun, leveled it at Paige's back. *At least she won't see it coming,* Jake thought.

The world turned off briefly. Jake heard the gun cock. The world turned itself back on. Drew's body was airborne. Darkness slapped Jake in the face again. A gunshot.

Paige's body fell heavily against Jake. *She's dead. The bastard did it!*

The lights did a spastic dance, then offered Jake a view of the horror unfolding before him. Tiny didn't mess around this time. He hit his target like an old pro. Dead center in the chest.

Paige clawed her way up, frantic, wrapped herself around Jake's neck like a young Nikki did whenever she felt scared and vulnerable.

Jake stared in disbelief at the sight on the floor.

Drew was dying. His brother, sprawled beside him, was going to beat him to it. Competitive right to the end.

Paige cradled her husband's head in her lap. His thick hair was streaked with blood. His face was ashen. He struggled to speak.

"I'm so sorry I hurt you," he managed to spit out. A tablespoon of blood leaked out with the words. "I thought if I could just put it behind me..." His eyes fluttered. Like the lights, he was on again, off again.

Paige tucked away all ill feelings and, for the moment, she was the loving wife, the caregiver, the woman Jake suspected she was before all of this began. She gently stroked her husband's cheek with one hand, firmly gripped his hand in her other.

Martin emitted a series of gurgling sounds. His body twitched. His eyes flickered, locked on Jake. He tried to talk, something profound no doubt, but his lungs swam in blood now and all he could manage was a wink. His hand twitched, slid itself over to meet his brother's.

Drew groped for it, perhaps thinking it was his wife's. He couldn't know. His eyes were awash in blood. Paige lifted Martin's hand and, in brutal fashion, tossed it aside like the garbage that it was.

Jake watched hopelessly as his old friend slipped away. Paige sobbed softly, seemingly forgetting Jake was even there. Still, he felt like a voyeur. He trained his glance on the floor. The lush area rug, once subtle shades of taupe, was a distasteful russet. Suddenly, Jake remembered something Drew had once said to him.

Drew told him that Martin used to say they weren't just brothers, they were blood brothers, made of the same flesh and blood. And no matter what happened to them, or how far apart they were, they would remain blood brothers. Forever.

The deep stain in the rug formed a bizarre sort of Rorschach inkblot in the space between where the brothers lay. Ice spilled into Jake's heart as he studied the stain that connected the bodies.

Blood brothers. Forever.

EPILOGUE
Spring

*"*I talked to Chip."

Jake pulled the phone away from his ear, as if the words had damaged it. "When?"

"Yesterday," Nikki's voice said. "At the prison."

"The prison? You went to the prison?"

"Relax, Dad." Nikki's voice was composed. She could probably hear the vein throbbing in her father's temple. "It took me a while to get the courage up to do it. But I needed answers."

Jake pushed on the thick cord pulsating in his temple. He feared it might just blow. He tried to sound calm. "Did you get what you were looking for?"

"I suppose so," Nikki said, sounding a bit unsure. "He said he was consumed with guilt over the accident."

"Accident?" Jake screamed. "The kid was drunk as a skunk."

Nikki sighed. "I didn't call you to get your blood pressure going," she said. "Just listen."

"I'm listening."

"He used to watch us at the cemetery."

The Tall Man.

"He said he couldn't bear to see the pain I was going through–"

What about the pain I was going through?

"–and he thought if he could do something to ease the pain..." Her voice trailed off.

Jake wanted to hate this boy for what he'd done. Now all he

felt was pity. "Are you okay?"

"He said he loved me, Daddy," Nikki said through sobs. "Do you think he really meant it?"

Maybe he did, maybe he didn't. What the hell did Jake know? All that mattered was that his daughter get through this. "Of course he did. How could he not?"

The sobs receded. Then Nikki said, "How are the McCauleys?"

Jake shrugged to the room. "Getting by, I suppose." He glanced at his watch. "That reminds me, I'm late for an appointment. Are we still on for dinner tomorrow night?"

"Same time, same place," his daughter said, a hint of joy in her voice.

"Okay, I'll see you then." Before he hung up, Jake said, "Are you sure you're okay, Nik?"

She convinced him this time. "I'm going to be just fine, Daddy. And you?"

A sense of calm invaded Jake's body. His shoulders felt lighter, as if the burden he'd been carrying for so long had slid right off like snow from the warm hood of an idling car. "I'm great," he said. As he hung up the phone, he had a hunch he was right.

And his hunches were almost always right.

April was nearly over, but the air still had a wintry snap to it. The sidewalk underfoot hissed and crackled like a pond warning you that it's not quite frozen, not quite safe. A puff of smoke shot from Jake's mouth. It quietly evaporated. Then he saw her.

Paige McCauley threw Jake a friendly wave. Downtown had not yet opened its doors to the onslaught of commuters and shoppers and Paige looked vulnerable, standing there on the empty sidewalk. The street was just as vacant. Still, Jake had to resist the urge to rush at her, just in case a car whipped around a corner and jumped the curb. He quickened his step.

"Good to see you, Jake," she said. She buried herself in his chest. That ought to take away any chill.

"Good to see you, too," he said. The moment was awkward, like that first date to the movies when you dread the movie ending for fear you might actually have to talk to the girl partnered up beside you. There was no movie to ease things. But there was always the weather. The perfect icebreaker, no matter what the weather. "How about this cold?" he said.

Paige's face softened. "I'm beginning to think Mother Nature is lobbying to do away with spring altogether," she said.

"Does that mean the Four Seasons Hotel will have to change its name?"

Paige laughed. Okay, so humor did the trick too. Combine weather and humor, and you're in like Flynn. If only Jake had known this forty years ago.

"I heard about what you did with the recovered money," Jake said. "I think it's wonderful."

Paige nodded, her eyes proud. "I thought the Center for Missing and Exploited Children could use it."

"You thought right. It was very generous of you."

Paige blushed. "So, how is your partner doing?" she asked.

Jake said, "Looks like our resident lady's man is going to be on the injured reserve list for a while, but he's expected to make a full recovery."

"That's great news. I'm sure he'll have the ladies lining back up in no time."

"Knowing Kyle, he has a few stashed under the bed beside his bedpan."

Paige's smile held less radiance this time. Then it disappeared along with the glint in her eyes. "We're leaving tomorrow."

"I know."

"I think it's best for the children," she said in an apologetic voice.

"I understand," Jake said. "Where is it you said you were going?"

"Chicago."

"I heard Mother Nature definitely eliminated spring there."

The sadness in Paige's eyes took a breather. "So I hear. Besides, my mother's there and her health isn't as good as it used to be. And my sister is only an hour away. She has a son the same age as Ben."

"That's great. How is Ben?"

"Oh, you know. Can't wait to get his driver's license. And the girls–"

"That isn't what I meant."

Paige bit her lip. "I know, Jake," she whispered. She lowered her gaze. "It's been hard. On both of them. Anna still thinks he's going to walk through the door one of these days and everything will be as it was. But Ben knows that isn't going to happen." She lifted her gaze and it locked with Jake's. "Do you think he'll be okay, I mean really okay?"

Jake smiled his big old, unpretentious, would-I-lie-to-you grin and said firmly, "Absolutely."

Paige dropped her gaze again and said, "You must think I'm a horrible person."

"Why would I think that?"

Her eyes remained fixed on the cold, unfeeling cement. "All those years I loved and lived with a man who was capable of that... and I never saw it."

Jake hugged her fragile body, mindful of the damage he could do if he squeezed too hard. "You wouldn't have seen it," Jake said, "because that isn't the Drew you knew, the Drew you fell in love with." He pulled her back gently, looked into glistening emerald eyes. "Drew wasn't a monster. You have to believe that. What he did was wrong. And he lived every day a prisoner, his own judge, jury, and executioner. But what he had with you and Ben and Anna–that was real. It was the only escape he had from the hell he'd created for himself."

Paige nodded. "There was a lot of good in him, I know that. It's what I fell in love with. And what I miss." The floodgates opened. Jake threw all caution to the wind and hugged her tighter.

The sun made its entrance, shimmering across the brick and glass facades that dissolved into the horizon. A spray of light splashed across Paige's chestnut hair, its warmth enveloping her.

Jake Hawksworth pressed his face upward, drank in some of that warmth for himself. Maybe Mother Nature hadn't vetoed spring after all.

CPSIA information can be obtained
at www.ICGtesting.com
Printed in the USA
BVHW070131050121
596833BV00003B/45